LURID & CUTE

LURID
&
CUTE

ADAM
THIRLWELL

JONATHAN CAPE
LONDON

Published by Jonathan Cape 2015

2 4 6 8 10 9 7 5 3 1

Copyright © Adam Thirlwell 2015

Adam Thirlwell has asserted his right under the Copyright, Designs and Patents Act 1988
to be identified as the author of this work

First published in Great Britain in 2015 by
Jonathan Cape
20 Vauxhall Bridge Road,
London SW1V 2SA

www.vintage-books.co.uk

A Penguin Random House Company

global.penguinrandomhouse.com

A CIP catalogue record for this book is available from the British Library

ISBN 9780224089135 (Hardback edition)
ISBN 9780224089142 (Trade paperback edition)

Penguin Random House is committed to a sustainable future for
our business, our readers and our planet. This book is made from
Forest Stewardship Council® certified paper

Typeset in Stempel Garamond LT Std by Palimpsest Book Production Limited,
Falkirk, Stirlingshire

Printed and bound in Great Britain by CPI Group (UK) Ltd, Croydon CRO 4YY for Alison

IN SILHOUETTE

Why should I be the guinea pig for the caprice of fate?
There was, after all, Pascha the second-hand book dealer,
& Hennechen, the steamship agent . . .

Knut Hamsun, *Hunger*, 1890

IN SUMMARY

I. MADAMA MORTE

in which our hero wakes up

When I woke I was looking upside down at a line of velvet paintings on the wall above the bed. Jesus was standing on his halo beside a very bright Madonna – I mean the religious kind, not the disco version. In between the two of them was a tropicana beach – it was a palm tree, a palm tree, a palm tree, some blue sand. I thought perhaps I liked them, these velvet paintings. I liked the very bright vibe. But also I knew that although I liked the vibe it was not the vibe of my usual bedroom, just as the girl who was sleeping beside me in what seemed to be a hotel room was not my happy wife. It was that kind of problem situation, and while I acknowledge that some people would not feel that this is after all so bad – and that waking beside a person who is not ethically your own is just the usual way most humans enter the moral realm and therefore, kiddo, live with it – still, I could not be so suave. For a long time now there had been problems in the atmosphere – small cracks and fissures, like butterflies emerging in autumn, a light tropicália everywhere and it made me a little afraid. Just as now I felt like my head was somewhere else and I also felt very sick. I knew my phone must be beside me and I knew that I should look at it but I really also didn't. If at this point you had placed me on a chat-show sofa and asked me how I was feeling, I'd have told you that I basically was feeling very sad. Because I really am no big shot, or hoodlum. I am no *player*. Always girls have made me shy. In this role of high-speed macho I was about as authentic as the white chicks doing gang signs for photos. It really wasn't normal for me to wake up and not know how I got there. For me a normal pastime was to be intent on mathematical problems, or models of voting systems – my pastimes, I just mean, were always sweet and meditative. Nevertheless, this new thing went on happening and I was powerless to stop it. My head was definitely very bad. In Brasilia they were coming off their night shift, in Tokyo they were having a first whisky sour. Four thousand miles away there were drones just very noisily hovering in formation above the mountain passes and valley gorges, and down here on the quiet earth a girl who was not my wife was lying there beside me. Her name was Romy, and she was one of my favourite friends. She was blonde and when you saw her in a bar her hair was this gorgeous listless mass to one side of her neck but now I had this inner knowledge that she wasn't a natural blonde. She almost had no hair between her legs but it turned out that the hair that was there, a tuft, was definitely dark. That's what I tried to concentrate on while the light began to fry the nylon curtains and Romy continued to sleep. Because even if you're bewildered or sad you have to carry on. I remember one bodhisattva phrase – *keep cool but care* – and that phrase is never wrong. It's most certainly a rule to live by and such rules should always be treasured. I hope that if I prove one thing in the writing of this account it's the importance of rules for living, which is perhaps why in this story of my moral life I have decided to begin with this episode of blood. It was I think the place where my usual categories disappeared. I got up and dressed and stood there just considering how I was going to go back home – I mean in what state and with what explanations. But it was also very early. It was both way too late and also very early so I thought for now I would start with getting myself some breakfast, because sometimes the only correct way to act is to take care of the ordinary things. You have to think things through in stages. So I walked out into the car park and along to the hotel restaurant where I sat myself down. From the booth in which I sat I had a very bright view. It was nothing special. Insects rotated slowly in the green dawn, they just kept developing from nowhere, from the bright and granular air. My car was in the parking lot outside our door, and beside it there was what looked like a Caddy Hearse but I ignored it. And maybe this was a mistake – to ignore what other people might consider a definite sign. If you're used to the unfranked letters arriving at your house, or phone calls where a man asks if he's got through to the chapel of rest, I mean if you're alive to the mafia ways of telling a man he's marked or savaged or doomed, then maybe it could be said that I made a mistake. Had I known then what I know now, had I been able to understand the full ranges of terror I would come to know, the gore and ballistics, had I been able to perform the kind of loop-the-loop this manner of talking now allows me, I might well have argued in this way. But I always missed the obvious. I don't know why. Other people appreciated the ordinary things like shopping-centre car parks and cafe parasols, or whatever – the coffee-machine coffee. But me, no. I was much better at my own ruminations. It was very bright and very sad inside this restaurant. The radio was talking to itself but I had nobody to talk to, so I sat there in my booth with a view of the empty signscape and read through the laminate menu. I waited. I looked out the window. I kept looking at my watch and then the landscape for ten minutes: my watch and then the landscape, my watch and then the landscape. I really don't like waiting. Finally a waitress emerged from the kitchen. Her name was on her breast pocket. This name was Quincy. In another font, another badge was wishing me a nice day. And it was a nice day, no question. It was CGI nice, if you had not woken up in a state of oozing anxiety.

— I was waiting ten minutes, I said.

— You said what? said Quincy.

— I'm not making a formal complaint, I said. — I just think you should know that I came in I think ten minutes ago. It's really nothing.

— Uh-huh, said Quincy.

I don't think she really cared but at least I'd tried to help. I ordered my vegetarian breakfast. My style of eggs was sunny side up, to use the outmoded term. The colour of my juice was orange. I did want the hash browns. I ate my fries with gusto. I added the ketchup and mustard. And when I'd finished, having dragged some toast across the red-and-yellow plate, I rubbed my glasses clean with a wipe that Quincy had provided for my fingers. It was kind of her because people's hands are often covered in germs. It's always good to be conservative. The wipe made my glasses smell pure but they now also stung my eyes.

I looked out over the horizontal electric lines, then the horizontal lines painted on the tarmac. Then I looked out over the vertical road signs. The world was as empty as that. I felt very trapped and very sad. Although of course in retrospect I was nowhere near as sad as I should have been because *in retrospect* Fate was about to juice me even more than it already had. Fate was all around me, like the crimping on a beer-bottle top. But then, it's never obvious at what point you can use this language of *in retrospect* or *too late*, for although they seem like normal phrases they conceal much more than is useful, so that one major problem with living is that at every point of dejection you generally think you have reached the lowest depth, and so like everyone I tended to imagine that this frazzled state in which I found myself was the very worst state possible, just as when indeed I was inside something much more damaging to my ideal as debonair and open-hearted, as inside whatever ride of death you enter at the funfair, a ride in which I came to know grotesqueries and savagery I never imagined I would need to consider, at that point I no longer cared about this previous knowledge at all. Whereas here, in this hotel, I was stricken.

to discover his transformation

Because I do not like to do things that are wrong. I am totally against it. And one thing that does seem wrong is to wake up in a bed beside a woman who is not your wife. Or let's say, no, because in fact there are better or worse ways of doing the very bad thing, and in general as I examined this situation with as much scruple as possible,

I had to admit that to do this with a woman who was in many ways your best friend was an extra mistake, because I think I would happily argue in whatever saloon you put me in that sex with a mutual friend is probably worse for your adored wife in the hierarchy of wrongs than sex with a momentary stranger. Or at least I would say it was possible – but I wasn't thinking about these moral issues as methodically as I would have liked, a distraction which is so often a problem in this busy reckless age, because also I had a heaviness in my bowels and it was preoccupying me too. As I walked back to this hotel room where Romy was presumably waiting in some sleepy spaced-out manner, with eyeliner smudged in a way that would no question be appealing, I was suddenly regretting not using the bathroom in the restaurant. Because while on the one hand I didn't like going back inside the restaurant just to use the bathroom, on the other hand the thought of returning to my room and sitting down and exploding in the small hutch next to where Romy was sleeping . . . This didn't please me at all. But then I thought of a solution that made me proud. Before going back to the room, I decided, I would do the necessary checking out, and then silently take my backpack – for I am rarely without my backpack, partly because there's no end to the possessions I need to keep on my person for luck or voodoo or habit but also it's just the most useful method overall, I think, for taking objects with you if you're thinking about your future health – and then steal away. And afterwards I would go and get a coffee in a diner somewhere else and use whatever bathroom they could offer me and that was where I would more charmingly plan how I would return to my wife Candy in such a way that she didn't entirely hate me. This wasn't obviously usual for me – to leave a girl in bed without saying a proper goodbye. I would definitely admit that it seemed perhaps impolite. But in the end you have to choose among politenesses – and after all, I saw Romy very often. We would have many moments to discuss this and other aspects of our history. And also although I was in a very dark panic there was in me a sense that this manoeuvre did have a macho charm. It's not easy to admit it but as I stood there at reception, reading a calendar for the wrong month and the wrong year, I allowed myself this grizzled moment of glory. You, I was thinking, are paying for a girl to sleep. OK, she was no narco moll or Latina pop star, but still, it was something. It also occurred to me that if this was definitely happening then I might need more sustained medical attention. I needed more consideration applied to my pills. But that was only a parenthesis. And I would like to also assert at this early highpoint of pause and idyll that while it had its perhaps reprehensible machismo, this way of thinking, it surely also showed concern, for what can be kinder than not waking someone up when they don't want to? – and this concern was always something that my mother and father liked me to develop. They liked it when I thought about other people. They had a theory that one should work hard in this life. *You are so impatient, booby*, my mother said to me on many occasions in my life, like wanting to be more glorious than I am. *Why do you never do things slowly?* This was how she always talked. *Wake up, darling*, my mother would continue! *If this is what you want, then you need to take your time to get it. What did I do wrong to make you so impatient? You want things always to be the big bright blue sky?*

— I do not think this is what this is, I said.

— Of course, she said. — Keep arguing.

I think mothers are the atmosphere in which you have to live and I guess I do like that but it's also a miniature form of persecution, in the most lovable way possible. But still, I tried very hard to do as my parents would have wanted, which at this point meant considering the less fortunate lives of other people. The man who was at reception this early in the morning seemed a little sad so I thought about him with affection. He had a difficult job, I was thinking, an arduous job, which presumably necessitated answering phones to the people supplying the kitchens, as well as kids calling for a practical joke, and a woman arriving at four in the afternoon needing a room right now, and so on, as well as the preparation of check-in and check-out forms, and the monitoring of the pool maintenance team, and also the use of the credit-card machine. It was not easy at all. His name was Osman, and Osman, I was definitely thinking, seemed to shroud a deeper pain. He turned round to find a stapler or other office accessory and there was a dark scar behind his ear, as if from some bayonet or sabre or machete. Maybe in the heyday of Osman he had once been a fearsome Caucasian warlord, but events had so conspired that Osman was now here: in a chain hotel, taking calls. While at home he kept his videos, perhaps videos where he surveyed his troops and I hoped that he did, because it's important to keep some kind of link to your past.

— Have a nice day and come back soon! said Osman.

— You too, man, I said.

I did mean it. A woman wearing headphones was swabbing down the wooden decking outside the rooms. I wanted to give her a gentle smile but she didn't see me. Then I thought I saw my dead grandmother walking towards me, at least it looked like she looked in photographs. She seemed relaxed. It was very troubling. But when I was closer she was no longer my grandmother. She was nobody at all. So I tried to forget it. I could see the exit route back to something that I could call my ordinary life. It was very close. Inside the room the light was now brightly bleaching the curtains. I tried to turn off the ceiling fan because it was making this blurry kind of noise but instead I only turned on the bedside light. Romy didn't notice. I walked across to the desk, where my bag was propped. And although I was anxious to make what the pulp fictions must once have called *the perfect getaway*, I also wanted to kiss her goodbye. I don't know if that's pulp, or if it is then it's a different variant of pulp, the romance pulp, but still isn't that right – to kiss a girl goodbye while she's sleeping? Isn't that what the passionate do? So I walked to the bed, and bent over her. Romy was sleeping on her front, and beside her nose on the pillow there was a thin dark slick of blood.

whose reality he tries to doubt

Everyone thinks they will not be there when someone dies, I mean when someone dies who is not their endless and married love. Everyone thinks that things happen in regular sequences but of course they don't or not always.

Time, as the fakir once put it, has this malicious ingenuity in the invention of affliction. In the end everything happens. Savage combinations are always possible and in fact I'm not sure they're combinations, so much as aspects of the same thing. This was the knowledge that was being forced on me while I stood there. I was fading in and out. I was like a hologram or optical illusion. Or like a neon sign. I was switching on and off and I was sinister. I looked down. *What kind of big shot are you?* I was saying to myself. *A fucking small one.* I looked up. The ceiling fan was still going round and round. That was basically a version of me too. I looked back down at Romy. Yes, everyone thinks they know the order in which things will happen but in fact this is not true at all. And also whether something has happened or not is rarely obvious. I think we tend to over-exaggerate the idea that things are real. Or at least I was trying to think how real something was when it was so far entirely private. I mean, do your own mini quiz. When a gorgeous girl tries to kiss you in the back of a taxi when you're both high on ketamine, do you go home and tell your wife? I do not think so. You keep the gorgeous blonde to yourself as a stereoscope slide for winter evenings and therefore she does not exist at all. Or when your husband knows you do not smoke but you do in fact enjoy a secret cigarette, why do you upset his peace of mind? You find some chewing gum to sweeten your breath and go home as if nothing has happened. And if you act as if nothing has happened, if nothing in your behaviour ever hints that something has happened, then has it really happened? That's my question. That's what I mean by nothing happening, or one of the things I mean.

At this precise moment this situation was only known to me and so it was maybe not known at all. Although it's not so easy to really think this when you are inside the situation itself.

with blood all over the picture

The blood looked red to me but in close-up the blood seemed black. It was a red liquid that was turning black or a black liquid turning red. It seemed to be flowing more and more – how to say this? – *freely*. I think *freely* is the usual word for *flowing*. Then I tried to say Romy's name, but it wouldn't – my voice. It did nothing at all. I tried to breathe and that was difficult too. It was like my heart was somewhere on the surface of my body. I could still taste the stale egg taste from breakfast in my gullet. In other words I felt very much underprepared, like the nightmare where you are giving a PowerPoint presentation but leave behind your laptop in some stranger's Chevrolet. I felt definitely ill at ease. Because if you imagine me at a speed-date session being asked to define myself then I'd easily say I was a model citizen. I don't think that's exaggerated. My grades in literature were good, my grades in mathematics were spectacular. I read the classical texts. I had a talent for exams. I am aware that not everyone has the opportunity for such talent and I am very grateful for that privilege. Do good, said my mother and father, and you will prosper. Take exams, be diligent. You are a prodigy, they told me! I used to think they had things right but now I really wasn't sure if this was, after all, enough. It turns out that you can have all the ancestors you want, they can hover in the air around you like candy-floss, but still, they cannot help you in your mania and distress. Inside the room, my thinking was as slow as the way dub music's slow. I was remembering an article about a boy who went to sleep and woke up to find a girl jumping out the window. I didn't really want to think that, with variations, that boy was me, but then the only other possibility that was not suicide was that somehow Romy had been afflicted by a seizure or attack. And naturally the whole narcotics business was the main culprit or cause for this in my head, and since I was the person who had supplied these narcotics, this was not something that pleased me very much. But also I wasn't now so interested in causes, I was more interested in *what happens next*. I'd never thought of a life like a structure but now it was exactly like that, my thinking, because I was picturing those videos where buildings get blown up, where they just curtsy or dissolve from within. And I didn't think I could be expected in this situation to know what to do. It seemed beyond the usual life skills an average citizen should possess. I looked out the window. The view outside the window was very still. The bathroom contained two hand towels, two bath towels, a bathrobe and a bath mat. In the toilet bowl some paper from the night before had inflated like a parachute or squid. On the wall there was another velvet painting: the naked torso of a black woman, with shiny breasts and sunglasses, against a turquoise background. While outside, my car was parked, oh outside where there was also sunlight and the sky and everything was ordinary. Clouds gathered. Clouds melted. If I'd turned on the radio I would have heard a voice explaining the effects of the weather system in our city, but I didn't, because I was running the hot tap, washing my hands. And I was thinking about Romy. For to think comprehensively has always been my genius. I had checked out without mentioning that there was a woman in my bed; I had sat in the restaurant unnoticed for over ten minutes. The neutral observer might therefore, I was thinking, draw the wrong conclusions. And although of course it was possible to do the ordinary thing, the legal thing, to go back to a man called Osman for help and explain, in abject supplication, that I'd found the body of my friend comatose in my bed, but that I was nothing to do with this situation, or only in the most minor way: yes I suppose I could have returned to Osman to discuss the problem of hospitals and police, but the voices in my head were not so normal. The voices in my head, they did their own thing. They tended to prefer I should keep this to myself.

which creates small traps and impasses

Her left arm was behind her back and her left cheek was squashed softly against the pillow. It was like a Kodachrome of a kid sleeping or a cherub but it also wasn't. First, I needed to mop up the blood on the pillow beside her, because it seemed the tender thing to do, and I always try to do the tender things. I don't think at this point I had finally decided on my total project. I took a bath towel and laid it on the blood. The white terry cloth became maroon. And I was thinking that maybe this was the first time I had ever seen another person's blood, I mean blood that wasn't a minor wound or a girl's period but proper flowing gore. I didn't want to touch it but I knew I had to. I had this fear of someone else's blood, like I had the vaporous fear of coming inside a girl without a condom. I don't think that's unusual. I took the towel up and tried to rinse it in the bathtub – which meant that I was leaving a tiny trail of blood on the bathroom floor which was tiny, sure, but also gruesome and repulsive. Then, kneeling on the side of the bed, I gathered Romy in my arms, from behind, and gently lifted her chest and it felt wrong, touching her breasts like this, and the paradox was momentarily intriguing but then a cry of horror overtook me. I couldn't help it. It came out of my mouth much quicker than I knew. I was trembling. I held her there, as if I were performing some slow-motion Heimlich manoeuvre: first gazing at the pillow, which was a mess of polyester and vomit and possibly more blood, a total horror show, then gazing sideways at what once was Romy's entire expression, but all the expression was gone. I held her there. I bent to her face and her mouth smelled like vomit but also it was warm and that, I had to admit, was a very good sign. If I concentrated very hard I thought that also she was still breathing and I wanted to concentrate on this more, but I couldn't. Because, to return to you, Mr Chat Show Host, if you want to know what Fate feels like, it feels like this. You are holding a body in your arms, and then you hear a brisk knock, followed by a key card being slotted into place. That's how it feels. I would possibly argue that maybe it would be nice if just one time Fate used a more original ringtone. So I dropped Romy, gently, to the pillow again, and ran to the door. The maid was facing me, with her headphones in, and carrying a mop and brushes. I didn't have time to check if I was bloodstained. I probably was. Maybe people don't care any more. Maybe in the modern world blood is no surprise. But me I was always old-fashioned.

— Housekeeping, she said.

— But I'm still here, I said.

— This room is not occupied.

— But I'm here, I said.

I was trying to sound very hopeful, like I always do. She looked in and I suppose she maybe saw a pair of naked feminine legs. She looked at me. It was just about plausible that I was a mini donjuanish type, or at least I'd like to think so.

— They said you gone, she said.

— We're leaving, I said.

— Ten minutes. Ten minutes, mister.

It was probably then that my plan became obvious to me, which I still believe was a plan of carefulness. I was thinking that there were maybe two or three things that were true. That I needed to get Romy some medical help, that I needed to do this unbeknown to the hotel authorities, so that possibly it would also remain unbeknown to Candy and my parents, and that speed was very necessary. It was a difficult trio but maybe not impossible. I wanted Romy to be OK and I wanted to return to my ordinary life, or at least the possibility that such an ordinary life existed.

in the manner of many catastrophic myths

I suppose other people have their ways of thinking this through. I know that in such a situation my father would calmly acknowledge the presence of the Devil, for although he is not so devout he has his symbolic moments. For him there is a prosecuting spirit everywhere. I think this is in fact one of my earliest memories, standing in my water wings, waiting for my father to return from shul so that he could take me to the swimming pool. My father very softly and very secretly believes in devils, and while I have never managed to be quite persuaded, as I say this it does occur to me that I often fear many monsters. I call my devils *monsters* and in the end perhaps there's no big difference. I remember the ancient mutant monsters in the national museum and they make me very fearful still, those pictures of the green god and his dog-god of judgement, the devouring god with his crocodile head and the single feather of truth. Although at least the dog-god stays down below, in his alabaster hall. Whereas this scene in a hotel room felt more like what happens when the gods decide to lope up their ladder to earth, and when they do, they kill you. Have you ever met a god? It's like this. They just can't help themselves. They're very sorry, the gods, but they are going to fuck you up. Like the child-eating goddess who would very much like to but just cannot, really cannot stop herself from guzzling your little daughter. Or like the gods who once demanded that three temples should be built for them in one night. But dawn, so goes the record, came too soon – and therefore these aforementioned deities appeared and smashed the scaf-folding up, like gang-rape footballers.

but nevertheless he does his best

So I began the crazy project of delivering Romy's body privately to the care of trained professionals. It was kind of the time desperation of being on a Game Boy with the battery run down to zero when you're poised to triumphantly enter the Hi-Score table. But obviously also worse. It was like time was gone, but also stretched. As gently as I could I dragged Romy, under the armpits, so that her legs flopped onto the floor beside the bed, then lowered her torso to the ground. It wasn't totally easy but still it was easier than dressing her in her dress again. That was like dressing a difficult toddler, like maybe a toddler who's overtired and isn't wanting to leave the dance class. Her arms were difficult and her legs were suddenly longer than seemed possible. Still, I dressed her in a way. But before we could leave I realised that first I also needed to make the room look neat. So I slipped off the bloodied pillowcase, and also the sheet with its vomit and saliva. I think if I could have spoken my voice would have been much lower, a proper bass, like when they put voices in slow motion in the horror flicks, or when the batteries ran down, in the tape recorders from my childhood. I didn't know what to do with this sheet and pillowcase and the previously mentioned sodden towel. I had a shopping bag but it, I now discovered, was punctured with two holes, and I also had my backpack but if I could avoid it my backpack would not get bloodied and smeared because then I would have to abandon it, which did not worry me for the backpack but for its possible future existence as evidence against me in case Romy did suddenly die. I looked at the bin in the bedroom. The bin in the bedroom was a bucket of stainless steel. But in the bathroom the pedal bin contained an unused plastic liner, neatly folded. With my hand inside, I made it unfurl, like those bags for picking up dog shit. Then gently – maintaining the bag unfurled – I squashed the pillowcase and sheet inside it, and then the bloodied towel, but the bag was now gaping open and the blood was very much visible. So I took the shoelaces from my sneakers. In my worry and terror I couldn't tug the laces out: the laces stuck, the laces were dirty, and so I scrabbled at the interlacing and was going to cry. Finally two laces hung from my hands. My feet sort of wallowed slackly in my soft shoes. I strangled the bag with my laces, then gently placed it on the floor. And I know that in some way the theft of a sheet and pillow-case and towel was definitely a crime, and a crime that no doubt would be discovered, but it also seemed quite mini-ature, the kind of crime that just leads to something extra on your credit card – and this was definitely a better crime than the discovery of blood and then the consequential thinking on the part of the authorities. But with the sheet removed I now also noticed that not only the pillow but the mattress had this formless stain, a sort of horrible discoloration. It was like nothing I'd ever seen. I can't compare it. It's like trying to compare kapok, or tundra. That's how simply a kind of formlessness can infiltrate a life. And in these situations I think my mother would always say that you should just do the best you can do because that's all that anyone can expect, and so I decided that I would try, which meant that I would turn the mattress upside down. But a mattress is bulky. And I am only small. I do mean this. I am no Gorilla Monsoon, or Brutus Beefcake. Whenever I see a personal trainer, which is not often, they tend to regard me with tender awe, the way ordinary people regard ill-fated dwarves, for in the end everyone must consider their place in the endless chain of being. When moving a mattress, therefore, I sweated and heaved. I manipulated the dense sprung mattress so that it moved through a nondescript circle. I curled it up over itself where the mattress stalled, for a moment, on the crest of its sodden wave. Then it collapsed from under itself and flopped to horizontal. I dressed it again in the duvet. Which meant that the problem remaining in the four minutes I had left before the housekeeper returned was to try to manoeuvre Romy's body out of the door and into my car in a way that looked as normal as I could manage. First I went to the basin in the bathroom and tried to scrub my fingernails, but it seemed to have no effect. I still needed the toilet very much but this was no longer an option. Nothing in this room could ever help me again.

& disappears from the bloodied scene

I wonder if because this is the era of mass calculations is maybe why I managed the situation. There are so many calorie counts and fitness reps and email checks in the average day that in fact it's much less strange, this manoeuvring of bodies, than you might think. It's just a different way of thinking tasks through in detail. I dragged Romy to the threshold. I tried to do this gently but in the end of course I didn't really. Then I was having to make sure that I could hold her up to about the level of my shoulders and I was regretting suddenly the many hours of news aggregators and YouTube videos. The entire history of my wasted time seemed sad to me, like it turned out to be a menace where no menace seemed to be visible, and I berated myself that, vigilant as I always was for signs of menace, I had not noticed that the true menace was right there, when I had been doing nothing more than just existing. It was daylight and this isn't an easy condition for introducing a comatose body upright into a car. I was also thinking that in my usual attraction to the taller woman I had possibly overreached myself. But still, the maid was gone somewhere, to call her son or just stand and look at the cars on the motorway while rolling a brief cigarette. No one else was there. For one moment, Fate was off buying itself a burger or apricot juice. I was trying to open the passenger door of my car, and I could see the entire sequence of future events unfold and then it was like those moments in the stories of the saints when the sage who has lived all his life in the desert or maybe forest receives a lunatic bath of light, a deep revelation. I would like to call this vision love, or something like it. It was just as if very sleepily I could feel my wife breathe beside me and again I thought I was going to cry but I gradually didn't. There were a few dead trees around, possibly palms, and they were making dry clickings; the palmettos were a sequence of old clocks. A brand of butterfly I thought was long extinct seemed to shudder past on a sweltering breeze. I pushed Romy inside, with my hand over her head, very gentle, like a halo. Then a shoelace loosened on the bag that I was holding and the towel became visible, a slack red wet dense smear. I thought that the whole thing was going to fall open and it made me panic but in the most fragile way it paused. I sort of slung the passenger belt over Romy and fixed it and shut the door. And I was walking round the car and was just sort of paused when I started to shake. I couldn't easily match my hands to what I wanted them to be doing. I suppose, I told myself, this happens. This shit happens. Then I realised that Quincy was regarding me from a cigarette break. Because there's no reason why a life should not come complete with a laugh track, none at all. Although I say *cigarette break* but of course I have no idea. She was just standing there, at the restaurant door, and she was starting up this middle-distance conversation.

— Want a cigarette? she said.

— Sorry? I said.

— Want a cigarette?

— I don't know.

— You don't know?

— I mean no.

We paused on this obviously not satisfactory conversation. I was hoping it would mean she'd stop but she didn't.

— What's your name? she said.

— My name?

It's sometimes useful to look like me, or at least the way I look to certain people, which is younger than I am – I have this face that's wide-eyed and also innocent, and this was one of those occasions when it had its useful aspect. So I just stared at her. I let the silence enlarge itself until it began to freak her out.

— Well. No harm done, said Quincy.

And she wandered away in this weird dazed perplexity while I was left in a state of envy or melancholy for her condition as a blissful and morally unstained employee, even if this state of mine was also still totally panic. By which I mean: was it right for me to be so punished? Events will become much worse but still, I think it's right to posit this question now. All I'd done was wake up – for the very first time in my life – beside a woman who was not my wife. Is this so untoward? I really didn't think the grand things are real – like murders and death and destruction – it never occurred to me that such things could really happen in a life, and now that something like this was happening it was making me amazed and also confused. Yes, I think it was about then that the first inkling began to occur to me – like the way you see a cat drift through some amateur porn footage and just sit there, it occurred to me as backgroundly as that – that I might be doomed. It was like the moment you look up in the air at some distant passing plane and just think for a sad moment that its engines might possibly be failing. I really did feel that this was unfair. I dislike harm in all its forms. I became a vegetarian because I had a vision of a bleeding cow, stripped of all its skin, and bleeding, and bleeding from the eyes. My favourite meal I ever had was this vegetarian goose dish which I appreciated above all for its noble ingenuity. I am trying to teach myself the banjo. Reading want ads makes me sad. *I have no meanness in me.* Whereas just make sure, Fate was telling itself, as it contemplated the picture, like a connoisseur, that no level spot of ground isn't trampled over with blood. I don't think this is an exaggeration. It fits the facts as I see them. I would have preferred it if Fate had concentrated more on the future of – I don't know – Aldebaran but it seemed that no, it preferred me. And in response I would like to say that this was in no way fair. Or I mean, no, this is what I was thinking. Elsewhere they are in their black ship somewhere, your enemies, the pirates are floating out there in the port, and drinking champagne. They are in the dark tanker. That is everyone else. But you are here and you are on your own. And you are no longer into the poetry of the Buddhist sages, or movies filmed on hand-held cameras or whatever. The whole culture is not the point. It is no longer yours – the culture. Because now, against your will, you have undergone a metamorphosis. I was feeling suddenly empty, like I was the Windsor Plantation that with just one careless cigarette gets suddenly converted and becomes the Windsor Ruins. I was pulling out of the car park in a car whose steering, I was now thinking, was shonky, and needed to be seen to, before something went haywire on the road and then I died, but if this was a problem it was not as much of a problem as the possession of an unconscious girl with whom you may be illicitly in love. And I was saying to myself: Kid, you are currently the least talented gangster in the world. Or, in other words, you were always way-out innocent. Your mother used to say it was your sweetest characteristic. And now look at you.

into another world

And so it happens that someone falls from a window or into the sea and into another world. They just fall and are transported. Like my friend Wyman who one day woke up and discovered that his life had made him superfat without him quite understanding how, so that in his anguish he just cried out in supplication to the Virgin and any other deity whose name he could remember, even though of course there were many reasons why Wyman should be so lavish in his size, reasons which Wyman preferred to ignore – namely the penchant he had for Wuxi-style soup dumplings and disco fries, or a meal consisting of LaMar's Donuts as a final flourish after three Schmitter sandwiches – not to mention the demise of his legal career, and the garish side effects of his various uppers and downers . . .

an occurrence possibly more normal than it seems

In fact, the more I thought about it, as I drove to the hospital with Romy slumped beside me, and I kept putting my hand to her mouth as if to silence her but really to check that she was still continuously breathing, the truly strange thing is that when you wake up in the morning you do generally find things exactly where they were the previous evening. That's the deeper freak-out or at least it should be. Because in sleep or more precisely in dreams you find yourself, or at least you think you do, as the zaddiks of sleep description have observed, in a state fundamentally different from wakefulness, and when you open your eyes an infinite presence of mind, or rather quickness of wit, is therefore required in order to catch everything in the same place you left it the evening before. Waking up, I just mean, is such a terrifying state that it's a wonder anyone survives it. So easily you could be taken back to high school, or accused of an impossible crime, or discover that your wife seems to be now a shy Alsatian. Not that everyone wakes up every morning as a donkey or beetle but still, everyone will some time – because to wake up as a donkey doesn't always mean you wake up feeling groggy in your new big flappy ears, or turkified and in possession of six scimitars. It can happen in whatever hotel you pass by every day, with just the merest inflation of a thought balloon – and there you are, in bardo. In fact it's not even necessary to, let's say, wake up beside a girl who is bleeding from the nose and unconscious. It can be even smaller than that, I was thinking. Recently it happened to me more and more – I would wake and feel just minutely transformed, simply by waking beside my wife, with a miniature dog between us. I understand, to you this is possibly not so psychedelic. But was I really so wrong? Show me the married man who is still living at home with his parents and neurotic dog, who is putting his clothes in the wicker tub of a laundry basket, as he has done for more than thirty years, so that his mother can once a week take them downstairs to the washing machine, and then tell me if you think it might not be acceptable for this man to be given over to feelings of catastrophe. Not to mention other complications of hospitality which I will come to very soon. At this point it's only important to consider how this was not the basic situation that my ambition would have imagined for its future self. That's maybe why every day now I woke up and was just dazed by reality, like any cartoon character who is supine after a fight, with many dingbats circling his bulldozed head.

especially for a dauphin or delfino

The only thing that's made me unlike other people is that me I think much more. It was because of such excessive thinking that in my family I was adoringly known as a prodigy. But when you think more than other people, although that difference might seem small, it can end up enormously expanding and you finish with different results. It certainly meant that I felt just slightly separate from the world – whenever I saw an object, the consciousness that I saw it remained between me and it, like a halo, preventing me from ever knowing it directly – and that's a dismal condition to inhabit. All I'd ever wanted was to get on in the world! – that was the only glory I had in mind. And in this I was only being faithful to the values of my family. I think every family has its myths and ours was that really anything was possible. My mother assured me every day that I could do great things, like she was my astrologer. We were the courtiers of the inner life! I don't mean that we were super-rich or the owners of vast factories and estates, but we were definitely among the powerful, those with sparkling waters in the refrigerator and unusual fruit from the supermarkets. Obviously as usual on the outskirts of other countries there were wars – small wars, absolutely, but wars nevertheless – in which our armies were involved, but they were far away and so for us instead it was the time when everyone was owning strange pets, not quite possums or small lemurs but almost, and meanwhile it was incredibly chic to eat small pastries imported from various locations, and in every garden people hung those elegant paper lanterns. While me I was a prodigy. I know because my mother said so. In book-stores she told the assistants that my reading age was hyper-advanced, then she bought me histories of the pharaohs and I read them all. In the luminous pharmacies and department stores, people always smiled at me, and I believed very much that when they smiled they did it because they liked me. What happened next was that the money of my parents bought my education at a secluded school, and later a secluded university. Afterwards, because I was a devoted son, I worked in an office in the city. I suppose what I'm trying to say is that everything was very soft and delicious. The juggernaut of meaning, let's say, was not parked heavily on our lawn. When I married – and we married very young, my wife Candy and I – we remained living at home, just as my parents preferred. You see? I always wanted to be a pirate and I think I basically was, if by pirate you mean someone who has everything they want. So OK, I had no eyepatch or cutlass, I wasn't truly a corsair, not in the clothes, but everything I wanted

I got. Before school every morning my mother styled my hair with a hairdryer and delicate brush, as a servant might have cosseted the curls of the inbred Habsburg prince in his knickerbockers, the prince with his outsize chin. But if this seems like a basic paradise with fountains and gentle rills I should also add that such happiness rarely remains happiness for long, so that in fact at the moment when you are realising that what you feel is happiness it is probably transforming itself into something much more slithery, whether you know about this transformation or not – the way a demon might extend his slithery arms, or you might open the back door one morning and not notice the cat entering menacingly below your gaze. I was possibly seven when my mother said to me that there was no one who made her laugh more than I did. Would you like to be such a dauphin? I do not think so. It's lovely to be the only child – it gives you privileges, the privilege of being adored, of being the only one there, and if that happens it does last your whole life, I think, or at least it has for me, nobody can do anything but take care of you, that is the way I was and this is the way I still am, just as also it means that whereas for everyone who has siblings, which is nearly everyone, the issue of superiority is a very important one, the issue of who is better and who is more loved, instead I have always been more equable, serene in my own serenity, as if Buddha had been born right here in these delightful suburbs, just contemplating the monkey-puzzle trees and mechanical sprinklers: yes, all of that is true – but still, to be the dauphin has its disadvantages. My mother drove me to school every day and while we drove I entertained her with my quips. What a weight for a child to bear! That's why when I talk, I still tend to talk very hyper. To be destined for higher things has this effect. You find yourself in some silent isolation tank, apart from other people – like you're training to go into outer space and there you are, alone with your dizziness and nausea.

who lately has been anxious about his achievements

But then, of course, everything that once seemed grand in conception soon seems only small, the miniature realisation of a dream that itself was not ambitious enough at the moment it was first conceived: like, for instance, I don't know, the freeway system in LA with its beautiful intersections – and this dream of my higher glory was no different. I got older, and there was no glory visible. I did not, let's say, *impose*. If someone walked towards me, when walking down a street, I was always the one to move aside and into the wet gutter. In the local bars and mescal diners, no one nodded to me or knew me by my name. I was like a trick of Photoshop, the way I tended to be camouflaged by my surroundings. It made every day a trial because in the end it's important to have a certain sense of self, I don't think that's an outlandish proposition. In fact, such outlandish propositions, and other general maxims on the way to live a life, were why in the end one morning when I woke up and once again, as so often, discovered myself in this unreal state which did not in any way match up with my ambitions, I subsequently realised that I could not do this any more. I could not continue wasting or losing so much time. For a long time now I had been meaning to write to a friend in the country. My friend Shoshana had married, and moved into the provinces, and subsequently Shoshana was obviously sad. Her husband, she said, did not understand her, and she was imploring me for pity. But me I shied away from the sad, in general. In general, I preferred the glad. I sat down to write to her and suddenly I could not, and for the same reason that I could not write Shoshana a consoling email I also that very day walked out of my office and did not ever come back. How could I write with any consolation if there was no sincerity? That was the question which perplexed me. For in the end if you are destined for greatness it's a worry if it seems that greatness has passed you by. I was worried that I had never found the true form for all my gifts – and certainly that form was not, as my mother and father assumed, the world of the office and its liquid financial vocabulary. I mean, think about it. In my impressions of the world I am super-subtle. Were I ever to be a superhero, I would be a superhero of thinking.

MY MOTHER
Let's not try to analyse everything to death, shall we, just this once?

ME
But what else can I do?

And it was out of consideration for this anxiety that I made the determined decision to respect such inner grandeur and leave the world of work. Or the world of as they say *steady work*. Instead I wanted to pursue my dream of art. Exactly what form that art would take, I did not definitely know. What I knew was that I needed to resign from this outer world. After all, it was the time for it. Others around me were being made unemployed every day. So why shouldn't I make myself unemployed of my own volition?

& unemployment

And yet I did have to admit that I could understand why my parents were now concerned. Gradually, I felt it too. I have been a son for ever, it has been my best career, which is why I say with some authority that one problem of being a son is to persuade others of your worth. As the weeks went by, it didn't seem like I'd chosen the ideal time to begin a new vocation. Each morning with amazement I watched the busy people filling the pavements with their cortados and umbrellas and other accessories. Perhaps as a result of this general panorama I also returned to the hospital for another short period of rest, the kind where they give you pills to restore you to your former self. It always seemed to work and this time was no different. I came back home and while for the moment Candy, abetted by my mother and father, was supportive of my ambition, we all agreed that I should have other ways to spend my time. So to keep me extra busy we bought a dog. The dog had very sad eyes. While Candy went to work in the city, where she looked after the international financial affairs of a charitable and radical organisation, I took this dog to puppy class or also walking in the park. Or I made conversation with the woman beside the road selling fruit from laundry bags. The sky was grey and it was like the sky wanted to keep on raining and so it did. It was a cold but monsoon season. As for me, I suddenly had no salary or status at all. I could understand what our puppy felt like. Although sure, I had my activities. I don't think I'd realised how much work you could invent for an average day, what with washing and talking to the plumber and developing the dog's personality. I was hyperactive and a slacker both together – a hyperslacker! And although very little of my time was watching Troma studio trailers or surf videos, I knew that my father wasn't quite convinced by my concentration. Maybe nor was I. I had developed this problem thing in conversations of getting maybe too emotional. My mode right now was the *rant*.

— Why, I said to my mother, — does everyone say that rant is such a bad word? Isn't it good to have high expectations?

— Perhaps, she said. — I just don't know. You shouldn't be going making youself so sad.

— Who made me this way?! I exclaimed.

When I woke up every morning now strange beings were advancing. All the thundercats and griffons I had never believed in were yawning and stretching their unwashed wings in the empty air, and in fact they appeared not just when I woke beside Candy in the dawn, but also at other moments when I tried to distract myself – whenever, for instance, I was taking my many drugs to keep me excitable or serene, but also in more healthy places, like when I was on my bike in the early mornings on my way to the private gym and spa complex. For by the way I do think that biking should happen more often – to protect the environment, definitely, but also because it has an old-world charm. And me, as I think I have mentioned, I like to preserve the outmoded things. That time will destroy all things is something that upsets me every day.

harried therefore by a sense of catastrophe

If we posit an ideal heaven, and in that heaven place Candy, answering questions about me, I think she would almost definitely argue that this catastrophe thinking was just an unfortunate illusion of such a mood, my whole dark cafard thing. This melancholic mood she tended to see as the fault of my inheritance.

> CANDY
> You slept all together in your parents' room! You slept beside their bed in a sleeping bag! This is not in fact normal, my darling, my kook.

But after all I was the heir. I existed to continue our major line. So what if the heir was screwy? And so what if our throne was just a carriage clock with foliage engraved on the face, a prayer shawl and an escritoire? As I said, we were not the super-rich. We were the moderate rich and that's a more delicate form of existence. With such a burden on me, no wonder that I suffered attacks of terror in the night, so that I would sleepwalk and be returned to our bedroom by my father. Always I was warding off disaster – I had many lucky charms that I carried with me, just as in the evenings, when some light was still seeping under the curtains from the garden and the street lights, and in the twilight the orange netting of my soccer goal in the garden was developing into a bruised green, I would sit up in my bed and pray. These prayers were very detailed lists of worries and future problems. I wanted my million gods to concern themselves with my music practice, or sports reports, or perfect my knowledge of verbs in any language on which I might be tested.

— My problems are psychosomatic! I once said to Candy.

— Psychosemitic, added Candy.

My prayers were very fearful of the world's approaching disasters. If whatever power was in the heavens would solve these problems or avert these disasters, I would promise the heavens my good behaviour. I do not think I am alone in this condition. I performed some good deeds, others went forgotten, and in this way the undone good deeds piled up. Still, I kept on promising. I was loaded down with unfulfilled promises. The last I still remember was a series of good deeds I promised to do, if it didn't rain one afternoon. It didn't rain – but I still didn't perform the good deeds. And yet I went on praying. What I'm saying is that I was born into my family as previous heirs might have been born into some eighteenth-century library, with all the marble busts of previous luminaries and forefathers gazing down on me with blank concern, even if my own were pedlars from the eastern shtetls or yeshiva accountants. It's definitely true that my parents scared quite quickly – whether the cause was drug-taking in the young, allergic reactions to nettles, correct dress etiquette for bar mitzvah celebrations in the ballrooms of grand hotels, the traffic systems of global cities to which they had never been. To them the world was fearsome even if that world was where they wanted their son to be, and I suppose it's therefore only natural to inherit such a feeling, a general tone in which you see things – that everything's unknown and ever so delicately hostile. I go outside and things upset me very fast. In fact I don't think that's so mad when you consider that outside the fascists are enjoying a boom, and everyone hates everyone. But still, perhaps without such phenomena I would have been the same. I was like that figure in the old dialogue, crying out always: *Madama Morte! Madama Morte!* I gave up therapy because I was scared my therapist would die. Even the dogsitter makes you very sad, said Candy once. And it was true. I suppose it has to be admitted that it's a problem. But then just think how lonely people can be! Our dogsitter is a lovely man but when I sometimes think of the life he lives, to be with the cats and dogs whom other people love and yet love them in some secret way like maybe a mistress loves a husband – I mean there is something secret and unregarded about his love, when perhaps he loves these animals more than anyone else, but still he is forced to leave them, he is forced to say goodbye in a totally casual way, the way a woman might say goodbye to the love of her life, sitting at a cafe table with some acquaintance from the bureau, as if she can hardly remember his name: when I think about him, I do think that this existence is a sad one. I can't help it. When I step into the world, all I hear is a catalogue of sighs.

but catastrophes do recede

But also it was true that as often as I perceived disaster it somehow also receded. Mornings over this maritime city often began powdery and blue. Even as I drove to the hospital, Romy's breathing became deeper and more regular and I therefore thought that, while unpractised in medical signs, surely this had to be better than nothing. It surely indicated life, rather than death. And this habit of life returning was not for me unusual. All my fears were undone by day that I had woven in the night. I liked to fall asleep considering the moment of my death, but whenever I tried to think what it would mean to be able to say the sentence *I am dying*, as in some baroque tragedy, the truth imposed itself on me that in order to be saying such a sentence it would have to be just ever so slightly in the future to be true, and therefore, at the moment of its saying, not true at all. *Madama Morte! I die, I die!* You see the basic problem. Everything I ever thought might be irrevocable somehow beautifully dissolved. Just as in the end I left Romy – sedated, true, but definitely alive and out of mortal danger – in the care of trained professionals, and my subsequent getaway from the hospital was very stately and unperturbed. As usual the world was powdery and blue, like a rococo miniature. I was driving underneath the tree canopy and behind those trees were mansions and their many vehicles, gently arranged on the drive. It was the world as I always had known it, when being driven by my parents to music lessons or football practice or the first ever parties of my youth, the ones that ended at dawn with everyone staring at each other calmly in a field, feeling tired. That was how I always lived, out here on the outskirts of a giant city: the world occurred to me as a series of impressions seen from the windows of a car. Previously, there were chauffeurs: in this landscape, we made do with parents instead.

MY MOTHER ON MY FATHER
He's not a chauffeur, cookie. He's your father.

That atmosphere probably makes the world overall a very difficult place to enter. If everything is happening with the sound cut out, it probably makes it easier to imagine that scenes can be deleted and rearranged, when in fact they maybe possibly cannot. Further out were the motorways and warehouses and the hypermarkets with their empty parking grids painted onto flat surfaces of tarmac. This was the landscape in which I made my getaway, a getaway which did not resemble any frantic speedchase I had ever seen on screen. Because according to the cinema theory, as recorded in those films with the dash-mounted cameras and synthesiser music, a getaway is where the reflected lights slide up and off the windscreen and you go careering through the zigzags of the street lights of LA – ballooning and bursting security fences, upending squad cars, *and all that*. When in fact getaways are much quieter than anyone thinks. You just move on out of the hospital car park in the early morning having left a girl at reception, while still worrying a little for the state of your steering, and no one wishes to delay or blame you at all. And I was glad of that because while I would have been happy to have stayed with Romy if she had been in any major danger, like certainly I would have done that and taken the consequences as any other hero or giant-slayer, still if I could avoid those consequences then I definitely would take that opportunity. What I wanted was this unusual situation to entirely and totally subside, just melt like a vitamin tablet fizzing in a glass of water. And in one way it was definitely possible to argue, in the manner of some warehouse supervisor with her clipboard and radio mic, that so far everything had gone very well. On my way from the hotel to the hospital no police or other spies had stopped me. At the hospital itself, there had been no insistence on any exchange of names. This all seemed very promising and like the ideal state was possible. Absolutely, I would be monitoring Romy's progress and doing everything I could to make her happy. In secret I would visit her with the glossies and other treats, and definitely we would be discussing our history and future. Right now, however, I wanted to reduce my life back down to something no bigger than a tape cassette, or memory stick. Although of course to do this I had a final task and the execution of this task was making me perturbed – for while I may have looked like I was calm, inside me I was as ever like an undertow in the big deep dark sea, like I had grand glowing jellyfish and floating fish skeletons of anxiety. I was trying to imagine the conversation I would have with

Candy – because I have these internal gifts of hyper-vision, like I have this gift for imagining other ways in which a scene might happen, even when it has happened, or is happening – and yet somehow it seemed difficult to imagine how precisely I would offer explanations. I could not quite envision it, and this absence of any explanation made me anxious and also a little furious, not only at myself for creating such a problem, but also at the world for always demanding so many confessions. I wish confessions did not ever need to happen. Confessions, it seemed to me, were a total illness of our time.

until blood pauses him once again

Before I could continue in this way of thinking, however, these anxieties were overtaken by a single and present anxiety – and that anxiety was blood. I was bloodied, totally. When I'd parked the car at the hospital I'd looked across at Romy and in that one moment of quietness I noticed that while the bleeding from her nose or mouth seemed to have stopped, which I assumed could be only good, still there was a selection of bloods sort of smeared across her face. And the reason I was now considering this image once again was that the only way of getting Romy into reception, after which she could be tended by doctors and nurses and surgeons, had been to gather her under the shoulders and lift her out of the car, because although she was breathing and conscious she was still very much in a narco state – and as I did this it was once more very obvious that a body was a larger thing than anyone can reasonably be expected to manoeuvre, which meant that in the end we kind of shuffled tenderly and gracefully, cheek to cheek, on the pavement of the forecourt towards the gently opening and closing electric doors. We performed this stunt until a paramedic, who was smoking a single cigarette of leisure, in what I imagined was a state of opiate paradise, very generously – because I know how much such minutes of leisure must be prized, in the middle of a busy work shift among the saws and bones and pulleys and all the other ambulance accoutrements – helped me to locate some stretcher, on which Romy then entered the hospital. But therefore these few difficult moments had meant that there was now blood not only on my cheek where it had rested against Romy's but also on my hands and teeshirt – and it was this gunk that was now worrying me, in so far as I was overall worrying how it was I could return home to my parents and to Candy, my adored wife, and resume everything that I had left behind. Because while simply not returning until the morning is one definite sign to be explained, this is going to be much more difficult if also you return with blood sort of steeped in your clothes. That's what I mean by catastrophes being endless. Every time you think the day of judgement has been averted, it returns. And yet, however, you can still avert it, after all.

& so he detours to a superstore

For there are advantages to living in the modern world, and in particular the suburbs of this modern world, and one of them is that the suburbs everywhere are an expanse of buildings for shopping. Also these stores are very welcoming, you do not even need to seek them out – instead they announce themselves with the crazy bright joyfulness of a collection of very tall signs, that's all you need to see to know that soon you will find some business park, or collection of inflated stores. The graphic sign in space – that's basically the architecture of this landscape I call home. And in these buildings there's really nothing you can't discover if you just try hard enough, you only need to enter them with the appropriate strength and determination to succeed. In fact this task is often made easier for you than this might imply because inside there will be men and women who are pleased to help you, who may even approach you with a smile – and it's definitely true that a smile brightens up any day, that's just a fact of life. They will come up to you and ask you something like *May I help you, sir?* And underneath these lights I did think as I stood there locating the aisles for clothes that the best way for anyone to help me would be to ignore the fact that just possibly I had gouts of a woman's blood on my otherwise also crumpled clothes. But then again, they did – because that's how they've been trained and it's very useful. That's what it's like inside these superstores and I think that they are responsible for some of the happiest moments of my life, whether it was in the toy stores where there were so many games that the innocent kid had no idea what to do with them all, or the hypermarkets with imported food where all the sauces I could ever want were lined up for me, waiting. Because I like sweet things very much, and especially I like the sweet sauces – the red ketchup and the yellow mustard, and other liquids and suspensions – but suddenly there did not seem enough difference between the red of blood and the red of red sauce and so with purpose I moved among the aisles, which is an easy thing to do because these places are like geometry, they are very organised and patterned – as if someone has taken one mini bodega, the type where the window is a flat arrangement of many cereal or cracker boxes or candy, and then multiplied it zillionly until it's gigantic. Then also the objects talk to you very much – *Let me tell you the story of how I am made!* they say. *Let's consider ways to be kind to our surroundings* – and I appreciated that, the way each object is its own sign. I appreciated the way they had of advising you and hoping for a better world. In that caressing state I bought a grey marl teeshirt and a very blue bright pair of jeans. By which I suppose I also mean that just this once the usual effort to curate the way I looked had to be for a moment abandoned. Because I try very hard to care about my clothes, even if lately, if I wanted new clothes, then Candy had to buy them – and while I know that at this time so many people have unusual household arrangements, still, I did care about this, after all: I did feel that my identity was in doubt. But in the end the desire for style was greater than the desire to be me, because to style yourself, I sometimes think, is the only way of proving to yourself that somehow the future will be OK. But for now the future was this pair of jeans and grey marl teeshirt which could have benefited, let's say, from at least some quirkiness in the stitching. I left the superstore and returned to my waiting car where I undressed, which isn't easy when you're sitting with the wheel in front of you – you have to wriggle and do strange shimmyings which to an outside observer must look comical indeed. Yes, there I was in the midst of an endless grid for absent cars, and as I paused with my teeshirt off that I used to wipe my cheek with the cosmetic aid of the rear-view mirror, I was struck as I always was by that sad look your torso has when you've only got jeans on – a sadness I suppose made more sad if you've just left a girl whom you care for very much in hospital, but equally you do care about your wife, as much as if not more than this girl who is currently in a hospital bed, and now you are sitting alone in a car park with your wife almost definitely waiting for you, in the company of your parents. I suppose this is reasonable, to find the situation sad. I don't know if I any more knew. Picture a blue expanse, then double it, that's where I wanted to be. I had this image of a place that had no humans in it – as if you pinned up a flag or sail against a wall like a windjammer and then let yourself look into it, as into the deep blue disorganised sea. That's how tired I was, how woebegone – but also I could see the cosmic argument. Even at my moments of great pleasure, always I could sense a coming insurrection and revenge and punishment. Because one thing I do believe is that people should rise up against me. They should overthrow me, like they would overthrow some psychopathic plantation heir. Had I been able to exist in two places at once, I would have carried out the punishment myself.

before returning home & lying to his wife

If this ability to live with her husband's parents has made you assume that Candy was a quiet girl then I assure you this is not correct. My wife is very cool – and I think it shows in a certain downbeat sarcasm. Her vibe is tough.

Candy trained every morning with a punching ball. She had dumb-bells which I could not lift. And I thought then and still think now that this was very cool. That's basically all you need in the way of a description. She is tall, and her beauty is austere. It is high cheekbone, and delicate eyes. But when she does drunk she also does a kind of lowborn hair-flipping in the kid-from-a-movie manner, which always is good for amusement. Easily she could go to some party in a slap bracelet and rag dress and flats and also some pastel plastic rosaries like she was the queen of the supernatural, a white chick Pamyu Pamyu. She has this smell about her which is like if you imagine the most carnally elegant thing, a sort of lubricant stink that's also patchouli or rose. For Candy therefore the atmosphere in our house was definitely more old-school than she would have liked. She no more wanted a dauphin for a husband than she wanted recipes from my mother, or to be stared at very quiet by my father, in his ancient pop-star glasses with their yellow lenses. What I'm trying to say is that I had no high hopes for this conversation with Candy. I saw no tearful scene of forgiveness. My only hope was to invent another world. Therefore as soon as I had passed through the fake white pillars guarding our ancestral suburban house, and I was standing there in the hall where Candy was also standing, I began to talk very fast, partly because I think without fast talk we are nowhere always but also because whereas Candy was standing there saying something ordinary like –

CANDY
Where were you? I had Hiro call you too but he –

I had my own plans for how this thing between us would now be scripted and I felt it was important to immediately begin with the absolute invention. You have to, I think, if you want to succeed in these sometimes difficult situations.

ME
So I was at this party, but I felt just really *down* so with some other people we went to another party but I left that also because it was making me sad too, and on my own I went to a cafe and just sat there, like in some cafe, and had a coffee.

CANDY
All night?

ME
I didn't know if I'd wake you and I was just: sort your head out, bro, keep cool.

CANDY
You didn't think I'd be awake already if you weren't home at like six in the morning?

ME
Dude, I truly am sorry. You are totally in the right. I was just like feeling totally I don't know *benighted*.

CANDY
Benighted?

ME
That not a word?

That was how I tried to preserve the plausible and the real
and I don't think it was so bad. I'm not saying at all that
this was perfect but in the end there are always limits to
one's inventions. Each invention is followed by another,
and that's very tiring. Next, for instance, she was asking
about my change of clothes – for these of course were not
the jeans in which I had left the house the night before
and she was always sensitive to such things.

ME
A superstore?

CANDY
Sorry what?

ME
I thought it'd make me happier.

CANDY
What superstore?

ME
Out on the motorway, the twenty-four-hour one.

CANDY
So you are currently kind of freaking me out right now
because –

ME
But why?

CANDY
Because – if you just let me finish – either you are lying like some crazy person or you are in some kind of breakdown situation.

ME
Is it really so bad? Like really?

CANDY
You know it, no?

ME
Know what?

CANDY
This cannot happen for ever.

And it was like the way a wave uses the water in the sea – the way the wave moves but the water doesn't. That was how Candy stood there and was overtaken by her painful thinking. It passed through her, like a wave. And I felt for her because it's always painful when you doubt your confidence in other people. If she didn't actually say anything it didn't mean I couldn't imagine what it would have been if she had.

for lies are one way of inventing another world

But I was also thinking that nevertheless it was undeniable that such silence had its beauties. I had noticed this before. In my infancy I liked stealing from my mother. She used to keep a supply of stickers featuring international foot-ballers and other treats in her handbag, as bribes for her difficult son – which then meant that one day I realised that since she bought in bulk she wouldn't notice if gradu-ally I removed a chocolate bar, or single packet containing the portraits of my favourite soccer stars, the Brazilians, with their single names. Or I realised that even if she noticed she would never mention this out loud. I wonder if always this is what happens in the families of dauphins. There Candy was and she was willing me to find the tone or story that would allow us somehow not to mention my strange behaviour, or examine its real causes, to exist in a world beyond the actual, and I wanted to be worthy of that performance. At last I came out on –

ME

I'm just not happy. I think that's what this is.

And I was pleased because at that moment I could see she was relieved. Yes, I could see she was thinking that if we played it at that pitch then she could play it too, like we were in the nineteenth century and I had performed some difficult transposition of a bassoon piece to the trombone, or some such tour de force. I do mean tour de force. It's often not acknowledged how lying needs such total impresario talent. The problem with lying is that you are told not to think about the truth while you are lying, to believe the lie completely, but what else will you ever think about when you are lying except the fact that you are lying? There's really nothing else to think about, it imposes itself, absolutely, so that even as you begin your first speech you are considering its shadow speech, in which you tell the truth, and when you are then embarked on your second speech the shadow first speech is still there, but now accompanied by its twin, the shadow second. And that Candy understood it was a tour de force needed no more proof than that she was looking at me with such love. It occurs to me that in my family history there were other such performers, I mean people who could bend the world to their desire, like those hypnotists bend spoons. By this I do not just mean the strongmen like my father, who could found business empires, but also the more devious strongmen like my many uncles, among whom were those who found it useful to present themselves as kooks. And if this coincided with your wife discovering one of your secretarial affairs and preparing to leave you as in the case of Uncle Marvin, or that your wife, in the case of Uncle Milo, wanted another child, or other sundry catastrophes, then this couldn't be helped. In a similar way therefore in this conversation with Candy I very simply became the person I needed to become in order to make the lying plausible, which was therefore someone whose life was not going so well and who was depressed, which wasn't after all so difficult because in the end this is not a role that's unavailable to most people. And in particular it was available to me: being a) unemployed and b) often seething at home in my pyjamas with all the rank smells you care to mention. I think you can see how easy it is for such a subject to lie to his beautiful wife, to tell the world that he is in a deep unhappiness when really all along he is also contemplating the picture that is a naked girl bleeding from the face, or that same girl's face not bleeding but looking up at him with sweat on her nose and above her lips and the light beginning to filter through the curtains as she comes.

CANDY
Zezette, what's wrong?

ME
I think I might just always be about to cry? You know? I think I'm maybe I'm unhappy.

CANDY
With us?

ME
With – no, with everything. Not us.

& can happen very casually

Because, to put this another way, it turns out that in the perfect marriage where you are absolutely trusted there is no end to what you can do. For lying only distils its gorgeousness if you are doing it to the person who wakes up next to you every day, who believes they know your inner heart more than they know their own, that's the perfect person to lie to because only when you lie to someone like that can you create a perfect lie, the kind that opens out new possibilities of other lives and other worlds, as if you'd made a voyage to the moon in your own home-made jetpack. You just do something with panache and anyone who loves you will believe you, if they have no other reason not to – and most of the time they do not. Although the problem with lying is that if what I wanted to do was consign just one aspect of my life to unreality then I think I was mistaken. Unfortunately, it leaks all over the picture. Sure, terrible things may well be often said in conversation but much more terrible can be the way that nothing is said at all. In either case there will be consequences, so that what looked like nothing but silence and absence may well turn out to be a grand event. For on reflection I do have to also admit that it was the particular way that Candy and I constructed this nothing that was in fact important for the future story I have to tell. That there were no consequences in the immediate future turned out to be the darkest consequence of all for the genuine, more long-distance future. It was the way we silenced each other that had the explosive possibilities inside it. And I do say silence. Because let's say that however cool a person is, very few are the people who definitely enjoy the row and the argument. I am certainly not one of them. If what you want to film is sharpshooting in the bars of silent towns, with shotguns and other props, I am not necessarily the ideal star. Nor can I do the shouting in restaurants thing so very well – those scenes with women who upturn tables and scrawl lipstick on their faces like bloodstains or bad clowns. Such scenes make me scared. In fact, brawls scare me in every form they take. The only other person in the world who dislikes conflict like I dislike it is Candy and maybe this is one reason why we will love each other for ever. We prefer there to be silence between people, even though of course there is no such thing as silence, for even as you move your head or hand in a certain way you are offering communication – which is maybe why there are so many possible art forms, because while film is possibly the greatest if what you want to do is silence and the many truths of gesture, then also you need an art form made of words for all the elaboration of the inside thinking. Just one of the art forms is not enough to do the entire cosmology, the vast interior and the small exterior. And in this case the cosmology was how much truth a man must tell his wife, in the early and suburban morning of a giant city. I would not say I totally yet knew.

ME
You go to work all day and it's difficult –

Yes, the only problem is that lying has to be managed with care, and for a moment we were careless.

CANDY
I only do it for us – I mean – I just want you to have your space –

Suddenly this was a more difficult place for me to argue from and so I paused there. But also I did try to make the right sort of noise because I totally agreed with her.

She was in no way being cruel and in fact the opposite, which often happens. It was like my mother long ago berating me in some Chinese restaurant for not wanting the salt-and-pepper chicken feet when I had ordered them myself. But there I suppose I can be excused by my youth and inexperience. Almost definitely it was catastrophic harm that I was causing but I don't know if harm should be the only or even main criterion for judging any of one's actions: what about for instance glee or marvelling or simply the grotesque? For there it is. Lying is lovely. True, to make that discovery is also very troubling. If you have a desire for moral outcomes, if your aim is the most ideal society possible – and that is always what I try to achieve – then lying has its fearsome aspects. But it just happens very softly and fast, like I'd just discovered that all the leather-bound volumes along one wall of a stately library were false, and then the wall swings slowly open and you walk on through, into another book-lined room. Somehow, I was thinking, it was now a situation that was true and not true, at the same time. For once again Candy regained the acceptable tone.

CANDY

But maybe do you think you should get a job? Would that be good? Do you think you're just getting bored? Is it good for you to be around the house all day? I mean doesn't your mother get you down?

ME

Like a job like where?

CANDY

I've always thought you'd be a good teacher – like a good primary-school teacher and you'd work with kids and I think it'd just be great for you. You'd still have time for other things. I think you'd enjoy it.

ME

I think, no. I think no way.

CANDY

What's happening with your work?

ME

I'm not sure.

CANDY

You think that's why you're not happy?

ME

Is possible.

CANDY

Why don't you write a horror flick?

ME

A horror flick?

CANDY

Something with gore –

ME
You think?

CANDY
I want men bleeding from their eyes. Or at least I want something *happening*. Why doesn't anything ever happen? Like make a movie about a massacre?

ME
I don't think you can show it –

CANDY
You don't?

ME
I do not.

And so we chattered on. And once again catastrophe had receded, just receded into the blurred and pastoral distances.

even if the gore remains, as a token, or proof

Always I had felt about as moored to the world as that airship was moored to the landing stage on the Empire State Building – and that's probably to be expected if you live a life where catastrophes are infinitely postponed. To be a stevedore or farmer is no preparation for a life like mine, where the real is more like sherbet. That feeling is enveloping – so that even as I turned and Candy asked what I had on my teeshirt, I was not perturbed. I looked down and with a surging recognition, the way a surfer must recognise the wave that will pull her under and cause the wipeout to end her days, I saw that in my hurry I had simply put back on the teeshirt with which my evening had begun. It was, therefore, a teeshirt with a range of bloodied stains.

— That? I said.

— Uh-huh, said Candy.

— I don't know, I said.

And once again we paused there. As I said, we are no sharpshooters, Candy and I. We let the pause suspend itself, engorge itself. Because it's really not so hard, to ignore things. And so it was like – what was it like? It was like that story of the man who passed through Paradise in a dream, and had a flower presented to him as a pledge that his soul had really been there. And indeed, when he woke up, he held a flower in his hand. That's one sort of similar story – or no, this is what it was like. It was like the story of that prince in the eastern realms who once upon a time dreamed he no longer lived in his palace but in the city, and was very poor. In this new life of his, he had no servants or cooks. He only had a wife, who went out every morning to work as a sales clerk in some department store. They lived in a house in the suburb favelas of a giant city together with a single hound. His life was shanty town and barrio. And then one morning he woke up and was back there in his palace with his courtiers or flunkeys, while the second hand on his gorgeous watch was perhaps just describing a minutely more obtuse angle –

Well wow you just dozed off there for a moment, sir –

but the prince still in his heart knew that something, like definitely, had taken place. What happened therefore next is that he ordered the whole court entourage to go out driving with him in a minor motorcade, and sure enough when the SUVs entered the plastic outskirts of that giant city, with hotels and other details, he recognised a street. Calmly he left his limousine, where in the road a woman came up to him. And she said: *Zezette, where've you been all this time? Like what, you got arrested?* – How should he put it? the prince would say, years afterwards, telling this disturbing tale. – *Imagine that you are the* enfant terrible *who wakes up to discover that he is in fact the creation of some pen or quill or keyboard that he cannot see. That's how I would put it. It's not a good feeling at all. But enough of me. What this party needs is more negronis.* And so the story ends. I mean, it was like that, sure – this bloodstain: just back to front, or upside down.

2. UTOPIA

at which point his double Hiro

— Why did you get married if you're totally unhappy? said Hiro to me some time later in this neon epoch.

— I never said unhappy, I said. — I never used such a word.

— Talk to me, said Hiro. — Explain yourself.

— I had a vision, I said.

— What did the vision say?

— The vision told me not to get married, I said. — So I got married.

— Totally logical.

— It's not easy to get visions right.

— Maybe, said Hiro. — What kind of vision?

— A kind of voice? I said.

I did mention other complications of hospitality. As deftly as some tapas stooge presents you with a dish of chicharrónes without you knowing that you'd ordered, or a djinn appears in one of the old fables, Hiro had suddenly appeared in what you could comically call *my life*, and there he stayed.

is revealed in the suburban panorama

Everyone who describes anything has this problem of what stays and what doesn't. Walt Disney had this problem and so do I. In this little murder ballad there are some things which already exist that will play a part in its future – like Candy, and Romy, but some things do not yet exist, like firearms or the time since I have last seen any of the people I am describing. Some things have just arrived, like Hiro. And some things exist and will still exist, like the setting. The setting is the one permanent phenomenon. At night, Candy would say, I almost like it here, when there's just the street lights and the citrus smell of the garbage trucks, but in the grey days it can be very hard. Don't you think so, chico? I knew the lyrical problem she was describing. There's nothing less homelike than the place that is your home, a place of memories, of dejection, of pettiness, of shame, of deception, of misuse of energy, however much you try to feel affection for it. I think a lot of the difficulties some people have with life are caused by the fact that you only come from one place – or maybe that's only a problem if you grow up in this panorama, with autoroutes and quilted plains, but since nearly everyone grows up in a place like this the problem must be almost universal. Take your pick wherever on the globe you like, in Kabul or Santiago, the same landscape is there before your eyes. Because in fact most inhabitants of Kabul do not live precisely in that city but instead on its edges, where Kabul disintegrates into vast light and vacant streets, the kind where the pavement is listless and there are only a very few street lights, maintained by random generators in concrete huts. That's where most people are nowadays, and it means that when you travel to any city of your choice you can find yourself at home, just so long as you get out far enough, not too far but just enough. I think these places are the most beautiful in our time: the tennis centres, lorry depots, chain restaurants, and also the hyper-markets and wholesale units. But whether these places are good for happiness, I do not know, if you consider how much suburbia is also a kind of absence, without a focus or a centre, like the verdant So-Cal foothills, just a succession of high streets and outer roads. It's basically grass, or lichen, the way it spreads to fill in all the gaps between the rail lines and the autoroutes, just spreads itself with multi-lane parkways, burger kiosks, banks, pharma stores, crematoria, temples for various religions and other faiths, insurance offices. In such a place, it's only natural if the boredom tends to expand like cookie dough and stay there, a sort of sense that you cannot connect all the pieces of your life together – like when you're in an endless security queue at the airport and therefore have no way of going either forward or backwards, but must just simply submit. And if in particular what you want is people to live together, to live together and adore each other, which is always my ideal, that suburban vagueness is maybe not so good as a locale.

with his utopian instincts

In this story I have to tell, people try to live together, but mostly they're apart. In this story people try not to be separated by money or love but mostly they are. And yet we did try, after all. To take Hiro as an example: when he got a side of turnip dumplings in the Thai cafe by the tram terminus he shared them, and with enthusiasm, for not only did he talk utopia but he tried to make the world as charming as he could. Whenever we walked down the street, Hiro took my money and gave it to any tramp we happened on. And I was always very impressed by this because me, I give very little to the poor, not out of any selfishness but just because I find it difficult to know how to interact with the less fortunate. It tends to go badly when I do, because I cannot talk with the free abandon I employ when I'm alone. Like only recently I had been in a burger place at whose counter a woman was being asked by her many small children to buy them fries, and it was very obvious she was embarrassed by this problem that she could not afford to buy them all food, so she bought one miniature portion for the horde of them. And therefore when I came to purchase my own fries and chocolate milkshake, proudly I added the appropriate number of multiple fries to my order and brought them over to her table, where she looked at me in hatred. *They've already eaten?* she said with that total disgust intonation. So I retreated with my many fries and in my shame I ate them all, then hated myself for eating them. Utopia, I just mean, is not so easy to recreate, and it maybe showed in a certain manic quality also to Hiro's thinking – his letter-writing scheme to aid prisoners in the west, or a mobile kiosk for granitas, in flavours ranging from lavender to chilli. On one day when we had maybe drunk too much beer iced with imported orange soda, we even had a dream of an office for these schemes and went so far as to investigate one, in a building whose other occupants included any number of other businesses, like opera newsletters, foreign-language lecture bureaus, highly specialised travel agencies, small-time currency speculators, perhaps a private detective or two, because it's never good to be isolated from the world. Had there not been such difficult matters as rental payments, or insurance certificates, perhaps we would have taken it. I was thinking very often in this manner, as if really you could do anything you wanted if you only tried. Weightlessness was the element in which I lived – whether I considered Romy, or Hiro, or my basic unemployment. That's what I mean by these suburbs being a problem. A landscape like this tends to make the world as flimsy as those old movies where you see the hero romancing the heroine while driving, and behind them unwinds the pre-recorded road. And the further problem is that when you enter such an existence it's like when you return from a million miles away and are jet-lagged, and all the things you thought were import-ant just seem to have been not removed entirely but just slightly rearranged, like life is some espionage officer who enjoys playing with your mind – reordering the books when you're at the supermarket, taking out your garbage, until eventually you start to doubt your own reality.

& manic tone

Even if very possibly such unreality does perhaps improve your moral code, in that it makes things possible that other people might be inclined to ignore, like forming this gang that we then formed, this trio of Candy and Hiro and myself. Especially for instance my father and my mother did not quite understand, perhaps because for them the only desirable group was the very definite family. At home, there was one constant conversation –

MY MOTHER
And when do you think that Candy will be wanting children?

In this way my mother would sit down and just very casually discuss things with me, mainly in our favourite floating restaurant by the docks, eating pockmarked old woman's bean curd, and pickled duck's eggs with ginger sauce. And sure, if I could please anyone, I wanted to please my mother. She was always my best confidante, to whom all my secrets could be entrusted. But in no way had Candy and I begun to think about this possibility of children at all. We were beyond such usual thinking.

MY MOTHER
But of course you should do what both of you think is right.

ME
Uh-huh.

MY MOTHER
Talk to me. I am just trying to understand. You want to find yourself?

ME
Not quite.

MY MOTHER
So what then?

ME
What are you, Ma? Chang Apana?

MY MOTHER
Don't muddle me. Don't make your jokes.

The people as old as my parents – they understood nothing!
Because there are in fact many other ways of being together
that are not a family at all, but something more like a
troupe. And a troupe I think is a lovely and elastic thing.
Those who have never been in such a troupe have missed
one of life's most desirable experiences. It makes you feel
like nothing is ever boring because there's suddenly always
someone to talk to, it's absorbing like that, which has as
one consequence that you spend more money in general
at coffee shops and/or brasseries because the sitting in such
places becomes a total treat, the way you develop conversations and just generally consider the world situation, so
that the money you might spend is easily recompensed by
the amount of ennui that gets destroyed. That's how I tried
to explain things to my mother, even if according to her
such reasoning was only anxious or hysterical, and in
retrospect I can understand why she might have thought
that. I could sometimes think too quickly or impatiently –
not that thinking in itself is such a bad thing but it does

matter when it occurs. If you do it too much before an event, then either nothing gets done at all, or what does happen is in some way too loopy or inflated. But I only learned that later. For to have turned Hiro away, as I explained to my darling mother, would not have been possible according to my moral code. And after all: Hiro and I had *past*. We'd known each other since the smallest of infants, then throughout the stages of our education he had been my comrade and accomplice. This was partly because in these suburbs and sylvan idylls we were similarly prodigies, but also because to us mathematics or chess teams were equally dismally boring (— But don't you *want* to join in with something, sweetness? my mother had asked, when presenting me with a turquoise satin tracksuit as a corrupting bribe). Instead we were much more into the pharmaceuticals and narcotics. It brought us, as they say, *together*. I was basically Hiro's double. Although admittedly Hiro had more charisma. If we were a commentary duo, then I was the play-by-play and Hiro was the colour guy. But still, *double* was no exaggeration. Especially if you also considered the way we talked, all quick and chancy with a polyglottic drawl. So together we had planned our entrance into the adult world. I would say that this entrance had gone differently for both of us. Hiro flew out to the skyscraper districts of various harbour cities, in the manner of the success story. While me, I remained in these horizontal environs. Sure, I sometimes called Hiro my crazy friend but I didn't always know how seriously I meant this. (— All your friends are your crazy friend, said Candy to me once. — Dat's because they *are* crazy, gringolette, I replied.) Like I knew that he took the various drugs from weed to coke but this didn't mark him out as unique in this generation, just as I knew the rumours that swirled around him like winds blown from the trumpets of naked cherubim in the ancient pictures, that he'd eventually left his job out east because he'd spent some time at a rest cure or nervous retreat, like a nobleman with syphilis, but that didn't make me doubt him. Me too I had my periods of melancholy and stabilisers, but did that also make me crazy? And since Hiro was the person who had known me for longer than anyone except my mother and my father – who do not count as people who know you, being parents, and therefore existing in an orbit of knowledge and obscurity known only to them – and since such childhood friends are the ones you cannot say no to, they are the ones who when they want to re-enter your life you cannot refuse, I therefore did not refuse Hiro. As much as possible you must try to be *appealing*, is what I'm trying to say, and be as likeable as you can. Just as anyway: always Hiro had been as energetic as a dot-matrix printer. If his chest had been adorned in wool-knit jumpers with intarsia penguins I don't think anyone would have been surprised. Even when he was five, Hiro was inventive, and now that he was fully grown he was as loaded with wishes and plans as a musket is with grapeshot. I find that kind of personality just totally seductive. So one monsoon day Hiro arrived with a suitcase and installed himself in our spare room, and from then on we spent our days together – in the local dim sum cafes, the afternoon cinemas. Against the blank horizon, Hiro's silhouette stood out, like a cowboy in his ten-gallon hat doing tricks with silver pistols at the very far end of Main Street.

capable of world transformation

Not that Hiro did so much standing. His general posture was the *recline*. A small pot he kept with him contained his little contribution to the pharma economy: the antipsychotics recommended by his doctors, then pills he had bought online from high-rise compounds in other countries, herbal remedies – and this sometimes led to comical situations, like he would mistakenly take both sleeping pills and antihistamines, then sleep from midnight until morning, wake up, but still keep falling asleep, until finally he would wake for good just in time for a late supper with the family, and so to bed again. How ill precisely Hiro was, I did not know. To be taking such pills, for instance, in no way made him special among the people I knew. We were all of us ordering remedies off the Internet. If things seemed possible to Hiro that did not seem so possible to other people, I tended to find this only charming and not sinister. Like he would happily talk to strangers and offer to drive them out to the airport, little kindnesses like that. For why should a person always have to waste money on vast taxis? And therefore why should I judge such brightness as a craziness? Perhaps, absolutely, now that I am maimed and aged and all alone, I now think differently, but at the time I was trying very hard to make the world a better place. And so we continued buying drugs off the Internet for our private use and these increasing narcotic entertainments did make the way I thought perhaps a little blurred. I don't mean by narcotics the semi-precious items like peyote or crystal meth, which I tend to associate with ill health, but items you can find in your local general store like ketamine or uppers. They give you a sense of confidence which is really very important in your entrance to the adult world. For if your friends all dress like children, with their sneakers and sweatshirts and goofy hair, and so do you, this can definitely mean that the overall tone feels gruesome.

— The problem is not, said Hiro,— that the adults wish us harm.

— It is sadly not, I said.

— The problem, said Hiro,— is that they wish us only good. We are the first children who are everyone's dream children.

— Is not so good.

— Is not, he said.

To think of the problems that can occur to one person, or two! To be a troupe is so much safer. But of course such troupes cannot be maintained at every point in the day, not in this sadly serious era, so that when Candy wasn't there, which was of course the usual situation, when Candy went into the city to her office, her high office in the fraying clouds, Hiro and I continued the troupe as a duo. And often this duo was a seminar where we examined my moral philosophy.

— You, said Hiro, — are in one strange position.

— Say it, I said. — I can take it.

— Flighty with your only love, dependable with everyone else.

— Flighty?

— Is the truth, said Hiro.

It's true that Hiro is my best friend but I nevertheless didn't think that he was right, or not right entirely. I knew, of course, why he said it. Romy had called me the day she left the hospital, and immediately I had gone to see her. Naturally I was very relieved that she was OK, but I would say the greater emotion was that I was once again excited, as I always was in Romy's presence – how quickly feelings succeed each other! – so that just as recently I had been terrified of total catastrophe, I mean of Romy's death and the death of my marriage and the total wipeout, now that such a scenario was no longer happening it was as if it had been cleansed from my memory entirely, and I only cared once more about Romy enjoying my wit and company. The new catastrophe, perhaps a wit could say, was the catastrophe of her survival. Everything continued as before – like I was the dazzled driver drifting happily between lanes on the autoroute – and in a way this episode of blood in its terror and suspense had made me feel even more tenderness and obligation towards her. Had I never come across her bleeding form, and had we simply got up and had breakfast and left, I suppose it's possible that we might have determined to remain just happy friends. But the blood was a form of drama and it made us very close. Not that we had slept together again, but we did write messages to each other very much and talk on the phone, for such ties are difficult to deny – and yet also, nevertheless, I loved Candy without end. And this is why, I tried to explain to Hiro, I think that marriage is the most confusing state, it is our greatest enigma, like suicide was in the previous absurdist times. So what if our problems seem sweeter than those times, those times of wars and also pestilence? We are sweeter maybe, but also deeper. For basically I think true magnificence is in the maintenance of as many relations as possible. What else could utopia mean? *Whenever I go to a party I always think it's going to be the best party ever*, Shoshana said to me once, before she disappeared deep into the furthest regions of this country. And I still have never heard a sentence that more made me fall in love. But if you really do think that way, and I think I do too, it is going to mean a difficult burden will fall on you. You are going to submit yourself to risks of other people that most people do not approach – the vast wisdom that any person who has once entered your life should never be dismissed from it. Those who no longer talk to people they slept with even just once are cowardly or strange, I think, while if I were ever a Communist and wanted to resign from the Party I would do it with a gentle grace – because why antagonise for no reason? That's why marriage is such a grand and permanent problem. It is the purest of moral conundrums – like the largest urban sprawl in the world, so that whenever you think you have left it you are just in another concentric garden suburb. Or, to put this the other way round, in the end you cannot be only talking to your wife, and once you talk to other people then where will things ever end? You will, for instance, find yourself not only sending tender messages to other women, but also looking after your best friend and trying to keep him happy.

— Oh *I'm* the problem? said Hiro. — Is that so, chico?

And in a way he was. What I mean is that I think it often takes a person to make a philosophical problem obvious, it can't be done with just the abstract thinking in your escritorio, and my friend Hiro was such a demon. For while it's normal to say that the rule of the overall reality is that nothing happens – well, what do you do when something does? I think *something* is a whole unexamined category of philosophy. And it was Hiro who had this gift for inventing something where usually there was nothing. He was the opposite of the way people sit in deckchairs in the shopping-centre forecourts, as if they can make these weird spaces normal, which they can't. Hiro could make a bingo hall or chop shop seem overgrown with unbelievable orchids and green vegetation. And even if such behaviour had its causes, and was perhaps a form of suffering, that didn't mean the consequences weren't real or even joyful. With Hiro it turned out that the difference between the ghoulish and the usual was maybe very thin, like about as thin as the difference between two sides of aluminium foil.

where crimes can be virtues

To consider small crimes as larger virtues was one such innovation. At night we would drive around the city – the quarter where the butchers had lately been placed, the beaux arts buildings, the cricket stadium – just slowly drifting past each little row of kiosks and illuminations, e.g. Kasey's Chicken, a late-night milkshake bar, the gaming centre, a store that was advertising Cube Ice & Ice Cream, with underneath *24 hour* scribbled in neon – and although I wasn't sure if this all-hours claim was true I still liked that whole modern sentiment, because I think it's good to know that always while you sleep you can get up and find people and also buy things, not that you ever will get up for cannoli or the like at five in the morning, but still, I

think that's an important reassurance. And then occurred –
if that's the right way of putting this, because I am finding
often a problem of verb forms, I am finding it difficult to
have the right tenses at my disposal – this moment where
we were in one of the further suburbs, on one of our
roaming sprees, and we wandered into a bodega, just to
look around or consider buying lighter fluid or the fashion
magazines, and I delayed looking at some blown-up cover
for a society journal, just staring into the dead face of a
supermodel or heiress, and so I was therefore maybe a few
steps behind Hiro – which was why when I found myself
definitively inside this place my first view of Hiro wasn't
him bent over and examining gelati in the freezers, no, not
doing whatever else might be normal in such a setting, but
instead with one hand he was holding a maxi bag of prawn
chips and with the other he was holding out a horizontal
pistolet or gun. And much later, when we described to
Candy this tableau, she was certainly perturbed.

— You are kidding me, said Candy.

— Ignore him, said Hiro.

— I am telling you, I said, — we were totally in an
armed situation.

Not that at this time I examined the precise nature of
this gun, partly because although I know that guns are the
most modern thing available that still doesn't mean that
it's easy for the average Joe, and by Joe I obviously mean
me, however modern this Joe or me might be, to be *familiar*
with the items. I think it's no exaggeration to say that
being wised-up is no easy matter. And yet Hiro was making
it feel very restful, to enter a bodega and pull out a
blunderbuss.

(— That reminds me, said Candy. — You remember my friend Epstein?

— Epstein?

— My friend Epstein, she said.

— Darling, we're telling you a story here.

— OK, she said. — OK.)

It was all the more exciting because Hiro's look is not obviously brutal. This is another thing we share. That Hiro was brilliant or goofy or both together you only needed to look at him. He sported square spectacles with black rims, and a dark brown corduroy jacket with a shawl collar and various zips, underneath which he wore a brown plaid shirt, but the detail that marked him out was that on his feet were two tan deck shoes but without any socks, like a riviera mogul. He was a pure product of modern chic. That was why the picture was a little outré: in the background, the television behind the counter was on a rerun almost definitely of the famous cat-and-mouse revenge saga, for everywhere you look there are cartoons, it's unavoidable, and meanwhile Hiro was slowly backing out of this very bright kiosk with the horizontal gun in one hand and the vertical prawn snax in the other. And I at least agreed with this idea of an exit because I was wanting to get right out of there and demand an explanation from Hiro as to when precisely he decided that holding up bodegas in our area was a way of spending time. I do accept that in theory there are no better or worse ways to spend time, the point of time is just to waste it, but also there are limits.

— The fuck was that? I said.

— It isn't *real*, said Hiro.

And he showed me the blunderbuss which on examination I now understood to be a water pistol, and plastic, but very realistic. And I guess that did calm me, to discover that no harm was intended. I had no idea how little you ever needed to be a convincing copy, and not only was that knowledge reassuring but it was also, in retrospect, very tempting and seductive. I wonder if everything that happened from then on happened because of that seduction, the realisation that it doesn't need to be *much* to be the thing itself – so that even as we looked up and down the silent boutique vista, even then we were transformed into watchful mafiosi. The threat to us, I had to admit, was small. There was one lone street sweeper in the distance, paused on his cell phone. It was as if the street were a beach, like the blank beaches when you come heavily out of the sea among the plastic seaweed, and you stand there, and look at the crowd and suddenly you can't find anyone. Above us koalas or pigeons were playing in the jacaranda trees. And so we walked away, while Hiro gazed pensively at this pristine bag of prawn chips. Then generously he handed them to the first infant we went past on the street.

which is a seductive knowledge

Surely this was a form of utopian thinking, this small improvement to a person's life? I found it very charming in my friend. Maybe in some far-off century if you wanted to reinvent the social contract you would have done it with more squalor, living underground in isolation, and losing yourself in crazy monologues and financial worry and hunger; but in this very bright time it also seemed that you could do it more softly – just in this desire to create a more adventurous existence: with friendships, love affairs, extra or extended families. Because I guess that although we now have so many forms of utopia, we have computers and space travel and TV and telephones, all the impedimenta of the recent future, still, there is more utopia available. It's just maybe now it's in something smaller, like the distance between thinking of something and in fact doing it – like tying up your boyfriend, then using him until he cries out in dark pleasure – or even smaller, just in the beginnings of sentences, like *if only it were so* . . . or *something's missing* . . . You have to start small, I suppose I mean. And if your best friend was recently out of the hospital for difficult emotions and very vulnerable and with nowhere obvious to go apart from on his own then I think it's only logical that we had a duty to take him in. For really what you adopt can be loved as truly as what you create and in fact perhaps more so. Or at least it always seemed to me that adoption of foreign elements was one proof you had a soul. Long ago, when I was much smaller than I am now, I was in some store with my mother and was apparently very intent on pointing out an ugly person, who had dark hair that was distinctly bushy inside her nose. My mother took me away and for ever after told this story as a very bad thing I had done. So what was I meant to think? From then on I thought that you should definitely not be mean to other creatures. Not that my thoughts were always on the oppressed of other nations, but I did try not to be cruel to those around me who did not have as much as we did.

We are not rich, my mother argued, but I think this was because around us were houses with rose gardens and swimming pools and when that happens your perspective might get scrambled. Whereas when you start to think about things a little more closely you realise how limited you might have been in defining what you think of as the good or beautiful or charming, you realise that so many things you thought of as not possible, like sending messages to a girl in the middle of the night who is not your wife, or removing items from a store without permission, can also have their beauty if you only consider them right. That was how I now reasoned – as if previously I had inhabited some happy gated compound, that protected its inhabitants from the drug-crazed depredations of the maquiladoras without, and now I was in the open and also pleasantly surprised. I was admiring the cactus trees, buying myself a mango juice and enjoying the blissed-out vibe. Transformations, it turns out, are possible. A lot of the time maybe you're doing something and it seems like nothing – just dense and pillowed like one of those per-fumed puffy Care Bear stickers and then BAM! it's mayhem.

DECEIT IS ONE BENEFIT OF LAZINESS

for everywhere it seemed like nothing was happening

Not that at this time it felt like mayhem, not precisely. It was only softness and the colours softness comes in: pistachio, vanilla, peach. That kind of softness was something I appreciated very much in those around me. Like one day we ran into our school friend Nelson. Nelson was often in the newspapers as an essayist in showbiz and the cinema. When the film stars came in by helicopter from the north or south, Nelson was there to greet them. And now here he was on some very sad backstreet, explaining to me happily how he very much appreciated that he could take part in his child's breastfeeding. It was beautiful, the way he described it. He held the baby very gently so it could suckle at his wife's breasts, because the one thing to avoid was specific roles for the mother and the father. As much as you could, he said, you should therefore do everything together. And I adored this happy thinking very much, and wondered if deep down this wide-eyed aura, the way this world we all inhabit is lit according to the pastel colour-palette of chemicals and candies, was an effect of our education. For our school was basically a country club, if by country club you can also imagine the hypereducation at a small Renaissance court. And also that it was devoted to the various halfies and mestizos, the octoroons and griffes: all the anxious children and grand-children of immigrant peoples. Everything we were taught was to erase all differences between people – and here were its fruits in front of me in the sadsack figure of Nelson, and in our bright environment more generally. There were trips to watch the sailing boats, or frescoball or snooker, or to the park with its lemonade stalls. While Hiro and Wyman and I pursued sprezzatura pastimes like getting fat, or fatter, eating peanut-butter waffles and vanilla shakes, or sometimes both together, in some deli-quescent form of sundae. And yet still, this was how the mayhem happened, as softly as it could, like the mayhem came in on tiptoe. Hiro for instance had taken to sporting a variety of wigs – the blonde, the retro, the goofily cre-ative. Personally I found his energy liberating but not everyone saw it that way: they saw it as *worrying*, or *dangerous*, or other therapeutic terms. He was spending time on the Internet and comparing kinds of firearm, and if Wyman expressed his worries at this development, Hiro was unruffled and unconcerned.

— You're such a perfectionist, said Hiro, making his coffee very heavy with much sugar, then swallowing some pills. — Chill out a little.

Or I would come downstairs and encounter strange vignettes and conversations, things like:

HIRO
I mean, what about when you've just had the worst haircut in the world before you meet someone for possibly the first and only time and you very much

want to explain that this is not your usual look although of course you can't? You are resigned to the real you being absent from the picture. You do not think the real you is the haircut but you cannot explain this –

CANDY
You OK?

HIRO
Well, sure.

MY MOTHER
That's excellent.

HIRO
I mean, I don't know how I'd know.

While before each party Hiro would arrive from one of his outings with a selection pack for everyone, and it's very possible the narcotics were primarily to blame for this whole sense I was having of entanglement and Fate. Like I keep forgetting to mention one strange message. *Is this Danger Mouse?* a stranger wrote to me, from an unusual country code. *Am I talking with SuperTed?* But then, you get a lot of mixups in this time with much available technology so I tried to think no more about it. Instead I made sandwiches consisting mainly of Kewpie mayo and around me happened the great arguments of the day.

MY MOTHER
He needs a job.

MY FATHER
Absolutely.

MY MOTHER
Why don't you go back to your work and ask?

ME
I did ask.

MY MOTHER
And?

ME
You know this.

MY FATHER
He needs a job.

For if you are very much *not* importing lapis lazuli to be sold in an airport concession, or supplying mini pretzels and other snacks to a hotel chain on the Pacific coast, then the time you would have spent in such activities will need to pass in other ways. Time was clumped and thick, like time was congee. It was a pocket or pause and when that's the scenario it's hard not to start experimenting with what's most available, like how long you can drink a coffee, or how many gore movies you can watch in a row. And while I know I said I gave up work for this dream of art, I suppose I should also admit that I had so many doubts in that regard – doubts as to whether this was in fact too late, that this was the end of youth, the end of stories, the end of art, doubts which will enter this account, but not just yet – that such a method of occupying time was only the slightest tremor on the edges of my thinking. I preferred the idea that a life might be a work of art instead. For my new leisure, it turned out, permitted also the invention of new categories of phenomena – dark possibilities of fantasy and deceit.

which allows our hero to develop new desires

No wonder that the principal way I spent my time when I was not with Hiro was therefore in pursuing my adventure with Romy. As a way of spending time it was definitely one of the most intensive, involving as it did so much composition of email and other messages, and framing of photos, and then the timing of how or when to send them. And then waiting for all the various replies. Or if there was in fact no reply, then obsessive consideration of the reasons for this absence. I understand, this way of spending time, in at least the language of the Churches or any other orthodox synagogue and ashram, does make me a no-good person. But show me the soul that is *not* a trash vortex, gathering its plastic in the otherwise bright blue sea. For the deep temptation of massive leisure time that is perhaps not obvious to you as you read this on the metro, is that leisure time gives you all the means you need to deceive other people: it is you who are commuting and hard-pressed with deadlines who are going to be luckily limited in your interior life, and therefore unavailable to temptation. Whereas the unemployed have so much time at their disposal. When a person needs a secret phone call or long meeting it is always possible to arrange. Not that I don't understand the potential priestly disapproval of such lies and infidelity. But once you discover how pleasant are the acts which hurt another person without them knowing, and how easy it is to do, then it's difficult to resist, for the knowledge is then forced on you against your will that the terms of this world are much softer than you ever assumed. I think that Romy knew this, too. She liked Candy and did not want to hurt her either, but why, we used to discuss with each other, should anyone ever be hurt? The ideal was just pure lightness.

shielded by the alibi of his sadness

Such purity in a boy! You generalissimos and judges who deplore this state of affairs, that I enjoyed myself in this rainbow bubble while my wife worried about me very much, and encouraged me to enjoy myself in any way I wanted, thus making her an accessory in her own cuckoldry, or whatever old-fashioned word is necessary for such actions – can you not see that we had no other choice? It was our general rule. If Candy ever showed she was worried about my domestic state, then it would show she did not believe me and my confession that I was sad, and since she had to show she believed me, that she was convinced that my sadness was so great that it led to me leaving parties and sitting alone as nighthawk or madman in the diners and cafes of this city, she therefore also had to be now all compassion and disquiet. She encouraged me to spend any time I wanted in nocturnal excursions, since she wanted me to be happy, and she did this with so much tenderness that I started to believe her, and imagined myself heavy sad. But then, perhaps this is not so insane. I mean, how ill is ill? If you imagine something afflicts you that is in fact not afflicting you, how can you ever tell the difference? Inside the thought balloon it is absolutely as bad as the medical textbook thinks. Just as when we try to itemise our feelings the problem is that, given how many feelings can be inserted between our thinking and our worst motivations, is it really dishonesty in a person when they do not acknowledge their obscene and gorgeous urges? In such an impasse I would stand there in the kitchen making doughnuts or other treats, while Candy stood there in her suits, trying to understand my difficult emotions.

CANDY
How's things, baby?

ME
Not so good.

CANDY
You think?

ME
I do.

Well, you don't rush yourself, OK?

Such power does lying have! It really can do anything. And maybe this word *power* is not untrue. I think it might be true that in this world I am blessed with an entirely unmerited power.

but which creates upsetting nocturnal fantasies

But while I did enjoy myself very much, exploring my conversations with Romy which were now heavy with the talk of apertures and openings, or if not direct talk then the intimation that such talk was on the brink of substitution, it was also true that there was this darkness I could not ignore, among the brightness, like the black circle left in your eyes if you've been suddenly just dazzled. To be thinking about two people at once was very difficult, and its effects could be seen in my secret nocturnal thinking. For at this time as well as picturing Romy in various undressed postures, I also sometimes pictured her dead or at least just gently disappeared. It happened not only in my dreams but also very consciously. Or instead I imagined it the other way round and it was Candy who was dead, thus leaving me alone with Romy, which was in some ways good and in some ways not so good. Although of course I have never really known any aloneness of any kind, nor ever experienced in any form what it feels like for the people you love to be dead; there is no major death in my family or among my friends or lovers or really acquaintances – until the events I am describing, my life had been marked by an absolute absence of blood – and I think that's also true for many of the people around me, like Wyman or Nelson and their cartoon families. It makes me comical and innocent, absolutely, but perhaps it also offers a perspective on the death of other people that usefully has no emotion in it. For although ever since I was young I was taught by my mother that you should never wish anyone dead, still, surely it must be usual to consider the death of someone else – it must happen even if you are a woodsman or bond trader? A death can be a definite solution for some otherwise impossible situations, and one such situation was this scenario where I pursued multiple lives when really you are meant to pursue no more than one at a time. I could not see how the various lies would be resolved and it upset me, and so I was often given to conversations with Romy in my head, where I would say: *Romy, qué pasa?* And she was tearfully saying to me goodbye, as I softly poisoned her. At the time I did feel guilty about this and thought that such thoughts were shameful, but I wonder now if the fault was really mine or instead belonged much more widely and to society, for should it really be true that such a multiplication of one's affections must be always circumscribed? All I was trying to do was solve an infinite conundrum.

given the obvious complications

And I think this was all the more difficult because Romy was my friend. Had she been an acquaintance unknown to everyone I might have felt a little more relaxed. Whereas to think of the many ways in which Candy might find out! – which would for instance involve Romy telling someone we both knew, but this would only happen if Romy hated me or wished me harm, which I found doubtful, but then another possibility was some tiny slip where I would mention some detail of blood or hospitals, or perhaps could have been seen at the hospital by someone else we knew who had perhaps overdosed or become involved in a stabbing or altercation, because it's difficult to know who might be anywhere. So I stayed awake at night and imagined Wyman or Shoshana – although Shoshana, true, was no longer in the city – watching me from the cafeteria, just seeing me arrive bloodstained with Romy and noting this, like some Gestapo stooge. And in remorse I leaned over in the night and kissed my wife very softly. Those were the thoughts I possessed in this time, and it requires a certain character to cope with them – for lying is a talent like any other, like eating or happiness or drug-taking, it's one of those things where you think you can just do it but in fact it takes training, intuition, physical stamina. And of course I do not mean at all that I did these things without guilt, it is guilt precisely that I am trying to describe, but especially for all my other selves, the selves I might be losing if I never continued into these adventures.

— You what? said Wyman.

— Listen! I said.

For what never gets said in these discussions of morality is the deeper problem of timing. If you have married so young, and Candy and I we did marry very young, in full innocence and sincerity, then what then?

— You stay together, said Wyman,— or you split up.

— Is not so simple, I said.

Because it really is true that everyone thinks they will not be there when someone dies, I mean when someone dies who is not their endless and married love. Or certainly I thought this was true about me. The only person I imagined ministering to at a deathbed was my adored wife, Candy, and even then I hoped I wouldn't because my preferred option would be that the person who would be dying would be me and in her arms. In every possible future I ever imagine, my wife is there. That's what I think inside although I know that on the outside it creates some difficult appearances, a possible carelessness about the feelings of other people – when in fact I think the opposite is true, I think too much about other people. If I can make anyone happy, I want to do that, however complicated the consequences, however much it leads to a way of thinking that expands itself in waves, or like the way the bees arrange themselves, inside their vibrating hives.

whose structure reveals a universal sadness

And sure, I said to Wyman, my most spiritual friend, as we smoked some preliminary chemicals in preparation for a night out, later on in this account, when I was nostalgic for such simple worries, I know that in human history the majority of sadness belongs to the dependent women. I know that the breakdowns have always been those of the bedridden woman – leaving the lunch table in hysterics, then setting up church bazaars and everyone pitying them. I totally know this but also now, I tried to argue, I knew what they knew. Me too I was the victim of my economic circumstances! I was like the heroine in the telenovelas. I was the woman cheating on her husband with her black gardener, and taking Valium or other pills while reading horoscopes in the tabloids. I don't mean those examples are the only other examples of sadness in human history. In the annals of the Song Dynasty I'm sure there were husbands and wives who were also perplexed by their leisure time. I just mean that when you have this vastness at your disposal then it's only natural to feel let's say a little hopeless or unhappy even if, having said that, I can do the next part of the interview myself, as something like: *But then what do you expect, kid, when you leave your place of employment?* I know this is the one-dollar question. *You also wanted meetings with your PA? You wanted to make art, sure, but also have a heavy schedule of appointments?* Sure, I understood. But still, it was upsetting. Life! I wanted life! And really, was this so unusual? More and more I was convinced that the most urgent task, in every megalopolis, was how to use your time – how, in other words, will you reveal it as grander than it seems? It's so easy to know what Beauty looks like in a statue or a painting, but what does it look like in a life? Me, I ask this question all the time and at least that's an occupation like any other. Lethargy, I think, is a difficult accusation. For surely it's possible to argue that the Zen master in his padded cell is doing more work than you. And if it is, well, sometimes so was I. I was very busy with my reflections –

the lost art of happiness

– like in particular one conversation with my friend Tiffany, who taught at the university, when she berated me for even hinting at the wish for other lives. *You ask for this and then you hate us for it? Is that it?* This was basically Tiffany's argument. *You want to be looked after and have this wife who brings home the roubles and rupees and then it makes you also feel aggrieved?* Well, maybe, snooks, she was basically adding, as she looked at me in scorn, you could just grow up for a moment. I totally did see the justice of how she was arguing but also I really did not, for the values by which she seemed to be judging were both unimpeachable and not my own. In many ways I feel let down by my friends. It's like that film which Tiffany loves, where the black and white people begin an affair and then go back to their husbands and wives. Why, she once said to me, when I was not at all talking about this, should a possible future happiness be worth more than the present happiness of two people? And I wanted to assert that I really could not understand it. About happiness I am often wrong but at least I would like to believe it is the only question. You want what, she then added – a life without regret, is that it?

ME

If I have a regret, it's that coffee with condensed milk in the Vietnamese way is not something you can have every day, because it really does fuck up your diet goals. If I have a regret then that would be it.

TIFFANY

Is like you're tyrannised, boo, by this fear of missing out.

She said it with this heavy wistfulness, as if just looking at me from far away and out of reach, an hauteur which I liked to think was possibly unjustified. In my defence I could imagine surely another perspective. I mean: *lowdown, clumsy, sly, underhanded* – can these not be values too, if happiness is at stake? And perhaps, OK, I therefore conceded to Wyman, my kind of listless paralysed atmosphere more usually happens in dictatorships and other totalitarian states, that's where moods like mine tend to breed most colourfully, among the presidential palacios and tear gas and lampadas – but I would say that paralysed states can also happen in a number of other guises . . . There can be this sense of unreality, I said, while Wyman nodded – although he may not have been concentrating, it's never easy to tell with anyone in any conversation – if things have just come to a gentle halt, like at the quietest country train station in the humid afternoon. Wyman, can you not feel this too? I'm only drawing a parallel, but I think in many ways my plight is similar to a lawyer or accountant from a bankrupt state who leaves everything to come and run a grocery store in a giant and clean city. The new identity is a shock, definitely, and in some ways a humiliation, but also it means that as you walk through the streets you do feel that you are walking in disguise, with all the hidden powers that a disguise might confer. You suddenly see meaning leaking everywhere – the way you might come back to some glamorous hotel in the late morning to see the used towels and sheets in formless damp piles in the otherwise perfect corridors.

— Leaking? said Wyman.

— It began with the orgy, I said.

— The orgy? said Wyman.

— I never told you about the orgy? I said.

— Apparently no, said Wyman.

— So settle down, I said. — You got a beer? Ensconce yourself.

a pastel atmosphere interrupted by a party

Gently it began like every other party, with ice cream and accordions and dubstep and whatever other accessory people felt would make them happy. From the corner of the room I observed with Candy some psychedelic band. If I did have any feelings of foreboding, like some extra sense that even now the black mamba was descending on me with its gooey fangs, those feelings were just unwinding out of sight – like those backdrops of lakes and fields in the ancient brothels that some viejo would wind by hand to give the loving couple the illusion of a wagon-lit.

— Hey, there's Epstein, said Candy.

— Epstein? I said.

— Hey, that's Romy, said Candy.

— Romy? I said.

— I told you, said Candy.

— Told me what? I said.

Of course I should have expected it, given how small the cast list is. Everyone in this account is a friend, really. I know them all. It's like a group portrait or maybe more precisely a self-portrait with models. That's how picayune this picaresque is and I think it's also the most truthful. Because it's not so strange, this smallness of cast list.

Everyone in general knows everyone you know, or at least in this landscape it can seem so.

in which melancholy revelations occur

And therefore I should not have been so amazed to see Romy engaged in amorous and intimate conversation with some beatnik schlub called Epstein, a beatnik schlub I knew as one of Candy's friends from her days out of university in anarchist study groups. It was just, it was still a shock, after all, because I only had a very short time in which to cope with the knowledge impressed on me by their general pose and vibe that in some way they were a couple or at least loosely together – but that is often how a social existence works, that very quickly you are forced to absorb distressing information. Yes, there Romy was, talking biopolitics or some other chic topic with Epstein, of all our beatnik friends the most beatnik, who was currently dressed in some exaggerated cardigan, while Romy herself was in her usual outsize glasses and boxing boots. For Romy had this thing that she was one of those people whose erotic allure is not in doubt but also not part of the immediate effect, like she went to such lengths to disguise her beauty – the dark blondeness of her hair, the way she had soft freckles all over her face, as if a tracing had been laid over her skin – that it now occurs to me if perhaps such a disguise was in fact a grander form of vanity, all along. Each of her efforts to disguise her beauty only served to make it more poignant. Like her hair would be just secured with a felt-tip pen in a lazed-out bun, it was that kind of drawly thing. She waved me over because she wanted to say hello and so I wandered to her, leaving Candy to investigate the range of drinks available, while feeling a little frustrated at myself because evidently, even though I was trying not to show it, a question or enquiry was still there in my gaze, because Epstein immediately began as if he needed to explain things:

— Yeah so we've been seeing each other for a while now, he said.

I wanted very much to look at Romy but I knew that was not allowed, for that would indicate too quickly a manic need for explanation, and in public I had no right to such explanation, although also I knew that if I were not to look at her at all then it would be in some way a sign as well, for this is how life is, you emit a sign by either doing or not doing something, there is no neutral space.

— I hear, said Epstein, — you helped this lady out.

— How so? I said, or somesuch dumbass phrase.

— When she had that thing, he said. — It's cool you could be there for her. In the hospital.

— Oh, yeah, I said.

— I called him that morning, said Romy.

— Naturally you had to get back to Candy, said Epstein.

— Naturally, I said.

I really did need to examine him further but also I needed to examine Romy, too, and it was difficult, this way of being, to be as insouciant as possible. I was trying to work out if this meant that she had been with Epstein even when we woke up in that hotel, and then afterwards, throughout all the correspondence and assignations of our tense and no more consummated affair – although of course she had no obligation to tell me, just as I had no right to assume that she would not be seeing anyone else at all. But in retrospect it therefore coloured the whole imbroglio and I did not know how I felt, in the way you might feel if you send a naked photo of yourself to a boy and then discover later that you sent it just as his girlfriend arrived for a night in with pizza and raki. Even if the present moment was pleasure, when it turns out to have been based on false assumptions that pleasure will just disappear whenever you think about it in your memory.

that prove the endlessness of receding selves

But then, this was just the universal problem. A person is a little sequence or bundle and you never see all of their aspects. With those you love, however, it's especially unnerving because they at least are the ones where you decide you do want to know them all, even if really it is impossible, and it makes people act quite strangely or unforgivably, or perhaps more precisely makes you realise how strangely people do act, all the time, it's just that it's only those you love who are scrutinised with the appropriate attention. And yet also I realised that if I was feeling this sense of estrangement and receding selves, as in some funhouse mirror, then Epstein was surely feeling it more. If he could have spoken to me in a private booth I knew how he would have been feeling. He would have wanted to subject me to an inquisition. *Where were you that night? What did you do? How can I trust you?* When of course he couldn't trust me and he knew that very well. He was suddenly discovering that he couldn't trust anyone, or at least he was perhaps not discovering this fact for the first time in his life, since he was surely old enough for this knowledge to have been forced on him at least once or twice before, but perhaps he had thought that with Romy never again would this sadness of hidden selves be revealed to him, but here however he now was, and I thought I could observe a certain exhaustion in his eyes at having to once again accept this difficult knowledge – and it made me sad. I mean, I was sad to be present at his moment of disillusion, or more precisely I was sad to be the agent of such disillusion, since mostly I think illusions are to be cherished and adored. But since always I am keen to be as noble as possible, when Epstein was telling me how grateful he was I did not pause, I accepted his praise as graciously as possible. These are the ways in which one has to behave to one's friends and acquaintances. I did it quickly, though, because I did doubt my ability to continue such a comedy indefinitely. Then I excused myself very gently and went back to my beloved wife.

& the dangers of every party

Everyone goes to a lot of parties, which must mean that mostly no one thinks there is anything wrong with that. Whereas of course the motives for ever leaving a house and entering society are often flawed or even dangerous – such as the desire to sleep with someone else, or to complete a sociological survey, like see inside a house or meet people you might never usually meet in the course of an average day, which was why I could sometimes be found in the houses of my richer friends, at their birthday parties in restaurants or salons with cinema producers and gallerists, even if the next day I would feel guilty and ashamed for my sudden love of social climbing, but also other seemingly minuscule motives like boredom or the request of a friend, because even such seemingly innocuous motives begged the basic question – that really you should not be having friends at all, you should only be accessing your own solitude and delinquency, and never leaving the seclusion of your room. How blithely do we enter these parties! Because it really is dangerous, to enter society, especially when you think of the possible danger to your various attachments. Everyone thinks that there is only one person in the world for them, this is how they are told to operate, and I suppose in general it works very well, whereas of course the truth is that there are many people whom you could find as charming as possible, not just sadly scattered at distant points around the globe but on every street you walk down, it's probably true of nearly everyone you have a conversation with – which is there-fore why those couples who talk with wonder about the extraordinary sequences of chance events that unbelievably have brought them together are sadly comically wrong, I mean they are not taking into account how many people they could have fallen in love with at the same time, or before that, or could in the future, too. Perhaps people know this, after all. Perhaps that's why so few conversa-tions do ever happen, we try very hard to avoid ever reaching the point of conversation with another person, usually contenting ourselves with a quick greeting and negotiation, and also why if indeed a conversation does occur it has to be so guarded with politesse and business skills, with indirection and guarded thoughts – precisely to avoid knowing the other person at all and therefore inevitably falling in love.

for parties lead to difficult conversations

And there they were, my contemporaries – eating Hawaiian pizzas in Hawaiian shirts and I didn't know if this artistic irony belonged to them or Fate. True, there have been more definitive signs in world history, like it wasn't as specific a pattern as the one experienced by my father's associate, a man called possibly Alvin, who got shot through his car window in a pattern of bullets while sitting at a traffic light, just shot very neatly in his shoulder, and the next day in hospital received a card with the same pattern neatly inscribed inside – at which point this Alvin left town for good. But still, it was something.

— I still have draw, I said to Candy.

— And so I'm rolling? she said.

— But if you could –

— I'm only checking, kook.

I did say my wife was cool. She was way-out severe when she wanted and I liked that very much. So Candy made our joints and I stood there trying not to look at Romy, which meant noticing that Hiro was already here, watching a screen playing reruns of that ancient trash series about the prettiest slayer of vampires.

— Yet again I have rolled a shit joint, said Candy, exhaling.

— Is not so bad, I said.

For I wanted everyone to be as happy as they could be, which is always my ideal but at this more tense moment had a special poignancy.

— You think this weed is sprayed? said Candy.

— You think? I was saying, but then I was interrupted.

— Hola, shifu, said Romy, who had come to talk.

— What's up? I said.

I was trying very hard to gauge the general tone. It seemed like everyone was happy and that I did not need to worry – and I suppose that's what happens when you're deceiving people: conversations become a surface you always suspect of being a depth. Any pattern at large seemed possible, whether numerological as according to the ancient sages or just the patterns of the weather or the flight of swifts, if I could identify a swift, which I think I can't. Pastoral is not my habitat.

ROMY

You are such a Mickey Mouse creature.

ME

What's wrong with Mickey?

ROMY

He's only got three fingers on each hand.

In private I would have been able to reply, and with some eloquence. It's true I can sometimes seem not worldly enough, I would have said, but I would also point out that I have social issues, I am very shy, and perhaps were it not for these social issues I think I could have achieved great things, but there it is, I cannot help it. But in public I was not sure if I were meant to be taking part in this conversation, or if in fact more probably I was instead meant to be teased with a quiet grace, and so as silently requested I stayed silent – because I understood what Romy was saying with this dialogue: *Let's just talk as if nothing is happening, and therefore nothing is happening.*

ROMY
Did I tell you I saw your mother?

ME
My mother?

ROMY
We talked for seventeen minutes about you. It was really something.

HIRO
Everyone's so worried, it's crazy –

CANDY
I'm not worried.

It was like those moments when you touch down in the middle of the night and have to make some connection at an interglobal airport like Houston or Chiang Mai – not that this has ever happened to me but I can at least imagine – so you basically are manic with scanning for signs. That was the anxiety I had held over me in this conversation, like a parasol against the endless sun, this conversation where everyone I loved was just chatting among themselves, and one answer to that type of feeling is just to get even more wiped out than you are already feeling, and so I was glad to see Hiro become absorbed in doing his stacks – cutting a tablet of Modafinil into quarters, then Cipralex and diazepam. For not only did I in general applaud the fact that this was the new digital age of narcotics but also I needed very much at this precise moment to be distracted.

— You sure, cookie? said Candy as she saw me snort enthusiastically.

— Yeah, maybe that's enough, yeah? said Romy, too.

I understood that she had only recently been in hospital and very scared, so she had her own private fears, but really I did not care, because if I needed these narcotics then it was not without good reason. I was standing there, thinking very fast about Romy and my wife and Epstein and my desires, and so it was only kind of woozy the way I realised Hiro had meanwhile drifted away and then heard him gently say to these two kids on a sofa a sentence like:

— But what if we all had an orgy?

I never said I *liked* Hiro. I said he was my best friend. These are very different categories.

where the surfaces seep or leak

Every day – this was the lesson to be learned from the life of Hiro – you should try doing something that might help another person. Even if it's just guessing well when they play charades, that's enough. Or, another of his maxims was: a party is much easier than people think. It basically just needs beer and plastic chairs and music and takeaway food in plastic boxes. While the ideal drink is the minimum of alcohol with the maximum result.

— And anything else? I said.

— Then you just need to get the right atmosphere, he replied.

In everything he did, he liked to add to what was normal. And already two kids had got naked very fast. They had hardly been so dressed already, so the difference was arguably small. Just as I suppose I could at least envisage a perspective from which the difference between the clothed and the unclothed would be minuscule – but at this moment I couldn't quite believe in it. I still think clothes are a major difference, like the way skin is as well. I know once again this makes me as old-fashioned as an ice-cream van, in the same way as my inability not to begin and end an email like I'm writing out a letter, but there it is, that's how I think. It was about as soft and minuscule as the warmth a person leaves behind on a toilet seat, the manner in which Hiro proposed this orgy, and how it began. But then that's how things happen and it's why it's so difficult to talk about any event you care to mention. It was like if you imagine everything's a surface – and after all everything *is* a surface – but then something disturbingly still manages to seep through. These are the kind of actions I think happen most often nowadays, these kinds of small seepages or cracks in the general sheen. Everything feels so fleeting that it's almost impossible to notice an event when it occurs, like someone giving you a jacket they no longer like and it goes so well with your new pair of jeans, that's one way a story can work and when it stays like that it's fine – but also too late you can find yourself inside something much more supersized, like what is really taking place is Godzilla greenly emerging from the radio-active waves.

& become, for instance, an orgy

It was like I was looking at a scene from one of those envellumed Renaissance prints – the secret kind known only to the pervert connoisseur, with giant muscles and endraped beds. Had I ever thought about it, this word *orgy* would have been something very different, belonging to other ages, a time of swingers clubs and plumed moustaches, with a softcore piano score. But maybe the fact that this was so different was because this is no more the time of swingers clubs than a time when things are really obscene. As soon as you're in bed with someone you can do anything you like, that's the basic arrangement nowadays – there is no disgust or danger. Maybe that was why the scene before me was so peaceful and so different from my previous assumptions, and maybe this is true for so many words, for most words we happily use are in fact outmoded, or exaggerations. If the atmosphere was crazed, it did not seem that way. Whereas now, from this distance, when everything has disappeared, I wonder if I should have thought about it more. For the problem with happiness is how often it requires the cooperation of other people, and it's never clear if they're cooperating for the right reasons, by which I mean the same reasons. Sure, everyone has their reasons, as the swami has it. But the fact that there are overlapping reasons in a situation is no guarantee at all that the consequences will be overlapping, too. But at the time I was not thinking with such detachment. Instead I was just marvelling how different things were from how I ever imagined them, and I liked that discovery very much. This orgy was quiet and industrious, a whole *you wanna take over or – no no, I'm cool, you cool? – no problem, let's stay like this –* that salon talk, just kindly and methodical. I liked it, the way people were considerate of each other. They'd get up for water and sit around chatting and sometimes just take over for a little, if someone needed a break from licking, or kissing. It was charming, the way people went about it. It's so easy, I was thinking, to multiply yourself. I was the same person who had arrived at this party; the self in me was the same. This is not a surprising situation and happens very often. But now inside that self, occupying the space which earlier had only the haziest notion of how the word *orgy* might have been fulfilled, there were these two naked kids just shyly or lazily kissing in the most laid-back way, and a cigarette that the girl had put aside was unravelling itself unnoticed in an ashtray. And perhaps if it had just been this, a general escalation of a blissful vibe, then I could probably have accepted it. But this was to ignore the fact that an orgy among people with whom you have many secrets is a difficult social encounter. I did not blame Hiro for this. If Hiro was sweet then he was sweet like the most catastrophic kitten. If now he does perhaps seem to me like one of those space invader demons leaking down poison in pixels, it's not as if those pixels were luminously visible. I was very sure that Hiro had no malice in him, but still, it made me wonder if therefore I should have considered much more carefully the issue of Hiro's pills, e.g. the issue of whether his sporadic taking of the medical pills that were said to stabilise or ameliorate his general condition was in fact as useful for the common good as Hiro always maintained. There was no time, however, to consider this, I had to consider it only in retrospect, when it was in a way too late, when whether or not Hiro's manic behaviour was a danger had been proved beyond all measure.

surprisingly social

For what was happening in front of me in this the present moment was that Romy and Epstein were naked too – or at least Epstein was, and Romy was let's say topless. She came over to nakedly smoke a cigarette with Candy and me so I began a balanced conversation, one of those casual phrases like, oh I don't know, like *Romy, what the fuck?* There was a vein on one of her breasts I could see, and as ever I considered how odd it was that nakedness feels like such an extensive knowledge, that even if one has seen a person naked already their nakedness is always an event, and it was an event – the way Romy's breasts were there. So I just tried to make a neutral observation.

— Epstein is really out there, I said.

I think it was definitely neutral as talk goes but in fact I was thinking very specific things, the main one being a feeling of absolute jealousy and aloneness that I could never tell to anyone, for what right did I have to be jealous of Romy when I myself was attached very publicly to another woman? But still, I was jealous, after all, in this melancholy way, and I was sad that it turned out that she was seeing other people, or not just seeing them but loving them in a way that perhaps she did not love me. But then of course why should I be her only love, when she was not mine? Of which jealousy there was a secret compartment, as in some portable writing desk borne with him in the night by an aristocrat fleeing the workers' revolution, which was this vision I now possessed of Epstein's dark penis. I don't think I'd ever seen an aroused penis that wasn't mine, outside various screens, and it was very strange, to be both seeing a penis and knowing it belonged to a man who was fucking a woman I loved, or was about to, and possibly in front of me. Also I must admit, it seemed large or certainly not small and as well therefore as a sadness I also was interested to feel just kind of objectively impressed, so when Romy wandered away to return to this surprising athlete I just quietly pointed the fact out to Candy.

— You think that's cool? said Candy.

— I think it's cool, I said.

— It's big.

— Sure is.

— But will he ever know what it's like, said Candy, — to have a girl take his whole cock in her mouth and then look up at him gently with her big brown eyes?

I didn't know what to say to that. Elsewhere there were conversations –

— Are you up yet? said Romy.

— You can't tell? replied Hiro.

– but I carried on saying nothing, and just considered the interiors.

made painful by the existence of secrets

To say you have a secret life may possibly give some basic grandeur impression – as if you enjoy meetings in private cabanas inaccessible to the average person in their parka, that you are maybe attending suppers with cardinals in their palazzos and gossiping about presidents – but really secrecy makes your ordinary life so minute and heavy, it has this difficult effect that it forces you into braveries that no one really should have to bear. It sounds contradictory or kooky but secrecy, it turns out, is a form of exposing yourself to more things in this world than you should; it is to take your privacy into places that it should not need to go – like this moment where I understood I would have to watch Romy have sex with someone else, and with my wife naked beside me, and do this with the appearance of a bland curiosity. Porn barons or fascisti might imagine such things, but I have only ever been gracious in what I imagine. I am not grand enough to end all feeling altogether and see a person as only a body or form of pleasure. But then, I was thinking, this is what happens if you possess many secrets: you will have to learn something which perhaps other people are often spared, which is that everyone is inhabiting multiple universes at the same time – it's just that usually the various asteroids and supernovas of these universes never meet. But sometimes if you have more than one life then the present moment will unfortunately see these worlds collide, and at these moments the contemporary will therefore call for total poise and bravura, and always I have wanted to be equal to the contemporary. If I had to watch these awful things, if I had to be my era's chubby piece of heraldry, yes if I had to be its martyr, ecstatically poaching myself in boiling oil, sunning myself on a stake, then so be it. I would take on the demented consequences myself – even if in general it was usually in fact Candy, and not me, who found the contemporary easy and possible to accept. She was always good with stressful situations, like this one of taking off your clothes in multiple company – a situation I could not help but find extremely difficult, reminding me as it did of that moment in changing rooms, when everyone is naked but pretending to ignore the situation, the imprints of sock elastic on ankles, like toothmarks. But then perhaps this is also true when it's just two of you in a room – that undressing is an unusual process, because to undress is so exhausting, it requires so many movements and processes of thinking. Yes, taking your clothes off and putting them on again in front of a stranger, it's the most unnatural thing in the world. Perhaps that's why desire's necessary, otherwise no one would ever undress, not at all. Though as if in answer to my awkwardness Candy kindly gestured me underneath a duvet that someone had brought out – a child's duvet printed with elongated footballs – and once again it struck me how tender she was, how much she loved and cared for me, while we sat there on the sofa, in observation, and in return I felt a total tenderness for her, too. But still, I do not recommend it – being present at an orgy sitting beside your wife, while watching a girl with whom you have recently woken naked in a hotel room, and bleeding – unless you're some narco lord who is used to this condition of many wives and mistresses. Always my capacity for transgression had been very small. The usual transgressions of stealing scrips, or jumping the barriers of the metro, the manic machismo of dicking the help, I always thought these were beyond me. And so the nakedness I saw around me – because now more and more the atmosphere was happy and delighted and a large amount of people were kissing while in various states of nakedness, I say *large amount* which was maybe only nine or ten, but that I think is still a large amount of nakedness to observe – felt very intimidating, and in response I could feel my attention wanting to migrate, just stealing over the border into the empty wide fields. I often find it hard to concentrate on just one thing, and being here in this way I felt very much coerced or even trapped, inveigled by Fate and the very high stars – like the moment when the psychopath and his knife are claiming you, on the upstairs landing, and you know that the police goon in his squad car parked in the street below for a calm cigarro and empanada de carne is no way going to help you. And yet also I would say that, as in all things, predicting the precise degree to which you will be made uncomfortable is not an easy profession. I imagined that the problems of an orgy among close friends would be quite small, that they would be these problems of *spectatorship*. With spectatorship and jealousy I could make some exhausted arrangement. The bright disasters that were advancing, however, were something much more fantastical and suddenly I had this thought of my mother and my father, secluded in their bedroom, not so far away, my mother watching the late-night shows, my father snoring or in the bath, and I felt a total sadness or abandoned kind of feeling, like all I ever wanted was the miniature comedy of my parents. My father used to read the newspapers aloud to my mother, and they would comment derisively on the general scene. That kind of intimacy now seemed to me very distant and romantic, romantic perhaps precisely because it seemed so impossible and far away.

leading to difficult knowledge

As we sat there under the duvet, Romy had approached us in a kind and welcoming manner, with more drugs in her hand for us to take – and I was happy to take them because I needed to feel differently to this way I was now feeling. The problem however with narcotics is that if you take them with other people they will have effects not only on you but on others, and it's very difficult to control how other people will react. It's one more reason to add to these infinite files of papers why the ideal society is so far away and impossible. In a soft blurred cloud we sat there, maybe sharing jelly beans, maybe telling jokes, until I understood that what was happening beside me was that Romy and Candy were now kissing. And in my cloud and general blurred state I did understand that I was being called upon to exercise a grand restraint on my feelings – for if I had found difficult the simple sight of Romy, this interlacing with my wife was a new conundrum – and I was not sure I was equal to it. It was like watching a koan live before me. Not perhaps that this is new, not entirely. The basic effect of our many drugs is to enable things that were previously not possible, and while this is an advance I think it's possibly also the reason why loyalty is more complicated for me and my camerados than it was for our happy parents. It's one of the great achievements of the age in which we live, this oversharing vibe, but it also can be stressful. Already I had experienced similar dilemmas, like take something as minuscule as the general fact that if all three of us were talking and Romy needed the bathroom she could easily just naturally beckon us in with her, Candy and me, without anyone perhaps noticing that this could be novel. And once inside, it was like two time frames were overlapping. There was the old one where I pretended that nothing strange was happening, and the new more secret one where I was very softly getting excited as she did this – I don't mean anything's visible when a girl's pissing, they just lean forward a little while they talk to you and presto you could be on some sleek banquette in a lovely out-of-town restaurant, but the scene still made me excited and none of this, of course, could be demonstrated to Candy. Just as now I was watching her kiss Romy and trying to succeed in finding whatever gaze might be appropriate, which was after all the gaze appropriate to Candy, since I had no wish for the veil of illusion to be torn from our eyes. But since I had no idea what the appropriate movements might be, whether Candy wanted me to join in or watch or be unimpressed, for no one wishes to be married to the man who is a maniac, and has some seedy over-obsession with girls who also like girls, I settled for the most neutral possible tone. I sat there, trying to smile. Sometimes a smile is not easy at all, like crying isn't, but nevertheless I tried to do this for my wife, because I loved her very much. And in such a tone, it turned out, I think I could have continued for a very long while. I felt safe inside that tone. Candy and Romy were now naked together below me on the floor, with Candy's head resting on the edge of the sofa where I sat, ensconced in duvet. But it was after a period of some minutes that I realised Candy was now talking to me and gesturing to me to join in. And this was now a problem beyond any simple problem of tone, or expression in one's face – and one problem I have always had has been with my face, for not only is it one of the most youthful you will ever see, but also it is always so mobile and vulnerable to giving itself away. Thoughts promenaded freely all over it, fluttered about my eyes, reposed on my lips, then vanished completely. For how are you meant to make love to your wife, when naked with a woman who is your secret inamorata and obsession, too? It's a difficulty and one that is not without its wider meanings. Or at least I thought it was. For I could not see how else I could have acted. I had seen no way in which I needed to tell my wife about what was happening with Romy, since I did not want anyone to be hurt, and yet it was precisely this good intention that was why I was now in such a false position – and it was this moment, I now think, that marked a before and after in my life, as definite as the difference between a telephone ringing or not ringing when you're waiting all alone in a hotel room. My definition of what was possible was being stretched just very slightly, just distended until a whole new world emerged. For everyone thinks they know how things happen, they think they have reality understood, but that's only because the portion of reality they experience is so policed by themselves they never think how easy it might be for gore to overflow. They never think that they will have this exercise of making love as if for the first time to their paramour or mistress, while that aforesaid mistress is pleasuring their wife. It's an incredibly stressful situation and I think that deep down I was not successful – for in the end it's very difficult not to show some kind of knowledge or just comfort with someone's naked body, it's very difficult to conceal that you know how to touch them, just as it's also obvious in the way two people might stand together, or talk to each other, with just the minutest changes in their syntax. So that whether I was licking the inside of Romy's thighs, while sometimes pausing to kiss Candy who was there beside me, or I was putting my penis inside Romy while Candy's hand guided it in, there was this ease or accommodation that I did feel must be obvious to Candy if she only wanted to look. But it did however seem that she wouldn't.

a category that is complicated

It's really difficult, to know what should or can be known. One thing that had always been true of Candy and which we argued over was this degree to which a person could ever confront or hold the truth entire in their head. Candy always believed in the expression of everything. She was this wild tricoteuse tough guy. Personally I found the horror movies and the Holocaust shows upsetting, I thought that never should we be shown the images of bodies being burned, or lifted lightly into wheelbarrows and other farming equipment, but Candy was sterner than I was – she thought that all the world's pain was like the old Electronium, with all the massacres pre-recorded, and perhaps she's right, perhaps it's just laziness to think the way I used to think.

CANDY
So for example you have some Nazi planning how to kill people. Like how do you burn a hundred bodies if you only have the coal for ten?

ME
You cannot do it –

CANDY
You are just not thinking right. Like why not film a gas chamber?

ME
Darling –

CANDY
You think the gore isn't possible to show? Like what about the porn? You think they are worrying like you worry in the porn shoots?

ME
Possibly not –

CANDY
I don't mean you do the normal shots like women going into a shower. You want it like the porn moguls would like it –

ME

Hey, why not just starve all the extras?

CANDY

Now I like that. There'd probably be regulations but you are getting this, Toto. You are beginning to think intelligent –

And after all, this was one reason why I always loved the erotic home movies that are now available everywhere, I loved them because they showed everything there was, right down to the smallest bedroom ornament, the My Little Pony collection and sports medals, they couldn't help it – at last there is this art form where not everything is artistic, where chance is an element of the absolute design. In films things happen and you do not cut away, or at least that's what you want in an ideal movie, whereas in TV people cut away just when you want them to linger most of all, like all the execs are in some small cabal to frustrate all your noble instincts. And yet despite this tough-guy wildness that Candy taught me, I would also say that in our life together Candy had this gift for somehow not seeing things as they were. From our suffering she turned away, so that here we were in some increasingly harmful setting and something vast was not being said. But perhaps that's normal. We tried to see the good in each other and wanted it to be true and in some way therefore it was, however imperfect it seemed. For obviously, despite our grandest efforts, there was still a doubt in Candy. She wanted and did not want to believe me, in this period when I often disappeared, or was preoccupied, or silent. I could see this in her. I knew that what she was saying to me was: *Please do not become a monster. Please do not do the harmful things. I want to believe in your existence as a moral being.* What else would any wife want? Very much therefore she wanted to think that everything could be explained by the sadness of my unemployment, rather than other loves, and I think in fact that she was right, that my behaviour was indeed much more explained by a sadness than any delinquency with Romy or with Hiro, and therefore this offer to join in here was perhaps a test, the way a knight was tested in the old stories. And if it was such a test, I wanted to pass it with courage. So to please her and to explain that really I would love her for ever I continued to lick at Romy while Candy lay back and watched. If it was gruesome it was no more gruesome than the rest of life, I was telling myself. Most of the time we are not saying the reasons why nothing should happen, why everyone should sit tight in their space bubble and let themselves be whirled around the sun. There are false positions in every moment of your day, when you are not telling someone about their untenable tattoo or you are telling your ex-boyfriend that absolutely one day you will travel together to Tahiti, just as friends, although you know that never will such a voyage occur but he seems so totally sad and lonely even six months after you left him. I just mean: up in the air there are planes taking business people to meetings that are doomed because their business partner is in fact corrupt, and also wives are travelling to be reunited with their unfaithful husbands. That's just an average day in this small planet's stratosphere.

by what is visible & what is not

Elsewhere the room was marked by an awkward messiness, the horizontal problem of chair legs and lamp cables, and I was sad when I had to think how awkward bodies can look when there isn't a civilised amount of room. Sure, there were possibly only nine people involved, but still, the basic feeling was that everything was everywhere entangled. A girl was just lying there being licked between the legs while idly toying with a penis that had been offered to her hand, but her head was resting on some popzines and I worried for her neck. The question of common hygiene also worried me but I knew that if I raised this with for instance Candy she'd just dismiss it as even more uncool than usual, so I dismissed it on her behalf. I'm just saying that a lot of thoughts and counter-thoughts were occurring in this time, so many that it turned out I needed the orgy for distraction, and so I watched, like it was television – if television had become something extreme and also malevolent. Because now what had happened was that Epstein had returned to our group, after getting a glass of water. He lay down beside my wife and they were talking in the manner of old friends, but this time old friends who are naked, which of course was what they were, and he was nuzzling at her neck, and as he did so I could see his penis sort of just gently move and rise in this slow fashion, and it was painful, to see this happen and not to be able to do anything, to have to accept this as the price you must pay for your ideals. And I was aware, not totally, just slightly – kind of like when you're trying to reach for a dream when you wake up, or for the ping-pong ball when it's been smashed off the table and it's squirming away in spirals – that if I looked like I was happy with this new state of affairs, then it would have one good effect which would be that it would very much serve to show Candy that in this orgy I was not possessive of or focused on Romy. It would show me to be a libertine of absolute unimpeachable openness. For Epstein was looking also at Romy and they were smiling, and sadly I watched them watch each other. Everyone was exchanging these looks and glances to reassure each other that something drastic wasn't occurring, whereas of course this scene was drastic, absolutely. And yet perhaps it wasn't, after all, if we could still smile. Never had I felt so much tenderness and painfulness coexisting. Always I had wanted a troupe, I was trying to tell myself. It had been Candy and Hiro and me, and now here we were, extending it into vaster regions, like discovering the estates and empires of the moon. Romy leaned forward over Epstein and I could observe the tendons in her armpit and the way the skin of her breasts where it met her ribcage seemed so thin and fragile, and such delicacy made me want to cry out with love, but I didn't, I tried to remain outside myself instead, and one way I could do this was by thinking about the smell, since something I don't think I'd ever imagined if I'd ever thought about an orgy, which I must admit was rarely, was that the smell of many people having sex was obviously the same as just two people having sex, but multiplied, and this was sometimes disgusting and sometimes alluring, depending on your mood: it was deep and vegetal and enclosing, like being in a hothouse among tendrils with condensation on the glass. Then Romy was letting Candy sit over her face and it was a very delicate thing, the way Candy was holding herself there, very intently, you could see that it was a pleasure but also painful to remain in that position. Or Romy was sucking Epstein's penis and just occasionally she'd minutely gag, which made me worried for her but then also I was thinking it must presumably be nice in some way, the choking sensation, or at least a pain that was part of the pleasure, or why else would anyone do it? Then I was looking sideways at Candy to see what she was thinking but she didn't seem to be thinking anything. She was just narcotically relaxed and I was happy to see her happy – and however sad I was inside myself I did have this vision in front of me that I had to admit had happiness in it, for in this orgy it seemed to be being demonstrated that there were as I always wanted to believe other models for people to be with each other, there could be a sort of caring that was almost impersonal and very sweet. Perhaps therefore Hiro was right, that such small adjustments to reality could create much more interesting and pleasurable scenarios. Or in fact, whether or not I agreed with him, I reflected, it didn't really matter, it did not affect how Hiro existed in the world: he was just there, the way wind is in a wind tunnel. Just as so for instance here he was, in front of us. He handed Candy and me an ice cream each.

— Let me, said Hiro,— for once in my life have the presence of mind displayed by the hero of that movie who in the middle stopped and said: *I just want to let you know that being here is one of the pleasures of my life.*

Then he walked away again. Hiro was hyper like a genki drink. And that, I think, was how the tropical confusion began.

with potentially dark consequences

For afterwards, it was delicate – like it's always delicate after the first time you've had sex or at least just touched another person, but now exaggerated. It was that type of momentous thinking when future possibilities are now in the air, ludicrous like demons, or rather that you yourselves are the demons, flapping around in your stale and outsize costumes. I think I knew that none of us was exactly invulnerable or impervious to feelings, and that if this was happening then we should undertake some responsibility to try to prevent the tragic consequences. But that knowledge was so far away, like the merest lighthouse in the distance. So that however much I was aware – as Romy began to lick my by now quite tired penis while very gently cupping my balls in her warm hand, in a way that I felt was her mute method of reassuring me, and failing, that something other than playfulness was happening – that we had put ourselves in this situation where everyone was at risk, I could not pause and consider the question why. And if a story was taking on more elements than I expected, who was I to stop it? If things were leaking everywhere, my only duty was to examine the leak with care – whether or not I was the agent of catastrophe. I kind of thought I wasn't. I tended to see Hiro as impresario in this case although perhaps to find an impresario or first cause is not important or even possible. Then a friend of a friend who was naked apart from a pair of ski boots wandered over and asked for a light. Her name could have been Gryphon or Maria or Kayley or something similar. I searched in my slumped jeans on the floor because I was glad to be busy with something that wasn't sexual and meanwhile she kept talking.

— It's been the worst comedown of my life, for like three days? she said. — My immune system's just this tiny piece of paper? I mean it's like I'm not myself any more?

That was the dialogue that was normal among my friends, with that whole offness and bizarrerie. In fact offness was the total territory we inhabited. That's the tone I think I'm doomed to record.

3. LOWDOWN, CLUMSY, SLY, UNDERHANDED

HAPPINESS IS POSSIBLE BUT DIFFICULT

leading to rumours of libertine exploits

The rumours that then circulated about our little band were gothic and other genres – the noir, the skin flicks, the hammer schlock – until eventually I answered my phone and there Shoshana was. *What shit is going on?* Shoshana would say, or one of those Fed-like questions. She wanted me to know what was being said – that we all slept together in the same bed; that we liked to sleep all day then spend the nights doing acid in some sexually combinatory situation; or that we would turn up at parties and instigate crazy effects that left people shaken and disgusted. It was also being said that I was becoming a part-time dealer, including various prescription and non-prescription drugs, with a sideline in web entertainments where Romy and Candy had sex, or Hiro and I would do anything we were asked by an online ensemble of paying spectators. Other people could swear that they had seen Candy at parties with her arms covered in bruises, or wearing handcuffs to which only I had the key. And of course, everyone, signore, is the subject of rumours, everyone exists as this series of misinformation and stories in the minds of others, this is what everyone knows all the time, but to *discover* that, to know it for real – well, that is an unusual fate which is usually only the merited preserve of the celebrity. To be notorious or scandalous in any way distressed me very much – not that I could deny, however, that such rumours corresponded with a certain new freedom in my way of life. To have been part of such a group activity seemed to have extended the basic thinking – this discovery that things I might have feared like orgies or infidelity in full view of my wife could happen as pristinely as the way avocados existed, or the postal system. I had finally realised that whereas I thought I was simply standing in the garden, among verdant streams and widespread birds, I had in fact pushed open a door and discovered the general abattoir, and everywhere there was gore staining the furniture and my delicate hands.

that are in fact more domestic

And so I continued to descend the minor scale – even if it felt like I was moving the other way, in bright ascending arpeggios. In this new atmosphere where I began to articulate myself more freely, my pleasures became more baroque, like some cathedral with its death heads encrusted in the stone, and candles in smeared jars. With Romy I was now much less circumspect and reserved. For if once again we had slept together, and in the presence of my wife, it was as if an ancient interdiction had been lifted, and so we sought each other out more often, and it was difficult to stop this. But what I want to emphasise is that also now at home the actions between myself and Candy became more feverish, as if in instigating this orgy Hiro had demonstrated how easy it was to fulfil the simplest fantasy. There was this thing we had where Candy would sit there on the toilet, and begin to piss, but first of all she did this very shyly, like it wasn't easy for her to be so abandoned and she needed to concentrate, she needed to shut her eyes or look away and sometimes it never happened, sometimes I never did hear that gentle sound begin from under her like a mountain tarn but when it did then she would take my penis in her mouth – because I was there, standing in front of her, waiting – and it undid me, it was so gentle, and so messy. Nor would this kind of exploit have continued if Candy had not been very happy too – because while she has always been this person of grave intellect and serious mien, she never wanted the absolute married existence. It was Candy who had encouraged me to ask my parents if Hiro could stay. Like me, she had ideals of a more expansive existence, and I think for her this had its very precise political dimension – for why should any woman be defined or limited? She was wild precisely in proportion to the absolute repression she wanted to refuse. And I know that nowadays the combinations of girl and boy are so infinite it's sometimes confusing and depressing and hurtful, but also surely it can be delightful, the new combinations of what's normal and what's marvellous? Our domestic tone, if there was a tone, was something like Ominous Funk. For while earlier I would not have contemplated, say, hitting Candy in bed or slapping her breasts, I was now so assiduous in my attention to her that something had changed between us. Now a savagery or violence was among us. Everything with Candy and the bedroom was newly gorgeous and ornate and yet even here I was troubled because to do such things in privacy with Candy seemed in some way

to be an injustice towards Romy. Such spirals! Such innocence! *That* is what you wanted, Mama and Papa, when
you sent me to my secluded school, by a lake, in a forest,
with many therapists and cooks? For there was this one
time when uncertainly or tentatively at least I twisted one
of Candy's nipples, and she gasped at me. I twisted more.

— Hurt me, said Candy. — Like really, totally.

And that was how I discovered this kink in my soul.
It came from Candy, not from me. *A kink?* said Wyman
when I got drunk and told him. *That's just a kink?* Well,
sure, I replied. Because when she had said this I was looking
in her eyes and meanwhile everything about me was getting
more excited. I don't mean just my penis, although sure
I mean my penis, I mean also my stomach and lungs and
heart, I mean my nervous system. It was the excitement
when you make a major discovery. So that in the weeks
that followed Candy's cry of pleasure in her own pain,
while my mother and my father sat downstairs at breakfast, eating their cereal, letting the coffee percolate, we
would be upstairs where I would be tying her up with
some rope I had bought in a ship's merchant in the city
(a course of action I would not recommend to those easily
susceptible to embarrassment, since it is difficult in such
a ship's merchant to order only for instance a metre or so
of rope without looking not at all like the tousled mariner
you are trying to impersonate, but rather, as indeed you
are – so perhaps it is no longer a case of impersonation,
for if you are a thing then how can you resemble it? – the
sexually deviant dauphin your parents have developed).
And then I slapped her and hit her – although skilfully,
so that my parents would not hear – until there were

bruises on her arms and legs, and forced my penis in her while she turned her head from side to side. Or sometimes I would simply tie her to the bed and leave her while I breakfasted downstairs, engrossed in the conversation of my mother and my father. But mostly we would find ways to do this anywhere else, in the bathrooms of friends, or hidden by walls in public places, in the unisex toilets of museums: for who after all would want to be fucked in bed, like the mother of a family? And I should say: I did find these longings very arduous. I have grown up only wanting to do justice to the women around me. In the films I watch, I try very hard to watch an equal list of films by men and women, even if that's not easy to maintain. But if your wife wants you to hit her, in the breasts, and grasp her nipples very tight until she makes some noise or moue that very possibly means pain, then is it wrong to do this? I don't think it can be, and therefore I felt no remorse, were it not for a remorse at this very lack of remorse, because I could understand how this might be seen in other scenarios, that I was in this situation being the old-fashioned man. And I really did not want that to be true, that I would be as male in my desires as my father's generation, for although my father is a gentle man I find his friends very dispiriting, with their desires for women that only encompassed possession and disdain. But I think what was happening was much sweeter. Many people think we have it good, the children of my era, all milkshake and ice cream, but the atmosphere in general was grisaille and snow, like there had been a putsch and all of us were the worried chinovniks in the ruins of the winter palace system. I had friends who lived in threesomes but they didn't do it any more. I had friends who tried to live exactly as rabbinically Orthodox as their parents but that made them desperate too. The stories of the freakouts of my friends, these tended to be now finished. We might as well each morning have sat down for tea and fresh xiao long bao. So that if now in this period where no employment was in sight I had happened on this secret abandon, well, who was I to resist? There Candy would sit, at her dressing table, doing her email in her bra and knickers, with her hair in a band so that later she could wash her face, or let the moisturiser sink in, and it was this very calmness and security and efficiency that made me eager to unravel her. Naturally therefore there were miasmal smells. But just as my mother had always ignored my thefts and implausible stories, so she ignored what was happening now. And it was very useful, this silence, when considering the fact that on our sheets there was now often blood and semen and sometimes urine, which my mother cleared up without advertisement, with just as much carefulness as she showed for our carpets or our clothes.

requiring muteness

That's what I mean about beauty. To maintain any ideal it may become necessary to sacrifice or abandon other, smaller ideals, such as the ideal of decorum, or telling everyone everything, or not inventing falsities and untruths and lies, and not becoming violent and realising that violence can be delicious – and the fact that this is true in no way means that the larger ideal is wrong. The straight line of every romance may always have to get clouded by the other rightful objects of attention, or in the kung fu terms of my childhood movies, you always have to do the things that honour demands. And after all, long before this experiment with other people I knew how fun it was to disobey your own rules – like in secret I would very occasionally go to some hamburger kiosk and gorge myself on meat, despite all my vegetarian principles: I would sit in the dark in some basement at three in the afternoon and eat a hamburger that came with neither plate nor cutlery but only the greasy wrapper it lay on and an assortment of pinched napkins. In everything I did, I wanted happiness at all costs, and maybe this is all my mother's fault. Because in the cinema when I was very young my mother would do two things: she would offer me a commentary to explain what was going on, and also she would remove me if any unhappiness seemed to loom – so the movies from my infancy, I have either never seen them, like the one with the giant shark, because she knew before they began that they were terrifying and sad, or I have begun them but not seen them through to the end, like the one with the alien life form, where the sadness took her by surprise, and she hurriedly removed me. That's a powerful lesson in thinking that the only state to maintain is happiness. Very probably it leads to you doing things that other people might find hateful, or obscene. How vast it is possible to become! It's like some invisibility cloak or superpower – this discovery of the world of the secret. Because of course as soon as you have your own secrets you realise that secrets exist everywhere, in every person who ever sits beside you or to whom you talk: it can be as small as needing the bathroom very much when someone is telling you something important to them and moving, like the story of their psychiatric problems or near-death experience, and you are moved, too, but also thinking how much you are wanting to be enclosed just very briefly in that cool peacefulness of ceramic tile and light and silence and privacy. So that in fact I was amazed how rarely it occurred to me that anyone was lying to me in their turn, even as I constructed so many lies in the average day. And I know that Tiffany for instance would be asking a question that goes something like: but what you do not see in this is that everyone has the right to all the information. You talk of gore, I can hear her saying, so let us talk to you about gore. Here is someone being sent to whichever death camp scares you most: and if they do not know this, if they think they are on their way to some vacation idyll or just labour camp, this revolts us more than the death that occurs with their conscious knowledge. And OK, yes, I understand this. But I would also then reply: Tiffany, just tell me this: if you are going to die, do you prefer to be told, or die at once? Because me, I would like to die at once, with no one telling me anything. For in the end I prefer more happiness to more truth.

delicate to maintain

And so while I continued my baroque investigations with Candy, I wanted to send messages to Romy so that she would feel loved and not abandoned by me – but of course I needed to do such things with assiduous care to prevent Candy from any discovery – and so I would rouse myself late at night, refusing the exhaustion, then enter the bathroom and with the rain around me or the small clouds being purple or black sit there with the iPad warm on my warm thighs, and type slow messages. It was like I was trying to construct a tunnel from my room to hers, like up above us were the usual pedestrians in the green sunlight while down below there I was, blindly tunnelling and making my presence felt. It was important that Romy should know that definitely I cared for her, that my desire for her was no idle lust or passing whim. The problem was that the more messages I sent the more I also thought that I was possibly in love with her and therefore I began to worry about how I might preserve our equilibrium, the perfect equilibrium in which no one endangers the other's safety. The equilibrium depended on only a certain kind of communication, and we were, I thought, in danger of disturbing it by these sudden moments of lyrical desperation. *Can this last?* she would write. *Can something last when it becomes so complicated? Do we even want that?* Or roughly words like that. And because always it's important to let people know that if they have done something that makes them vulnerable, such as offering you a worry or anxiety that's dependent on you, I would respond not with the utopian upbeatness I preferred but similarly fervent observations, and so I would say: *Where are you, Romy, in this night? I look at this screen and want to see your face* – but the problem with this is that as soon as you do that, as soon as you write such sentences, in that tone, you are entering a new realm of trust and also desire. It's very difficult to control. So that the more I wanted Romy to be happy too, the more complicated and vast her happiness became, or at least it did so in my head. I had no way of knowing what exactly Romy was feeling because it was so difficult to talk in any way that was calm, where by calm I mean just watching the sports results on a sofa in the weekend afternoon. Instead our conversations always had this background of high drama. While at the same time the very secrecy this engendered was something I then felt I needed to compensate Candy for, even though I knew that she was not aware of it – for if, say, your husband is sometimes going to the bathroom softly at three in the morning, that's not so abnormal, it might only be because of his new hydration regime in order to help him with his gym sessions in the morning, so that such absence and secrecy did not seem like absence or secrecy at all. And yet I knew it was, and so I tried very hard to create a calm environment for her, complete with flowers, or small gestures like taking the car to the car wash.

examples of a larger philosophy

In the most grandiose classroom you have ever seen, complete with strip lights and graffitied benches, let's imagine me giving you a lecture on time and up there on the whiteboard is my final calculation. Listen up at the back there! Stop kissing, kids! On the whiteboard you would see me split time into three separate categories: the *necessary*, the *superfluous*, and the *almost necessary*. This is what I have learned from my reading. And I would say that if I had to pick just one, the most difficult category of them all is that final category of the *almost necessary*. That's what I was learning from this maintenance of my friends and other amoureuses. The necessary happens every day; the superfluous generally once – and if only the necessary and superfluous were what existed, then I think there would be no need for philosophy. But sadly there is also this extra category because the *almost necessary* is what should definitely happen, except it so rarely does, but then it does sometimes happen, after all. The *almost necessary* is what so rarely happens that eventually you become tired of even planning to do it, knowing as you do that you will almost definitely find a reason not to do it, and yet it can happen, after all, if you make a superhuman effort. Sometimes I wonder if all human character could be revealed in a person's relation to the *almost necessary*, not therefore the rare events like whom a person sleeps with, but instead the vaster everyday texture – like, if you do indeed sleep with someone, then how do you afterwards maintain their sense of self-worth with small messages and gifts? These are the constant problems of intention for everyone in existence – the people with their self-help encyclopedias doing turns down the boulevards with their children underneath the acacia trees and palmettos, the kids who inhabit the burger emporia and jobcentres and the maté dens – and they are really where the true metaphysics lies. If I ever write a treatise of philosophy, such smallness will I think be its major discovery.

of minuscule intentions

Just look at me! I no more found it easy to preserve my secret life with all its obligations than a courtier might have found it easy keeping up the exigencies of diplomacy at the palaces of Versailles. My skin seemed to be dying – each morning there was something new, whether eczema, psoriasis, small unexplained rashes, and also teeth complaints, hair ailments. And by this I think my body with its weeping and sadness was trying to communicate, like our terrified dog in the illuminated night, that while of course I did very much want to preserve everyone's happiness, at the same moment I could also see how possible it might be to hurt people and to avoid that hurt required immense effort and devotion. Nor was it only my inner circle to whom I thought I owed obligations. If I felt that I let down strangers it left me woebegone and ill at ease, even those who came momentarily to our door. There was one particular day, for instance, of sunlight and sunflowers, when a man came selling dusters and other items in a plastic bucket. In such a situation, when people make demands on me when I am not expecting them, my shyness is often a problem. And on this particular day I was preoccupied with various projects I was trying to maintain, so that as soon as I saw this fatboy with his dusters in their wrapper, and bi-tonal scourers for the ultimate kitchen, I said we would not be needing anything and closed the door on him which was, I admit it, a perhaps abrupt manner of behaving but then I did not want these items, and also if you're in a pensive state it's difficult to treat interruptions of any kind with the correct gravitas and respect. And so it was certainly possible that inadvertently I closed the door on him before he had finished his first sentence, which I regretted but also hoped that he understood, but instead what happened next, as I was walking to the stairs, was that he then pushed the vertical letter box open and through it I could see his face like in some horror close-up, and only one eye was visible but mostly I was looking at his mouth, which was screaming a sentence like: *Fuck you, four-eyes*, or something like that, I don't remember now the exact phrase he used and I think the reason I don't remember precisely is that I was very shocked. For I had meant him no harm at all. But if he had a grievance then I was sorry to have caused it, very much, and for a very long time I dwelled on this matter, and how I might have treated him better. But in my defence I might have argued that on that particular day I had been trying very hard to work, for more and more I was understanding that the true way I was letting Candy down was not in any of my deceptions, but rather in how I was subsisting in this state of total unemployment and lack of money. Many nights Candy would begin to cry, if for instance she was too tired to come out with me to some cocktail drive-in or to the stadia for racing dogs, or if I once again tried to convince her not to go to her early yoga but instead remain in bed with me. And I knew that in my inability to be productive I was only adding to the list of Candy's tasks, but also I had this sense that I could not go back to an office, not just yet, that on refusing to go to an office depended my happiness and therefore also Candy's. It was possible that a lot depended on my writings, like my monograph on philosophy – maybe several people's happiness, you never knew. I told myself that it might turn out to be a great help to many young people. Never work! That's at least an idea with a pedigree. Whether Candy minded or did not mind my lack of occupation was a very difficult subject for me, and was maybe all the more difficult because she did not ever ask, and by that very lack of asking I knew that it concerned her.

— If you want to show me something, she would say, — I'm here, cookie.

And I am ashamed to say that I was irritable at such suggestions, only because the less I could produce the more such questions made me feel inadequate and insecure. So that eventually the question was never asked, and Candy would go to work while I sat there making coffee and regarding sadly with a heavy heart the dog. In the hair salon I quizzed my cutter about the possible thinning of my hair. She seemed to be cool about it, but then it's easy not to be anxious about the anxieties of others, I would say that is one talent possessed by every being on the planet, including the deadbeat algae and the less sensitive snails. Whereas for me, anxiety was my general medium. I was the connoisseur of failing your high ideals. Certainly I was often wrong, but at least I was always right about why I might be wrong. No one can say I have any illusions about myself. But also I think that if you become too easily preoccupied with the small impossibilities, like what to eat or how to get up on time, you never get to see the major impossibilities, and that's a shame. It's why whenever anyone attacks me for my drive for perfection and its seeming hypocrisy I think they are missing the point. Because of course one cannot be the perfect vegetarian or timetabler, although also you should try – but that's no reason not to understand that on the grander scale, like love, it's always going to be impossible to live right at all. Even if there is no other way of living. It tended to exasperate those around me.

MY MOTHER
Why do you always make such jokes?

ME
I think I'm sweet.

MY MOTHER
Snooks, you are. It's just that no one thinks this.

ME
But shouldn't they?

MY FATHER
He is a clown.

MY MOTHER
But if he wants to be, so let him!

MY FATHER
I'm not so sure.

That was our suburb crosstalk that gets the extra name of conversation. But I think my mother was right. For my mother I wanted to be the all-powerful conquistador.

to increase such multiple worlds

It was always very caring, the ideal I tried to preserve. So that if I was even in bed while Candy undressed, and sending a small message to Romy, which happened rarely, but did sometimes have to happen if Romy wanted an immediate reassurance, then as much as I lied to Candy about whom I was texting, I also lied to Romy about where I was – since Romy was no monster of depravity, she liked Candy very much, and if I had told her that I was reclining in the same room as Candy, among the pillows, writing violent gorgeous things to her, then Romy would have been upset, and with good reason. So that while the moralist may well want to argue that the reason lying is wrong is for its corruption, the way it turns other people into fictions without them realising, or, to be more precise, transforms the people to whom you are talking into ghosts and simulacrums, I think it's also possible to hazard the possibility that this very ghostliness is something beautiful and to be treasured. Suddenly the world is all macaws and garish. And even if for that ideal I have had to suffer terrible things, still, it's not without its beauty, or seduction.

for which his model is Hiro

Meanwhile Hiro was into so many tricks and schemas that I could not keep up. He'd come back late at night with recondite brands of cigarette, from various maritime countries, and tell me how tomorrow he couldn't see me because he'd made a friend who had potentially upsetting medical tests the next day and needed his support, and while I applauded his public spirit I had this twinge of maybe slightly feeling jealous, like thinking why should *this* other person get the attention and not me? Why should the illnesses of this other person be so regarded? I wanted Hiro always. To be a sidekick is no fun if the original maestro is unavailable, and there you sit all alone with your breadsticks in the chequered light of the trattoria. Perhaps such loneliness was also because I was having other problems with my phone: someone would call, and when I would answer there was no one there. I know this happens often but still, it was unnerving in the circumstances. Naturally in such an atmosphere I wanted *joie de vivre* very much, and Hiro was my model. I wanted to follow him in his obscure explorations. If it meant that we found ourselves in pleasure spots and night dives, it implied no seediness or exploitation of those less fortunate, but only a way of trying to spend time without becoming bored, and a possibly laudable wish to talk to people one might usually ignore. Through the night roved Hiro, and I wanted to keep him company. Definitely I was also slightly worried for him, and wanted to protect him. I was all solicitude. He was in one of those manic phases where sleep seemed to him an inconvenience, and if you do not want to go to sleep and also do not want to sit at home, in the silent bedrooms of suburbia, then the kind of place you have to enter gets seedier as the night goes on. It's impossible to avoid, so that it was only natural that one night after wandering from place to place we might be sitting side by side in towelling robes, conversing with almost naked girls. And always it's important to enlarge your perspectives, to make the background and the foreground less separate from each other. That's a basic moral law.

— Hey, we said. — Hey hey.

— Hey, the girls said sweetly back.

Sure, Hiro called this place a *sauna*, and of course I knew the reputation of such a word, and had I mentioned this moment to Wyman – who is always fearful of the world, like the platonic form of a photograph of Wyman would be Wyman in striped blazer and straw boater standing up in a sepia punt – I think he might have argued that I should have possibly been morally afraid. The word, perhaps, should have been as ominous a sign as if I were in some teen horror flick and had come across a garage in the rainy night whose electric lettering was sizzling. But always I was very brave, when considering my inner life. I would risk my inner life in any place of possible corruption, to gain the coconut slushie and the million-dollar prize.

whom our hero accompanies to a sauna

There was a changing room which was like the changing rooms in the swimming pools where I had learned to swim, and that I suppose is no surprise because presumably the capacity for variation in a changing room is very small. The atmosphere was strangely sports aquatic, with each of us bearing on our wrist a key on a plastic bracelet. And this was where Hiro and I had settled into our white spa gowns with plastic sandals – a uniform that I think is only ever humiliating, especially for the gutbucket male, not to mention the gutbucket miniature male, which was possibly its purpose, to emphasise the ugliness of the men in the presence of the women. Maybe it was a small humiliation to set against the greater humiliation of the women. Even if I am not so sure that the women are humiliated, in fact I am almost certain that there is no shame for them at all in such a place. It was more like those myths where nymphs hang out beside a pool and I now understood why these myths should end with the macho getting punished. I think punishment is only right for such a situation – to be in a salon, on a sofa, with a complimentary non-alcoholic beverage, regarding this tableau that was slightly reminiscent of the refreshment area at the bowling but only if you also admit that it had this glowing kind of extra that was the fact that every woman was naked, or almost. It was just another of the examples I was collecting of the replica that is not quite a replica, because it was so much like the portrait of a normal bar but the difference that the girls were almost naked was a total new discovery of what is possible in this world. I suppose I don't think ever before I've understood what money was able to do. I don't think I knew that this is what was possible. I had previously thought that just the greatest treats that money could buy were drugs or holidays. I didn't realise it could totally go anywhere. And I know the argument that there are so many ways of coercion and entrapment in this world and money is just one of them, but the business of show was also very convincing. I was considering something Romy once told me she'd had to say to a boyfriend, along the lines of –

ROMY
It's like you just do things because of porn. Like take coming on my face. I do not like it. I am not interested. I do not want your come all over my mouth.

And I understood her but we still argued because in my opinion there was nothing intrinsically wrong with making things all Coney Island, the way they kept on adding attractions in the old days: the Roller Coaster, the Shoot-the-Chutes. I still think Manhattan is not Manhattan enough: it could do more with the artificial man-made illuminations. To which Romy said something like, but her point was, had he ever asked her? Actually sat down and thought: what does this cartoon character with steam coming out of her ears really think about this? I did see what she meant by that. The problem with the greater ideals is that you must achieve them with other people, and that can lead to confusing situations. Like here everyone did seem very happy, just having their conversations. If I imagined anything more, it would have only been massages with bikini girls, or maybe some oriental soapland where the emphasis was on scrubbing. So it was only when Hiro explained that you could go into a room with any of them that the real mystery of this place began to unfurl. And I knew that according to the usual terms of Wyman I should leave right away, but my worry was how excited I was feeling. It seemed to indicate that there could be a different way of understanding the situation. Just somewhere in the corner of my vision like one of those cartoon fairies I think I had a vision of Candy but it faded, it was like the brief exposure when you're in the metro and it goes past another metro and for a moment you are staring at another person's face instead of your reflection, but it still in the end does fade – for perhaps whatever sadness I might feel would be worth it for the new sensations I would have achieved, and especially when I thought that it was very unlikely this would happen to me again, never again would I find my way back to such a location, and that to do nothing here was something I would only ever regret. If utopia could be achieved in multiple perspectives among your friends, as Candy had observed, then why not also here, with strangers? Also I worried that now I was here it might seem haughty or even cold if I only sat and watched. I tried to think about the future, like perhaps two hours' time. I think I thought that the worst I might feel would be that kind of sick hollow feeling the morning after you've drunk too much rye and smoked too much hashish. It was about as bad as that how I imagined it, the feeling afterwards. And after all, it's easy to think that something has happened when in fact nothing has. There's no reason everything has to be followed by a dark bad sadness, that would detach itself and stalk you like some mushy fetish with its matchstick hands and terrible toes. I think the brief occurs to us more than we sometimes think, as minute as the soft tearing sound the bubbles of washing-up foam make in the bowl in the sink. But I never quite managed to finish my moral calculations, because I was interrupted by Hiro smiling at a beautiful girl who was almost naked but not quite, who therefore sat down beside me and smiled. And as she did so my mind just went blank – like the way the wheels on a suitcase go suddenly softly silent when they move from the sidewalk's tarmac onto lavish hotel carpet.

where he finds himself ascending

I'm usually bad at smiling but I tried to smile for her. I wanted her to see how polite I could be, and wanted to put her at her ease. Also I am vulnerable to female beauty, and sure, if you saw her at a party you might not have been amazed – but there she would have been in the ordinary modern clothes whereas here she was dressed in just some sort of fabric around her waist and I do not see this so often. In fact I do not think I have ever sat and talked to a topless stranger. I think there is something totally sexy about a girl who is topless only, I say sexy but maybe there's also something sad. Let's say it can be sad or sexy, depending on the situation. For instance I love it when Candy is only in her jeans when she is half dressing or undressing, but there the toplessness can some-times seem maybe also vulnerable, as if something is simply incomplete, whereas here it was only alluring. And it occurred to me to compliment this girl and so I said something like:

— You're really pretty.

I'm not so good with words in social situations. As I said, I suffer from shyness. But she looked at me with affection, and told me her name. And I know that this name was almost definitely made up but still, like every-thing, a person needs a name, even if that name isn't real.

— I'm Caycee, said Caycee.

And we sat there. Hiro was now looking away, like he was a calm philosopher or mystic saint. I sort of understood. I think that he was nervous, and definitely it was awkward, this sitting with a girl whom you don't know and is almost naked, beside your friend, with both of you in towelling robes. It was definitely a new form of human interaction. But also I approved of this, because I am thinking that the future will more and more be all about these kinds of interaction, where everything usual is blurred. I was definitely excited. Her eyes were blue and her hair was blonde and her breasts were small, but I didn't care about her eyes or her hair or her breasts, I was beyond the entire physical, because I was in the pure cartoon, in the seventh sphere, like that man who dreamed he was looking down on the very tiny earth – I do have a gift for separating or levitating like that. I was feeling very separate and also like I wanted very much to make this moment happy, like it would prove my expanding ideals not by having sex or something like that but just by being able to maintain a gentle conversation. And because I think it's always odd to be without conversa-tion when a woman is naked in front of you, or almost,

because I may not be suave but I know the proprieties,
I tried to keep talking.

— You're lovely, I said.

I really do have no vocabulary.

— You are how old? asked Caycee.

— Oh kind of thirty, I gravely replied.

And as I said this it seemed a sad age. It just seemed
very old and very young together. Then Caycee asked if
I was married, or had a girlfriend, and for a moment I
worried that I had left my wedding ring on, but most of
all it was the innocent directness of this question which
troubled me. It surprised me in the way I suppose a fledg-
ling roué might be surprised if his mistress asks after his
wife. I didn't have the courage to say I was married. I
wanted her to like me. And yet also I didn't want to seem
like one of those sad people who come into a place like
this because they are without anyone who loves them, and
so I settled on a compromise and told her that I had a
girlfriend. But this then led to an inquisition from Caycee,
something polite like –

— Do you live together?

Then if we did live together, because I told her the truth
and said that we did, other questions followed, according
to Caycee's reasoning.

— So when are you getting married? she asked.

She thought marriage was very important. It was a very
difficult conversation, not only in the dialogue itself but
also in the fact that one of us was essentially naked and the
other one was not. I looked at the soft nipples on her breasts.
She looked at me looking. She pinched them into pertness
like that was what I wanted. And when I replied that it was

such a strange question, whether I would marry my girl-friend, I also wanted to add that I didn't mean she shouldn't ask such a question, and that in fact I was grateful for her proposition that if one of us was naked then a new honesty might be possible – even if I wasn't being honest, although in a way perhaps I was, and even if also it might be argued that this was not in fact her idea, the nakedness, that in fact there were rules, and commercial expectations, but I really did think that these commercial considerations were, as they might say in commerce, only *secondary*.

— You should marry her, said Caycee. — If you love her, then you should marry her.

And she was right, of course, and in fact I so agreed with this argument that I had already taken her advice long ago and married Candy, but overlapping with this feeling was another feeling that I think was closer to regret that I was almost definitely the only man to have ever discovered inside a sauna a spirit of established order. But this was itself overlapping with another feeling, maybe a lostness or lustness. I scented coconut oil. Or whatever scent it was on Caycee's body, I enjoyed it. I didn't want to. But I did want. I also wanted to give an answer to her reasonable question. I wanted her to like me very much and approve of me. My mother always brought me up to think that it's what you think that is important, and most especially in your dealings with women. I have a rich and sympathetic inner life! Isn't that something after all? And so I think that it was important to me that this girl might think of me as dainty, that I was swashbuckle, definitely, but also my friends all think I am very kind and I wanted her to know this too.

— We do have a dog, I said.

I do not know, however, what she thought of this – because she didn't continue the conversation on the subject of my hound, she only replied by asking me if I wanted to go somewhere more private. And it felt sad, this business turn, but also I understood. It was a business, after all. And in a way – I don't mean every way – I would have liked my mother to have seen this, the suavity with which I did this talk. My mother is always – in the hair salons and the floral outlets – questioning my relationship to money, like money is this cloud in which I rest like some putto with my trumpet, and I was proud that I could now rebut her, had I been ever able to tell her about this moment, which I possibly couldn't. I had reached the limits of my privacy. I asked the price. The money was calculated, Caycee said, in half-hour sections. I was paying her for half an hour alone in a room. OK, I said. We could do whatever I liked, she said. And then I paused. I asked if I could just think about it, just for a moment, and I think I might have been possibly doing something that reminded me of flirting, although I think perhaps it wasn't flirting, but only fear. I looked to Hiro for help but Hiro was now sitting at the bar, enjoying a second guava juice. My saint had abandoned me just when I did really need him. Then Caycee took my hand and it was very hot, her hand, and I felt very moved by her hand, the fact that it was real and hers and there. And perhaps I should have tried to think more clearly about what she was thinking, I'm very much aware that very few men, like, for instance, my father, ever tried to understand the thoughts of a woman, but also I had this idea that in the end these thoughts are basically the same as mine. Which meant that I did just trust her to see that I was overwhelmed with something that was perhaps not gratitude exactly but certainly close to gratitude. I mean it felt like this was some beneficence or other-worldliness, like those pictures of the Assumption, as if the world had been converted into a fine and golden light.

discovering urges of self-description

The reason I am telling you this is that this moment marked an important stage in my vocation. As we walked along a corridor, and Caycee took a key from a row on the wall, then entered a room and locked the door from inside, I was suddenly struck by a small fissure or split. It was definitely not easy, I reflected, to keep liking the things I did. If for instance things end up happening inside some casa of ill repute, well, the whole fluorescent question of likeability does impose itself. There is only so long, to choose an example from the life of my friend Kayvon, when your wife has happened on you being dildoed by another woman on your bathroom floor, that a person can convincingly keep on saying *it wasn't me*. And I'm aware that the entire history of the theory of art is about removing the issue of the likeable from the picture, it's only the philistine spectators like Nelson who say: *Jeez, there was no one in the movie you'd want to like hang out with*, but maybe sadly Nelson is on to something. I mean, why should anyone give you any attention? That's a good question. And if they do, why should you be an asshole? It goes way beyond the moral, this whole problem. It goes into the deep dark mania to please. There were many things, I had to admit, that my mother would not admire about her child, if she knew the total truth. Confidante she was, but not entirely. Like for instance, and I am aware that still this is maybe small, but in fact I am not so sure that it's really possible to differentiate between the small and massive in these matters, I used to watch gang bangs on the Internet. They turned me on. It's true that very sweetly once Candy tried to tell me that there was nothing wrong with this entertainment. But Candy was always very kind. In one of the tapes a lovely girl whose given name was Chastity was being interviewed before her gang bang got under way. Chastity was wearing a grey vest with grey marl shorts. And then the man who was filming asked her if she wanted to say hi to anyone, like *Hi Dad*. — Oh that would be so awful, she said with a serious smile. She was thinking about this seriously. She said *awful* really sweetly, like *offal*. — I've got three younger brothers too, so that'd be so offal as well, I just hope they haven't found out yet . . . And I was full of righteous fury. How could this man behind the camera make her feel ashamed? What right did he have? She was a nice person, a sweet person, this was surely obvious to even the most deranged viewer. In porn I mostly see tender feats of endurance on the part of these beautiful women. For what she was about to do was essentially altruistic for all her infinite spectators. I wanted to take her in my arms and let her rest. But I couldn't, obviously, so I took my penis and concentrated on that instead, while watching her be sodomised – for if I had to say what I most liked I would have to probably sadly say it was when fucking a girl's arsehole, how suddenly the tightness which had been the defining characteristic suddenly disappears: not that it loosens entirely, but it does. What I mean is that although the old-school problems of description are all about how well something matches *the real world*, maybe the future way of putting this will be all about the problems of getting over the nice and likeable. Maybe I'm exaggerating. I don't know. I'm just saying, as I walked along that corridor, an old joke was occurring to me: *This man looks like a corrupt idiot and acts like one, but don't let that deceive you. He* is *a corrupt idiot.* That's basically the situation, I was thinking, of every talker in the universe. And I think it was then that I felt this sudden urge to write these things down. I missed the tearful saints and the curtained confessionals! Had I had my phone or other writing implement with me, a Dictaphone or felt-tip pen, I would have used them right away. I had a sudden mania for making diary entries and sportive sketches. Listen to me, it was like I was crying, on my banjo! I was so much larger, it turned out, than I had thought.

like his behaviour in this bedroom

Inside the room, Caycee turned to me and released her girdle and motioned that I should undress too. So I took off my dressing gown, which was in fact not difficult since I have always found those towelling dressing gowns difficult, so that in fact I had been shuffling with it held together in my hand along the heavy carpets. And I felt quite feminine and odd. I wonder if this is what women have to often feel, this denuding and unsureness. I was still in my plastic sandals. I wanted to take them off but also I was a little unsure about the carpet in this room and the general hygiene. Caycee was in transparent perspex plat-form heels and was remaining in them. The inequality upset or perplexed me but I wasn't concentrating on my perplexity, I was thinking instead about her legs or rather between her legs, where there was a perfect smoothness. It was like the beauty of one of those drawings where in just four lines the genius artist has drawn a face. In the same way when she lay down there was only a smooth curve between her legs. So I lay down too, with my feet still resting on the floor, since while I didn't want to remove my plastic sandals I also felt it was wrong to have sandals on a bed. It was dark and the air was heavy with her perfumes and also cleaning chemicals. And I now think that I should have been amazed but I wasn't. I was only suddenly happy and it was like it always was when you are naked with a girl, except it was slightly not. She lay down and made various suggestions, and I realised that in fact I hadn't thought at all about what we might actually do, which meant that until this point I had in no way thought about the possible dangers of disease. And I think maybe I hadn't wanted to think this because the thought seemed to me to be shameful. But now that the thought was occurring I also really didn't want this moment to have consequences that would haunt me for ever. But then, maybe that ancient fear was part of the whole experience. Also I am nervous in these kinds of performances. In a new environment, I can get perturbed. Sure, she was beautiful, but I was definitely thinking that in fact she in no way wanted me, and in that kind of situation I don't think it's unreasonable to find it difficult to be aroused. Even if a girl just seems ever so faintly bored or tired I want to stop and this was very much worse. Because I was also compelled to admit that while I was probably younger and perhaps with smoother skin than the usual customer or patron, I was not uniformly attractive, like I remember Romy saying that it was strange to be with me because in general she preferred a more muscular physique and although I said it didn't upset me, still, I found it difficult to forget. So yes I was worried about the mechanics of my penis, and worried about disease, and worried that Caycee was really not wanting this to happen at all, and mostly I was now wanting to be finished so I could give her all the money I possessed and the transaction would be over. But on the other hand, I understand this, I could have therefore done nothing, I could have absolutely done nothing and just paid her anyway, and I suppose if I didn't it was just that I have this constant curiosity. Always I will keep looking. So I said that maybe just a blow job and then she looked at me with what I hoped was a smile that understood that I was somewhere in my heart an honest man, I would only demand the most minimal things, and then she asked me if I wanted it with a condom or without. And I said something which I think now in retrospect sounds a little too innocent –

— Well, what do you think would be better? I asked – like I was in a cafeteria lunch queue or massage spa deluxe.

— I think for the end it's better with, said Caycee.

So she did it with a condom. I lay down on my back and looked away, in the familiar guise of the nineteenth-century wife. I also wasn't sure that I had an erection at all. It was like I was in such a panic that I had lost all feeling or awareness of my penis, like the frankfurter must feel inside a corn dog. I just assumed that if she was carrying on, then some version of an erection must exist, but perhaps such an occurrence is all too common in these situations and Caycee was so civilised that she could cope with soft extremities, like the older woman in that old movie instructing a soldier in the definitions of *fiasco*. She was kind of crouching over me to one side and I asked her if I could touch, and she nodded yes. So I touched the skin inside her buttocks, the rougher skin and the wrinkled hole. Then I touched her where normally it would be slippery and wet but here it was very dry and very smooth. And I did feel a slight disappointment at this absolute lack of wetness. I know there is no reason she would be finding this exciting but there was a part of me that did, or hoped she might. I couldn't help it. So I tried to think about something else. At first I was just thinking that in fact this was the first time I had ever had a blow job with a condom on, and couldn't really work out what it was feeling like, but in so far as this was a novelty the greater novelty, obviously, was the fact that I was paying this girl to put my penis in her mouth, but before any of these thoughts could continue towards conclusions I had come. It was definitely the fastest orgasm of my life. Slightly I was relieved that therefore if I had come, presumably I had been erect. But still, I could not conceal from myself a disappointment. She tied the condom in the most lissom and minute of motions. She was very neat, and I thought that in fact there is nothing neater than coming in a girl's mouth. People think it's mess but that isn't true. I came inside a condom inside her tidy mouth. How domestic can you get?

— That was quick, she said.

I wasn't concentrating so hard on her tone but I think it sounded more like she was pleased than that she was being sarcastic or ironic. I think from her point of view I must have represented good value for money. It also added to the tone I was hoping we had developed of being friends, or in which I tried not to impose. And then I realised that while if this was real life, and it was of course, but if it was let's say another aspect of real life where we had met as normal in a bar and afterwards found ourselves in such an intimate environment then we would have developed in this aftermath a conversation, and this is something I always like, to develop conversation, because it did feel that maybe there were things we needed to discuss, but here she was wanting me now to just get dressed. And so I did. I didn't want to upset her at all. She was very nice and personable.

in which all moral values are revised

We walked back down the corridor and I went into the changing room while she stood outside, waiting, and I came back with all the cash I had, because I wanted to show my gratefulness. I tipped her what was possibly double the actual payment. But then I am always unhappy with tipping, because the tip is saying that the system of society has failed, that the price advertised is not equal to the service rendered, and of course, señoritas, the system has failed, of this we have no doubt, but the tip therefore becomes the place where somehow restitution will be made. Even if in doing so it struck me that I was committing another injustice, since this cash of mine that I had given to Caycee was in fact really my father's, because all the money I had right now was given to me by my father, and it felt a little wrong that I had used it for this purpose, rather than on improving books. That felt like the greater betrayal, even, than the betrayal of my marriage vows with Candy – and so my true feeling at the moment, a little like the morning I had woken up beside Romy, was more like nostalgia, like I wanted to call Candy right there and listen to her voice. She just seemed very far away, like I wanted to be talking to her, even if of course she was the absolute person to whom I could never tell this tale. I would have to make do with my voice inside my head, and other confidants, like Hiro. And so I went back into the salon, where Hiro gazed at me.

— You totally did it? he said.

— Well, not entirely, I said.

— Me too, said Hiro.

— What do you mean? I said.

— We were talking and she said that she was tired. She said she'd been working twelve hours.

— Uh-huh, I said.

— So I gave her a massage instead.

I envied him, I really did. Somehow Hiro had managed to have a sweeter experience than I had. But that's what happens when you hang out with someone way ditzier than Buddha. It destroys all your moral faith.

4. THE PISTOLET

the basis of larger schemes

Already I was feeling that in the matter of world-transformation, we were maybe quite advanced, we were extending new manners of behaving in every direction, stretching out the world, like stretching out the dough to make a pizza, but in Hiro's opinion we were losing ourselves in abstraction and inaction. We had no grander scheme.

HIRO
This could carry on for ever.

ME
You're bored.

HIRO
I am more than bored. I am frustrated.

Our analyses of feelings, and feelings about feelings, in which we specialised, thought Hiro, were not enough, or at least, while possibly amusing in themselves, they were not the proper way to live. We needed larger activities. Or this was what he announced one dark morning in a cafe, when we discovered that we could only pay for one tea, and one elderflower doughnut, for one of Hiro's aims was always to exist as gigantically as possible – and I had to admit that I agreed with him. When you have no resources it's not easy to create ideal communities. And recently my father had decided to end the money he was giving me, being as it was spent on so many luxuries and lazy pursuits – not that he disapproved of those in them-selves, he wanted to emphasise, he just disliked being the person who was funding them for other people. By which I guess he did mean Hiro. He tended to think you should fund your very own laziness, and while I tried to wonder if maybe the truest form of resistance to the world in its current form is to waste the money of other people, I did not have the heart for it. Possibly I agreed with my father too. For to be as dependent as I was seemed to me in no way a good profession.

MY FATHER
At your age I had already founded a business.

ME
But that's my point.

MY FATHER
It wasn't easy.

ME
It's not so easy to be me.

To have it difficult in your early years, I think, is a good recipe for self-respect. Whereas to have it good – to be the one on the sunlounger beside plashing fountains exclaiming *che beleza!* – is definitely to have it bad. Which is just a more general way of putting the sentence: *I live at home with my mother and father and wife and I feel as if in constant pain.* To come from a family is unavoidable, of course, but also it's a terrible affliction. There is no amount of white pills that can make this cloud feel better. And when life does this to you, it's difficult to react very well. I suppose depression would be one way of describing my ongoing state, but I preferred the more romantic terms that were once in vogue, like *melancholy.* My therapist said no. She said I should say *depression.* But that was long ago. I grew up in so much comfort I was totally dependent. To the zillionaire I suppose it wasn't much. I just knew that I could always go home, in a taxi, and there would be clean sheets on the bed, and maybe the window open slightly so that the small sounds of the city could be heard, and downstairs my mother would be making me hot chocolate. Elsewhere there were addicts to junk burgers or to malls or sleeping pills. Me I was addicted to my station in life's bazaar. Don't you think such comfort might not be so good for a nature like mine? I don't mean my parents meant to do me harm but harm as we all know can emerge through so many sewer pipes and gutters that there's no real way of keeping the harm away. Maybe other people could maintain their independence even in such conditions but I was not one of them. So although it was hard to bear, this knowledge that my father was now through with me financially, I could also see it as a bright occasion. Like I was the ball and this situation was the basketball star and now we were only waiting for one final element to arrive and slam me into the hoop.

with firearms for accessories

In Hiro's opinion, the first problem was the eternal problem of cashflow – and of course I could not disagree at all, it was the pure difficulty now in our lives – but also, added Hiro, the more difficult conundrum was this: we did not want to work for it. His basic thinking was: if it's possible theoretically to get rich quick, why take your time? Or, to put this more philosophically, the gangster in her desire to get rich quick is doing something of extensive resistance to the social order. She is very much bored with the world of work, and this is not, perhaps, to be despised, or at least certainly not so stupid. And Hiro now, it turned out, was also in this business – and to prove his point he then brought out a very gorgeous gun, not so much the Uzi or small-bore but some sort of petite Magnum, I'm not so sure of the category, and the sight of this machine on Hiro's knees in a retro cafe, with photos of dead stars from the worlds of snooker or daytime television, caused an excited response in me which is not I think unusual, because it's not so ordinary to have a gun in your life, or at least not if you are the kind of innocent prodigy and general person I am. But also I would say that if you have never held an object that looks like a gun in public you have not lived. Whether replica or real, it doesn't matter. The thrill is cool.

    — The fuck is that? I said.

    — It's kind of obvious? said Hiro.

And I did not want immediately to seem too reluctant or disapproving, partly because in the end the person with the gun in their hand is always very persuasive, but also because I had this theory that I could make at least some people very happy, and maybe in the end the only person this was true of would be Hiro, so how could I deny him? And also as I said, I was slightly sad and angry at my station in this life. I had this melancholy rage inside me and that's a destabilising condition to be in when trying to make your everyday moral decisions.

in a criminal plan

How little equipment do you ever need to be convincing! Already I had learned this in the bodega incident. The merest replica of a pistol is enough to make you feared and this was after all not, said Hiro, the true and crazy thing itself.

— It's not? I said.

— Man, no, he said.

True, it was more real than a water pistol. On the other hand, he pointed out, it was less real than a real gun.

— Is just a replica, said Hiro.

— It still looks real, I said.

— Well, sure, said Hiro. — Why wouldn't it?

How many doubles, really, does a tale need? For while it's easy to do things with water pistols and so on, argued Hiro, if you want to do something a little grander or more serious then you do need better props, or so he had decided, while roaming the lovely wide-open illuminated spaces of the computer screen. The water pistol was good for speed effects, but if a gun looks real, like truly real, with appropriate safety catches, finishes, sheen and so on – that's as real as it needs to be if you do not intend to use it, and most of the time a gun in civilised society is precisely not intended to be used, it's much more a general way of talking to other people, a sign like fishnet tights or lunatic lunettes.

— What, I said, — do you mean by more serious?

— Well, let's say, the nail salon? said Hiro.

I do think we live in a very dangerous age, I mean dangerous for one's moral life: for in the previous eras there was always a problem of materiel for the beautiful soul who wanted to express herself, I mean it was perhaps not so easy for the average bookish student in the marsh-land cities or slum conurbations to get hold of a gun, or other accessories, nor the many wraps of opium that their heart may have desired. But now so many things are available from the flat depths of a computer screen, and while that's surely an advance for civilisation, it's perhaps also a drawback, too.

— OK, keep talking, I opined.

When we had done that thing with the water pistol and bodega, Hiro pointed out, at no point had I complained, so why, he wanted to know, would this be different? If the prop was slightly more menacing, still, in its essence, it was not more menacing at all since in both cases the implement was not truly real. So that if my worry was for the safety of the people who would be threatened, I did not need to worry, just as if my worry was for our own safety, then there as well he thought I should be happy, since what security detail or panic button would a nail salon ever have? For after all, continued Hiro, it was just a place of harmony and perfume, to which no one with any aggressive intent ever went. Sure, there would be CCTV and so on, but since the CCTV is the worst cinema experience in the world, with only blurred and minute figures, that did not need to worry us either. While *morally*, nothing could go wrong because such an establishment would be very much self-contained, with insurance schemes in place for precisely this kind of sad and inevitable event. Every shop on every street must expect this, said Hiro, the way a woman must expect a man at some point to hustle her against a wall and explain stupidly that he loves her. So that in conclusion, I suppose, his basic argument was that so long as nobody suffered you could treat crime as a pure and singular event.

HIRO

Like, does it really matter if you hold up a retail outlet? I mean: who gets hurt?

ME

I no follow.

HIRO

The girl you point the gun at or whatever, the bayonet, is going to get her money back, the company behind that shop is going to get its money back, the only person who pays is the major insurance executive who is very far away and more importantly can take it.

And I felt a slight annoyance – it was inhabiting me very gently, the way the giant wind inhabits the tops of the eucalyptus trees and acacias – that Hiro obviously felt it would be so difficult to convince me, and if he thought that I would not be easy to convince I wanted very much to prove him wrong.

— Let's do it, I said.

— You sure? he said.

— I know it, I said.

If you have no way of demonstrating skill in the rest of your life, it's really restful to think that there may be one small way you will be able to succeed. And after all, I was thinking, as I took the last bite of my doughnut half, so many things were now different in my life to how I had thought they would be long ago. The old thinking seemed no use. I know the usual thinking is to separate the inner from the outer, to argue that OK sure there can be an aesthetic interest in let's say grazing the brink of horror in any number of thought experiments and baga-telles, in considering murders as so many objects deserving of aesthetic attention, like statues, pictures, oratorios, cameos, intaglios, and so on, but that if at any point you succumbed to the actual realisation of such thought experi-ments the feeling would only be one of repulsion and squeamishness. But I was suddenly not so sure. It seemed a distinction that was perhaps more useful for the general social contract than just true. And what I wanted was excitement in my life. The lack of excitement seemed a very serious problem and I would do anything, I began to think, to see that excitement return – in whatever zany form. Please interest me! I was imploring to the world. It was like being a lover of animal rights but still in the end having this total need to sit out in the dying sun while watching the matador kill the bull. Definitely I was curious as to what a heist might actually be. I was gangster, I agreed, in this: if you have to find money in this world, it's always best to do it quick. That's just obvious when you think about it. What's worse than suffering ennui?

to rob a very bright nail salon

Because, said Hiro, people have a very complicated idea of heists and other steals, like if you want to break into some major art museum it probably seems natural to think you will have to do something ultracool, like borrow the uniform of the gallery security, then make your way to the control room and shut off the surveillance cameras, then deactivate all the electrics in the rooms with gold-leaf art and have your sidekick do his sidekick thing with lifting pictures off the walls then smashing on the sprinklers. That's how people might argue but really, said Hiro, you should just burst in and do the place with assault weapons and balaclavas. You have three minutes before any Black Maria is going to turn up, and that's a lot of time when you know what you're doing. The most complicated things, in other words, said Hiro, are often the most simple – and I believed him. That was why we made no major plans or diagrams of entrances and exits, we just entered the nail salon like any other client wanting a quick colour and polish – except that we were in baseball caps, and sunglasses, against the afternoon light, because the time we had chosen was that absence of the early afternoon, a time which is really only known to those who are parents or unemployed. The receptionist was on the phone and very much engrossed in her efforts at conversation:

— So she wasn't two weeks late, I think she was a couple of days. And the reason she was a couple of days was she was stressing. Yeah *thank* you. She's lying. Ly-ing. This woman has issues. *Very* unstable.

There was then a pause then something like:

— The fuck that got to do with things? The girl thinks she cool because she married an Asian. She never liked a black girl in her life.

I mean, I cannot remember exactly. I'm just mimicking from memory. That was the tableau as we entered, and it was happy in its bright way and I did feel this regret that we might be the agents of lessening this happiness, of being causes of concern and fright which was why I very much wanted to be doing this for as little time as possible. Also therefore I was glad that we had such a gentle look overall, because although perhaps it was a problem of heist authority, it surely would go some way to allaying their natural terror and unease. Just as also, I wondered, it could add an even greater element of surprise when you do indeed pull out the gun than if you entered with a balaclava and menacing cries, and while the shock may be greater to other people, the nail technicians and single customer with one hand in a chemical bath, then perhaps the fear is less. And as Hiro did this, I mean took out the gun and raised it in the air, I realised that my heart was not staying still at all, it was gigantic inside my body. That was one more effect that I would not have predicted, when contemplating the event from the air balloon or weather plane –

and in many ways this event, as I now remember it, or as I now try to record it, was an entire network of unforeseen effects. According to our sketched-out plan in the cafe, my job was to be the lookout or sentinel – although were I to have seen a security guard with wolfhounds or some other police agent, I now realised, I was not sure I would have exactly known what I should do. Therefore I tried to ignore this gap in my knowledge and instead stayed by the storefront, with mannequins displaying their gorgeous nail designs. Their hands were very large, as if in some dream or other hallucination where your will is not in control. And it was at this point while I was observing these hallucinogenic hands that Hiro started to shout – in a way which seemed to me just slightly exaggerated, and it worried me, this exaggeration, because it did seem to give away that we were scared and not exactly in control of the situation. In fright the girl stood up and her chemical bath overturned, and instinctively I wanted to find a cloth to mop it up – because mess in any form distresses me – but then I thought no, I needed to stay still. And so I did. Instead of the pool of chemical, I considered the gun, because, I was discovering, it's very interesting what happens if you bring out a gun in public. A sudden stillness happens and I can see how the serial criminals operate, it must be such a delight to have this every day, and also addictive, to watch how you becalm people with a single heavy gesture. To discover a power you did not think you had, this is definitely an interesting feeling. And OK, yes, my friend Álvaro, I know he is used to waking up to discover that his children's kindergarten has been decorated with bullet holes caused by a passing machine gun, and is now accustomed to the bribes and threats and protection and whatever other ways the criminal activity reaches the average taxpayer – like the way the Broadway shows eventually show up at the quiet provincial theatres, like the ones to which my mother took me to watch the pantomimes – but me, no. Whereas now I was realising that maybe the criminal and dark could also involve me. It was a new metaphysical step. But still, I also understood that this was not the moment for my reflections, and in fact I am not sure even that these were indeed reflections I had then – it was more like they were there inside me, awaiting pollination.

which they accomplish hyperfast

Everything was happening hyperfast. Hiro was pointing the gun at the woman behind the cash register and demanding on the one hand that she should not move, because if anyone touched a phone then he would not hesitate to shoot, and on the other hand she should move, but very slowly, in order to open the cash register and deliver all its money. I suppose these things just happen because you've seen them happen, I mean in the usual miniseries. But what I was not expecting was how slow it was, this hyperfast activity, even this five minutes, or how outside the window I could see people softly walking their dog or doing other small things – there was a man having a conversation with a very beautiful woman, and I could tell that he wanted to impress her because he had taken out a cigarette, and also taken out a lighter, but each time he was about to light the cigarette he let it pause there, while he kept on talking, then slowly lowered it again, and it was really lovely to see, that attention to another person. Then I noticed that at one of the mirrors there was one woman and she was crying very much, not violently or loudly but tears were on her face and there were smudges of mascara on her cheeks, like she was smearing her face with ashes in the manner of an ancient mourner. I wanted to comfort her very much and also I was not sure if Hiro would approve. So I called over to Hiro something like:

— Hiro, I said.

— The fuck, he said.

I think he was annoyed that I used his name but I wasn't sure that really mattered, I mean outside the movies – but still, he was annoyed so I wanted to apologise.

— Sorry, I said.

— It's OK, he said.

I knew that he was angry but I guessed this was not the moment for apologies, and I did appreciate at least that he acknowledged my mistake.

— It's just, I said, this girl is crying.

Hiro looked over at me.

— We're going to be done so fast, he said to her, and he said it softly so that she might calm.

She was not so calm but I had done at least what I could. And I was sad for her because, after all, so little was really happening, just two hoodlums with their gun, and we were not even hoodlums really, just as the gun was not even a true gun, not some .45 Magnum ready to be fingerfucked by the coked-up assassin, but then I realised that the girl at the counter was seeming agitated too.

— I said don't move, I said.

— I didn't move, she said.

— OK, I said.

I wasn't sure. It was very possible, I thought, that I was more scared than she was, and I wanted to make some kind of conversation. It's what I do when I'm nervous, like when I'm talking to our cleaner or to children. On the counter was a small wood carving of a saint or holy woman, and suddenly this was all I wanted to think about – it was one of those oubliettes of slowness like when you're on amphetamine and it suddenly becomes very very important to be refolding the clothes in your wardrobe in a particular order, or copying out the to-do notes in one notebook which are now a bit scratched out and tatty into a new notebook with the scratched-out notes no longer there, even though really you should be going to a funeral, or your lawyer for a divorce hearing. They are ways in which your attention is suddenly diverted, but whether or not it truly is diverted, it's difficult to say – for in my case what I was also considering was a moment when I was very young and had come to this very same parade and my mother bought me a book about the greatest football tournament in the world, and I was thinking how happy the book had made me and also thinking that that smaller version of me could never have imagined that one day he would still be here, with friends with guns.

— That's nice, I said.

— She protects me, she said.

— OK, I said.

— You believe in horoscopes? she said.

— So-so, I said.

— She protects me, she said.

— Can I look? I said.

The woman in the carving had a halo that was multi-coloured and her clothes were multicoloured too. It was carved on a piece of wood that looked like some chess piece or intricate element of a fantastical building, by which I mean it had these arabesques and curlicues.

— Can I keep it? I said.

— You're asking? she said.

And I think it was at that moment that I really did understand that what we were doing was so much more violent than the usual world that she was absolutely correct to find this frightening. Because however much this crime might have seemed just very fun to us its perpetrators, totally I could see that to other people, I mean the people forced to act as bystanders or spectators or unwilling participants, like they are in the most upsetting piece of performance art and also against their will, it was something frightening and unusual. In movies there is so much violence that maybe it then doesn't occur to people how violent just the smallest alteration to reality really is, in fact it's very fearful just to see another person raise their voice, like if some holy man outside a pub is shouting at you and then decides to follow you as you walk towards a bus, it's hard not to feel just very threatened and alone. So that to introduce a gun, even if it was only fake or invented, was to introduce a much more unstable element than I had ever considered. This heist was swarming with sad particulars that I found difficult to react to in the appropriately violent way, or anticipate when they occurred at all. Instead I did just feel very gentle and bemused, so that softly I put the saint or holy person back.

— I'm sorry, I said.

— It's OK, she said.

with doubts of the inner life

I wonder if maybe in the end this is all about the whole pop concept of *nice*. The nice thing is the major problem. Because I totally do look nice. I wear teeshirts and jeans and sneakers like everyone else in the history of the multiverse. My hair is gently spiky. That's what I look like on the street or in the canteen. Also my eyes are manga large and my voice is soft. I pay attention to the way I speak which I hope is audible. And yet also for example I get way up high watching very bright pornography, where a girl's choking on a penis and her saliva's hanging down in strands like spaghetti or maybe more precisely spaghettini. I suppose eventually it does make me sad or ashamed or disgusted so I look away, but for at least a few hours, totally not. So *looks*, I'm just saying, are no guide to the inner life: *it's no joke*, to use a favoured phrase of my mother, as if only my mother understands the full seriousness of the world. Everyone I have ever met, their looks were nice – that's all I mean. If the looks were everything, then no evil could ever happen. But it obviously definitely does.

and large financial results

For slowly the girl at the counter was offering me all the soft notes from the cash register. And it was very light, the way this felt – like I had maybe imagined that money in such quantities was going to weigh me down like the swag sacks of the illustrated burglars in my children's stories, but no, it was about as heavy as a very light handbag, or not even. I marvel now at this ability the world has to sometimes arrange itself into scenes, to just pause there and coalesce the way a sorbet might, or crystal. That's the difference between things happening and not happening, and since so much of our time is spent arguing that nothing happens, that an *event* is basically impossible, I still think it's possible to see some lives as like the lives of the saints, where everything that happens, all the missed appointments and back problems and small mood swings, are really all fine details that form a wider pattern. For instance, just the weight of some old banknotes in your hand – that can mark a giant moment. Although at the time I did not think so. At the time I was not so sure that anything had really happened, as we ran outside, and I don't think this reluctance to believe in events is indefensible or even unusual at all – for in general people do tend to believe that life is just this overall foliage, like as dense and thickly populated as the tree canopy out in the Amazon, or one of those collages with a crazy sense of offness, where everything is just minutely unrelated. That's the general matte surface people think they live inside, like how the parties of this world keep on going, on and on they go, the fiestas, and it's the same people with the same drinks or with minute variations, Campari one day, Aperol the next, and you just think that this horizontal vibe will continue for ever – with no dramatics or splits or fissurings, yes you think that the whole concept of the dramatic *scene*, I guess I mean, is overplayed. I definitely tended to think so. I more believed that what was happening always was just the ongoing process of my thinking, and its difficult moods. But then something vertical does happen, after all. I can't deny it. We ran out into the quiet rain – back down into the noise of the normal life, and it was difficult, like the way it must be difficult for an astronaut when suddenly he's no longer in zero gravity, and oh the tortures it must be just to keep your neck supporting your head, or lifting your fork when you eat your longed-for messy plate of carbonara.

5. LONG FIESTA
(THE HOROSCOPE)

LONG FIESTA (THE HOROSCOPE)

which improves his unstable mood

It was a time of many fiestas. They happened at picnics or other locations, in the parks where the trees hid statues of generals and renowned pharmacologists, or busts of the great explorers, with pink filtered light and daisies everywhere, and then at night in disused factories or small houses. We were at them all – because however much in reality you only want to be in bed and delirious with another person, still, you will leave the apartment and go to every party to which you're invited, it's one of those strange mysteries, why constraints are so constraining. Even the fact that I worried for our dog did not stop me, although definitely it made me sad to leave our dog behind, since unfortunately you cannot take dogs everywhere, they are not tolerated in society. Presumably he would have liked to live in a pack, with other dogs, but he was forced to live alone, dependent on us and without the language that we used among ourselves, at these swarays, where we talked gossip and the daily topics. But fiestas do have many moods. For me, I was upbeat absolutely but also I tended to have this haunted gaze. At unappointed moments my hands would suddenly start shaking, and I think it had a lot to do with the trauma of my recent escapades. This transformation into macho and crime scene expert, I did not totally take it with aplomb. And yet, I did want to believe that I could be equal to this career, with its possible revenges and temptations. I tried to think that although the life ahead of me certainly was frightening, still, since every career made me fearful, this new fear felt like a test I needed to surmount . . . It's very difficult, after all, to make yourself proud of your own achievements. To pass exams is not enough. And so meanwhile I would interrupt these reflections with stand-up conversations.

ME
Did I ever tell you about this flight I once took?

ROMY
No, cookie, tell me.

ME
We were on the runway and it was taxiing and I totally knew that something was wrong, the plane's noises were completely unusual, and then I saw the stewardess in front of me mouth *What's wrong?* to the stewardess at the other end of the aisle, and so obviously I decided that I had to say something, I had to stop the plane from trying to take off, because it would only burst apart in flames, and so I called to the stewardess and explained, I advised her that the safest thing to do would be to return to the airport and have the plane thoroughly examined, to which she replied that of course she could do this, but first she would get me a glass of water and when she came back I could tell her if I still wanted

her to inform all these people in the plane that I'd been so worried by what I considered to be the unusual buzzing noise of the air-conditioning nozzle that the plane would have to miss its take-off slot and be examined for what might be a period of four or five hours.

ROMY
So what did you do?

ME
I kept quiet.

ROMY
Is not so bad.

ME
But what I don't know, do you get this? – was if my silence was due to an inner knowledge that I was in fact being hysterical, and that there was nothing there to worry about, or whether I was so imbued with vanity and the wish not to make a scene that I preferred to risk my own death and the death of 453 other people rather than subject myself to the possible humiliation of the stewardess's announcement.

For, aware as I was that I wanted Romy to love me, and also aware that the reason why I was so in love with her was the fact that she had such cool, still I could not stop myself encouraging her to laugh at me. It was the only way I ever knew to charm, and so I could not help it. To live impossibly is no pleasure and yet it seemed to be the fate for which I was created. I knew of course that I needed to make decisions and renunciations. My life with Candy was impossible, but then, so was my life with Romy. Each option had no future. And yet in me was this extra wish to create some crisis, nevertheless, knowing there was no hope. Perhaps that's just an effect of my character because I do have a drive to the future. I am always searching for a better me. But in particular I think there was one specific cause for this sudden concern for acceleration. I think I blame the new-found thrill which is created by any scene of violence with a replica pistolet.

in its new-found machismo

Not that Hiro and I had come back with a sea chest spilling with doubloons but still, it was something. To have money of my own was very pleasant. Qat, I suppose, would have been one option now open to us, we could have sat outside the grocer's with those fronds protruding from our mouths like the red-eyed geeks who sat on garden chairs and looked into their inner space on the high street, counting cars. But my wildness was more different and more sweet. Now, for instance, it was possible for me to take Candy out for dinner, or buy her small treats at the African delicatessen, and to be able to do such things, which I had not been able to do for some time now, made me feel at least slightly if privately enlarged. Sure, naturally it's very sad when violence occurs, in no way does anyone *want* to be doing violence, but at the same time these things do end, finally, nothing continues always, and there you are on Geranium Avenue or some such boulevard, and really things couldn't be prettier. And then of course there are still restaurants in interesting parts of town, and little theatre openings that people tell you about. You can't let the memory of violence overshadow everything, or at least that was how I liked to think. And also, I had to admit that there was even something pleasant, in talking to someone when making them look down the barrel of a gun, just a fleeting delicious moment of knowing you have absolutely gone too far. And the memory of that sensation allowed me this lazy largesse in my general demeanour. We sat there in the pomegranate pubs and in the small-size newspapers read about the fascists taking over everything, their triumphal marches in the TV studios and the giant slums. Then in the bigger newspapers we read about our friends. Because what happens if you're hypereducated is that in the newspapers you recognise many people from your childhood or early youth, which is a problem if you want to preserve a sense of universal respect and public optimism because it does reduce your sense of gravitas a little – that *there* is the parliamentary secretary who once bored you over dinner, *there* is the cinema critic in the sadsack figure of Nelson. It tends to lower your estimation of the social world.

that may require more violence to continue

Even if very quickly the issue of the social world did start to impose itself, in the need for making more money. For largesse cannot continue, not indefinitely.

— Still, we do need more, said Hiro.

— I don't have any, I said.

— That's why we need to make more, he said.

— Oh, I said.

— How much money you got? said Hiro.

— I don't have money, I said.

— Doesn't Candy make money? said Hiro.

— That's not why I married her, I said.

— I never said that, said Hiro.

— I don't have any money, I said.

And while to make someone stare down the barrel of a gun has its definite temptations, my preference certainly would nevertheless have been for less violent schemes, if they could also be pursued without exertion. One method for getting rich quick in comfortable surroundings seemed to be online gambling, and especially the online poker competitions, but this was not, we soon discovered, where our particular gifts lay. We did not have the temperament. Then for a moment I considered if the general global vibe could be our friend, given how many products there are in the world and how many disparities in their pricing, and wondered about turning my parents' house into some Internet depot or warehouse where we would buy up special editions of chocolate or magazines, or rare forms of sneaker, then sell them to foreign buyers for enormous profit. But the obvious problems of capital and distribution, of market knowledge and know-how soon defeated this idle dream. It seemed that at this moment the considered small intrusion on legality might be our very best option, or this was how Hiro tried to argue. It had a neatness to it. And I always wanted to see the best in Hiro's reasoning. Always it seemed very impressive. This manner of entering the world that Hiro offered seemed valuable to me precisely because it was so piquant and unusual. I saw no need for any other classroom – just Hiro and his arguments. Perhaps in addition I think I did feel altruistic, like in the creation of this troupe that was always my ideal, I wanted very much to assist Hiro in his effort to live well. If he needed a student or laboratory assistant, I could fulfil that role with ease.

this opaque mood

Definitely this was a time of many fiestas, but the scene I am trying to describe is much longer than any one fiesta: it is the whole time frame of my need to live in truth and perform grand theatrical confessions. For of course, it was also difficult explaining the source of my money to Candy. She worried that I must be once again borrowing from my parents, and did not like it, for if money was a problem why couldn't I just be content with borrowing money from her, if it in no way upset her? And I had no obvious way of telling her she was not right, because sadly it's difficult to be clear about the sources of one's wealth, and it made me sad to be doing violence to her wish only to be generous and considerate. I thought about confessing everything to her, but then, I further thought, she might be in some way worried or upset about my behaviour, and I did not want to be pressed on what I was doing, because I knew that in some way it would be difficult to explain, and yet at the same time I was very sure that at the moment this was the right way to act, if only because it was making things so free. Perhaps this was all that had been the problem, perhaps with this new sense of freedom we could use our marriage as the *enfants terribles* might use a playground? It did at least seem so. Because to be able to pay with money that I had come by, if not by my own efforts precisely, but at least through my own innovation, was a surprisingly emboldening situation. Even if the means were arguably very wrong, now that I had achieved the goal of some small largesse it turned out that I wanted to enjoy the benefits of that goal – I felt that I deserved it. In the night-times, I would reason with myself in this kind of way: why else achieve a goal if not to enjoy its fruits? Not to enjoy the fruits would be to deny that the goal had meaning, and I did not want to admit this of our complicated adventure with a pistolet. It could not surely be true that all that planning and anxiety had been for nothing? Not to mention the possible hurt we may have caused to various people who happened to be in that nail salon on that particular afternoon. No, I could not allow that possibility. And also, the fruits this event had opened out for me were the fruits of ardour and sangfroid, beautifully outside my normal thinking – like the way you might try to imagine something a little larger than the universe, not massively bigger, just a little. When that happens, when you have access to such things, it seems only magnanimity on your part to continue them to the end, and investigate the paraphernalia that are now at your disposal.

where greatness may be possible

That paraphernalia, of course, being how it might be possible to be with Romy after all. Not, of course, that it really was so possible. The impossibility of the situation, however, was what made it all so thrilling. Temptations floated everywhere in the luminous air, and so if I made myself laughable to Romy, I also liked to play the sexual buffoon. Our illicit and obscene communications increased. I would send her small photos, endowed with little captions: *Think about my tongue, in your legs, your thighs.* And sometimes teasingly she would reply, like: *Why do we now always talk about sex?* And I was expert at convincing her that this was not only about sex. This talking about sex, I said, was really talking about something else inside out. Perhaps you're right, she said. I only need to hear your voice, I said. Sometimes not even your voice, she said. Just to know you feel that about me, and I'm gone. These moments of small triumph for me made me very happy. Once, I wrote to Romy that I was definitely getting fat, to which she replied: Darling, imagining you fat just makes me feel even more tenderly towards you. That tenderness made me joyful. I felt totally the masculine, in a manner of which I was sure my father would have been proud. Of course, I also had my doubts. Was this right? I sometimes wondered. Could it be that happiness was possible? Because to mishear and come up on stage to accept the jackpot prize when you are not the one who has been chosen, that's surely a fate worse than death, or nearly? And what of the other cases? What of the person who might well have been chosen, and might well consent to such a fate, but is so busy with problems at home, so many problems of unemployment and multiple love affairs and skin complaints, that he does not have the time to devote himself to his appointed and necessary task? Is he still chosen, or not chosen? I did not want to be the one who missed my opportunity for greatness. In this suspended state I think it's therefore obvious that questions of before and after would perplex me – as if just maybe the chocolate egg of the world had broken and all its liquor was oozing out, like those stories where the future is folded in among the past, all heavily and thickly. By which specifically I mean that in this rainforest season I began to wonder much more than I ever had about my horoscope. In some milk bar, hiding from the rains, eating assorted blueberry galettes, I picked up an old Chinese newspaper that came free in the local kiosks. And on one particular day it said: *Something extraordinary will begin this month in your love life. A major change will occur, but it will be a good one.* I checked the date. The date was still good. But still, at this time, I doubted it. New fluorescent birds were screaming in the park. Things felt heavy and mysterious, as if *portents* could be everywhere occurring. Late one night I was walking down the street and suddenly saw Jordan, whom I had not seen for at least fifteen years. Jordan, I said. Jordan. She looked at me.

— Why, it's you, she said.

And we smiled at each other. I didn't know what else to say. I had never thought I would ever see her again, not ever.

— Hey you, I said.

We paused but also we did not pause. Very gently we continued to walk away from each other in opposite directions, and I could not really understand if she had really been there or not – because maybe, I was wondering, what I saw was not a real sight, and in some way she had at that moment died, in some other city, on the other side of the hemisphere. Perhaps she had. I never tried to discover, or knew how I would if I wanted. So yes, it's true that trouble was the general atmosphere, as if the general web of mana were just breathing in and out a little more deeply than usual, but still I really was not prepared to believe that my horoscope was right, and that there would be some new crisis in my amours. I thought that Fate had surely done enough already.

but only if he can talk privately with Romy

My one intent was to find myself alone with Romy and say what I urgently needed to say. I didn't care about the general fiesta background. That we should be here among a community of various immigrants, lolling on plastic chairs, while behind us was projected a film of another party simultaneously occurring in some favela town across the unfinished ocean, it perhaps did seem like some irony or dandyism, but at this point I was not analysing things with such elan. Chorizo imported from across the seas was being grilled and it made the air heavy and red. In a fluoro skater's vest a girl was grinding against her chubby amorato. And I suppose I also had to admit that if the people here were trying to combine what might be called work and what might be called a party, then they were in their way no different from what I was trying to achieve in my own miniature circle. Me too I was trying to make my life a work of art. For while naturally much good comes of parties, they allow the socially awkward – the kind who cannot meet your eye when they address you, who prefer to talk from behind the shield of a cupped and nervous hand – to blossom and feel more at ease, for me I would say they formed a kind of trial or even inquisition. Because the helium balloon that was this feeling I had for Romy was now desperate for release. It was very important that she should understand how much it was possible for me to feel, that she did not think that I was without feelings or without passion. It's important I think to tell people everything you can. Not that this was easy because at this particular party Candy and I and Hiro had arrived in let's say a flustered state – with Hiro in one of his wigs and not everyone smiling – and that isn't ideal, for the party atmosphere. Candy herself had changed her hair as well, like shaved the sides so that the oversweep was an imposing mane. I'm not saying it was so feminine but I thought it did look sharp. And we were all the more flustered when we discovered that what we had assumed would be a simple drinks party, the sort of party you just enter for two minutes and then leave, was in fact this demonstration and happening, with political discussion and installations – not because we disapproved of such demonstrations but simply because it's difficult, when your social expectations are confused: a little like turning a page and discovering that in fact the last paragraph you just read was also the end of the book, or like when you see a child walk past then notice she has breasts and is a dwarf instead. It's no problem, obviously, but it just requires a miniature replay and readjustment. Whereas there was no time for such a readjustment because already Romy was there in front of us.

— Hey, she said.

— Hey, I said.

This was how we talked. And it was how therefore we continued to talk for we had no alternative, there is never an alternative to the prevailing tone, and I resolved not to be upset but it was difficult, especially because Romy could see that I was sad and dismayed and angry or all at once, and then she asked me, with Candy beside me, what was so wrong. And I was mad at her because if you arrive very clearly in a state of some conflict, and also if very obviously you have this ferocious need to talk very privately with another person, and they see that you are in a state of conflict, which is not a state you would have liked to display, then the polite thing is just to ignore that you have seen what you have seen, whereas she was instead asking me what was wrong, with Candy next to me, and I disliked this not only because it made me feel uncomfortable but also because the fact that she felt she could ask such a question so casually and even blithely surely seemed to prove that for her there was now no conflict, that she was simply with Epstein and so the false position between us all was totally resolved. And therefore or nevertheless, at the same time I was also thinking that now it was all the more urgent to work out how to find myself alone with Romy. Very much I regretted that I had officially given up smoking, for smoking is one of the great ways of delivering yourself alone with other people, and most of life I think is trying to construct private conversations with other people. But that option was no longer possible, and in fact it seemed no conversation would be possible at all – so bleakly did Epstein stand there with his beautiful poise, or lead her away into a group around a beat-up stereo, playing ancient Communist canciones. I walked away, therefore, leaving Candy with Hiro to chat about their usual topics – tap dance, for instance – with the rough idea of finding a bathroom but really because I was very sad. I was overwhelmed.

prevented in a kind of fold by another girl

While I waited to find Romy on her own, I roamed the dark scene. In one corner of the room there was a television, and I find it difficult to avoid a television – not because I am so intent on the game shows and confessions, but just because a moving image is very difficult to ignore. If I'm trying to read on one of those ancient planes where they silently display the film on a screen at the front, I keep looking up at it and losing my concentration, just as in the airport lounge already I will have been distracted by the silent news, and the mini frenzy of its montage. So naturally I paused and began to watch. It was one of those miniature portable televisions, placed neatly on an upturned crate. I sat down on a plastic chair and looked at the label on my beer bottle, where a pink sunset doused a surfing scene. Then a girl whose name was Dolores was beside me, a name as outmoded and international as that – and immediately I was interested because there was such a contrast between this name and the way her face was like the most modern and erotic invitation I had ever seen. She had the most open face I ever knew: it was cartoon in its immensity and lavish eyes.

— This is what I think, she said.

And I did like this way of opening she had. Barely had I looked at her but she talked to me as if we had been talking all that evening, maybe all that life.

— Sorry, she said. — But this annoys me.

— Tell me, I said. — I'm listening.

— So OK, she said. — Everything you see on screen happens like a dream although it doesn't seem like that, it seems just entirely normal.

— OK, I said.

— Does that make sense, she said.

— Perhaps, I said.

No question, this was not the brand of conversation I was used to, I mean this abstract opening. However, if she wanted to talk television then I could do it, because in this era you spend a lot of time analysing shows. The screen is often on, in the background, as pretext or what-ever for conversation, the way a castrato might have been on, in the background, in the old theatres, while everyone arranged their assignations and bedroom tricks.

ME
You said what you said?

Because as usual I was narcotic already, being as I was supplied by Hiro, and it makes you much more pliable and intriguing in conversations. On the TV screen there was one of those series that go on for ever, like without any resolution but just a system of glissando events that never reach a finale. That's probably why TV is our most popular art form – but that will change, it always does, everything that seems unassailable and for ever descends into blizzard and desert. On this show it was either very dark inside a house, or outside and very white in the bright and desert light.

— Now look at this, she said.

& in this fold talks screens

This man, said Dolores, wishes to prevent a showdown between his friend and two dangerous dealers on a corner – but as soon as I even say that, she continued, I am already talking like a dream because the man has no way of knowing when or where this showdown will take place. He is relying only on his intuition. Because although in reality there are always many things that are possible, in a dream or on a screen everyone knows everything, their ability to predict other people is unerring.

ME
How so?

DOLORES
Just look at it. Look with all your eyes!

For in fact he does know, added Dolores, that tonight will be the night when his friend will try to kill these two men with a pistol, just as he knows the location where this stand-off will take place, at their usual corner, even if this again is not so likely since if such a stand-off was taking place you might well choose some more desolate location or at least an area which you knew better or where there was less expectation of ever being found. But instead here he is, making for the precise location and arriving at the precise time when this shoot-out is about to take place, not too early, not too late, when the guns are just being raised – because in such a situation there is no messiness but everything happens very slowly, as if waiting for the off-screen presence that is surely about to arrive.

DOLORES
You see?

I couldn't deny it. On the screen a car emerged and rammed the two potential killers so that they were crushed underneath its wheels. Then the man got out of the car and shot one of these corpses in the head, presumably to be sure, and this was filmed from a distance so that the spurt or splashback of blood was only graceful and not disgusting or upsetting. Of course, so much violence was now much closer to me, and it made me ashamed, if also very scared, if this was the world I now inhabited, but also I slightly wanted to tell Dolores this, to describe the entire scenario I had recently undergone. I had this idea which I knew to be wrong that in some way it might impress her, but instead I just kept watching. Very definitely, she was right. I had to admit it. This was all exactly like a dream: I mean it was completely impossible, this perfect timing, and yet now that I thought about the matter, I mean the general matter of television and other stories, I couldn't think how often I really ever questioned it – I don't mean in some insane way of ever thinking it was real because of course you never think it's real when it's on a screen and yet you do, though, allow it this whole meaning or plausibility and that, I think, is what is already crazy and irrational. Never, when it matters, does anyone miss an appointment or screw up or drop something or take the wrong turning or sit in traffic, and while I think this is not the most unusual statement it also seems to me to be something worthy of more attention. Like many small things it conceals its depths.

— You think it's true, I said, — of other things?

— Well, here we are, she said.

She had this manner of talking which sometimes seemed like teasing and sometimes seemed like it wasn't and it wasn't always easy to be able to tell the two apart. I liked this, very much. Suddenly I had a vision of myself and Dolores living together far away and everything was perfect. This is one illness of fiestas. They encourage these small vistas. What hilarity! Not content with two impossibilities, I liked to now imagine myself a third. I was the impresario of the impossible situation. So I just sat there, looking at her. Maybe that looked dumb but I didn't care.

— You're looking good, she said.

I was surprised by this, but then, appearances are deceptive. You can feel the exhaustion of a concubine in the sultan's harem just by mini-vacuuming the car, so perhaps I could have been looking good without in any way realising this was true.

before finally pleading with Romy

Most things are much more like seeds or weeds than anyone ever thinks, a whole dandelion gossamer thing just drifting like filaments in the air. Or at least that's something it's possible to think when you are drinking at a party. People come and go, so that while you have been looking for Romy but talking to another girl in your own private fold of reality, suddenly that girl has gone and Romy is offering you another surf-lodge beer.

— Talk to me, chief, said Romy.

And with Romy too I wanted very much to tell her all the excitement that Hiro and I were inventing but this time for different reasons, not so much to impress her because once again I doubted Romy would be impressed by the overall crime scene, but I wanted to explain my new hepcat vibe. It seemed the only prologue to the wild things I wanted to say. But obviously I couldn't, and for a moment I was therefore silent when I had most need to speak. This possibly happens very often. When the person to whom you desperately want to speak orders you to speak it can be paralysing and difficult, for suddenly the whole question of an opening becomes heavy and upsetting, like when at your analyst you arrive full of stories and are suddenly unable to begin. So that instead it was Romy who began to speak and I think that's a mistake, to let the other person speak first when you have something enormous to say because it distracts you from your true purpose.

ROMY
You feel bad, I get this –

ME
Who me?

ROMY

About us and –

ME

No but –

ROMY

I mean, it isn't the first time.

ME

It's not?

ROMY

I mean, that time you told me about, when that girl
went down on you in where was it Africa?

ME

That wasn't unfaithfulness. That was unfortunate.

ROMY

At least you're not one of those people who shoot girls
who go to school.

ME

Is true that is definitely worse.

ROMY

At least we've got some moral boundaries here.

It was absolutely not the conversation I was expecting to
have, like somehow I had just been deposited far away

from my destination by the most inexperienced if well-meaning taxi in the world.

ROMY
Like, what are you wanting to say to me?

ME
I don't know.

ROMY
So, then –

To be shy is in particular a problem at moments of great importance. I was trying to find the right sentences and it was very difficult.

ROMY
You don't need to leave Candy, you know this.

She said it very gently, like you might hold a girl's hair away from her face while she's drunk too much on a night out and is vomiting on the street.

ME
No?

ROMY
What is wrong with you? You think that romance is a kid getting nervous when he hears the telephone ring in the house and wondering if it's his girl. It doesn't happen like that any more, kittykat.

ME

But what if I want to be with you?

ROMY

Then leave her, if you want to, and we can talk. Is not
so complicated, no?

ME

You don't want this?

ROMY

You've still got me, after all.

ME

I want you for myself, though.

ROMY

What are you? Seventeen?

No, it was the equivalent of when the minicab or delivery
guy is said to be speeding towards you, but when the
fifteen minutes is up he is not there, and so you call
the Chinese takeout or taxi firm, but then you are told he
will be there in seven more minutes, after which time has
elapsed and once more you call the sad communications
executive and he is definitely on your road except he is
not on your road, because you are out there on that road,
analysing a lone scooter for evidence it could be a car, and
your gong bao prawn or vegetable jalfrezi is in some other
stratosphere where your house does not exist. You are
now inside a whole new physics, clutching your defunct

astrolabe. In such a scenario, it's difficult not to feel just very desolate. That Romy was not wanting me to leave Candy, I understood, meant only one thing, that she did not want to leave Epstein – and while I knew this was the mature decision I could not also stop myself thinking that I loved her, that I needed her, that all the romance I could imagine in this world was centred for ever on her. It was not at this moment possible, although it would soon be possible, for me to think that in fact I had found some kind of escape in this rejection by Romy – the morning had not yet occurred when, waking up beside Candy, I suddenly thought that in Candy's face there was such tenderness and nobility that I understood what it would be like to leave her for ever, I suddenly saw in her face the face I had first known when she was young, and it was so tender and defenceless in those moments that I could not see how I could cope with such pain – even if really it would turn out that this thought in itself was not quite enough, for when in fact we did separate it was not at all like that, it turned out that I had not at all imagined all the complications, even when I thought I had, because the thing I had left out of the picture, also, was myself, I mean the desolation we both shared. For while I could imagine Candy throwing things out the window, hacking into my email, the true pain would be in dividing our possessions, her entering our house when I had been away for some months, to take away a bag of her clothes, or me unpacking a box and finding in it beautiful presents she had once given me. At this fiesta, however, none of this stored future was real. All that was real was my present cloud of desolation, where Romy did not love me.

& then Candy silently observes a mute passage of communication

But before I could concentrate myself in this total sadness, Candy came and took me away to some table with sangria and plates of fruit.

— This guy, she said, pointing to a beatnik, — he seems to be saying that all the zoos should be opened and the animals let out.

— That's not totally what I'm saying, he said.

— No? she said. — Because that seems to me an OK strategy.

A sort of dance-move party began to happen, with the usual people standing on its edges, not dancing but trying to express through the very fact of not dancing their deep urge to dance – about as listless as the people standing at the edges of the coffee queue, who have placed their order, and now can do no more, and so they just stand there rechecking the same emails on their phone, waiting for the barista to call their name. I was looking at Dolores, who was looking into the eyes of some flaneur whose name was Benicio or Ahmet and that flaneur, I presumed, was the man she loved. But while I considered such things, Romy re-emerged. She had found herself an instrument that might have been a banjo – or if not banjo then distinctly similar.

— You think I should play? I said.

— Was just a thought, she said.

— Why not? I said.

— OK, said Candy.

— Shoot, said Romy.

But very soon after the moment when this banjo was very snug like a pet in my arms I knew I couldn't really. My heart wasn't in it. I had been neglecting my lessons on the Internet very much. But most of all I was looking at Epstein and Romy and the way they held each other, not that in any way I thought that Romy was trying to hurt me or be cruel but she couldn't help it, and it was making me make bad mistakes in my fingering, if indeed this was a banjo, which I was beginning just slightly to doubt, but I did not want to say this in case I was wrong and would therefore lose status in the eyes of others. From the way they were talking, it was obvious that Epstein and Romy were whispering beautiful things to each other, small endearments and sexual promises, so that to be there with the banjo in my arms was like being in a state of siege. And although in such a state of siege it's important to preserve a sense of hope, sometimes it's difficult to do the things you know you're meant to do. Definitely sadness was heavy in my heart. So that naturally when Dolores once again approached me I was glad to see her, and especially because she was looking at me with this brightness in her gaze that I found very welcome and opportune.

— That's cool, said Dolores.

— You're welcome, I said.

She was saying it with this miniature smile in her eyes that was very appealing, no question.

— You're good, she said.

— Well, I don't know, I said.

— He's terrible, said Romy.

— Oh no I – said Dolores.

— Really, said Romy. — It's all noise.

And something, definitely, was happening, but it was difficult to define precisely what. At the very least it was an interruption and as such was slightly violent, according to the usual social rules, like you have just burst into a serious seminar and stood there at the door while at the whiteboard pauses the professor with his smeared equations. That was how it felt, the overly fast way in which Romy interrupted – for sometimes an event is not even an event but the tempo at which it occurs. I was looking at Romy with an amused and anxious glare. While Dolores was in a sort of pause, as if the video of herself was buffering, not quite understanding why such sense of possession and anger was being directed to her by Romy, especially when Romy seemed very much involved with Epstein, whose butch tattooed forearms were entwined around Romy's neck. I understood it was an opaque situation that required an explanation which was sadly impossible to give, and that was all I was really thinking, if not also a small glow of pride that Romy in this way was demonstrating such a sense of possession over me and wish for Dolores to leave our circle. Yet also I therefore did perhaps have some small anxiety that if it was visible to me, this possessiveness of Romy, and was visible to Dolores, too, then surely also it would be visible to Candy: and if it was, then what would Candy think? And it seemed obvious that the only things she could be thinking would be heartbroken and sad, so I tried very hard to avoid this possibility while not really looking at Romy, even though once again I understood that this very not looking could represent the problem in itself, but in that case where could I go at all?

And while these thoughts were circulating, Dolores was looking just a little unsure, like not understanding why suddenly we were in some minstrel band and not telling her the tunes.

— So, see you, she said to me, gently.

— Yeah see you, I said, in the gentlest way possible too.

We looked at each other. And in retrospect I wonder if that's how deftly a horoscope can come true: it was just there in the background, like all the quiet clickings and swooshings of people's phones and laptops when you're sitting in business class – in one single mute passage of meaning. But then show me what passage of meaning isn't total mute. I would like to see such meaning.

which leads to a gentle but disturbing conversation

But at this time I was only really aware of the ongoing noisy surface. Very much I wanted the atmosphere to calm, but what was happening was as usual jumpy. Have you seen jumpy? It is the opposite of the old phrase where a joint is jumping. The joint was tense. Whether or not from jealousy or just the wish to keep the level of provocation up, Romy gazed at Epstein in what could only be called awe, and simultaneously I knew that if I were to be an allegory for one of the ancient humours I could only have been the woebegone dishevelled figure of melancholy. Melancholy was my only option in world charades. For I have this constant problem with comparisons, I mean this problem that I am making them and I do not think that happiness is to be found in the making of comparisons. Not only did I have a simple problem of possession when I looked on like this at Romy but also I was very struck by what seemed her total devouring love for Epstein, and could not help comparing this to the more divided state of my marriage now to Candy. I knew this was unfair and that nothing is comparable, but still, that's what I did. So that when Candy said she wanted to go home early, I was both happy to go with her, so as not to continue to watch such scenes of my distress, but at the same time in the haziest way possible I knew that I was angry or annoyed, that to leave Romy at this fiesta and with her happiness with Epstein left me very much dismayed and like I was as always missing out. I was missing out on the one true bright thing. *We could also stay?* I probably said, with my big eyes, or something. And then was nervously surprised, because Candy did in fact consent to stay, which I was not quite expecting. And immediately it made me suspicious, I mean suspicious of her suspicions, that if she was staying it was because she wanted to survey me, to watch my interactions with Romy and examine the surface for clues to a possible depth, whereas in fact just possibly it was only Candy trying to show that yes she could stay out late even when she had to get up very early for metro journeys and meetings, and even that thought made me sad, for why should anyone change for anyone? But still, here she was, and there was no doubt that something was about to happen, I mean one last event to somehow prove that this indeed had been a fiesta to remember – because what's a party if you do not question your existence?

— You know what your problem is? said Candy.
— Your problem is that you love me so so much you get confused.

— I do? I said.

— Uh-huh, she said.

— Well, maybe, I said.

In retrospect I understand that this response of mine was not enough, but it was the most I could admit to, because really at this moment I was not sure that I believed it, that I did love her, or love her enough, but also I liked her for saying it, very much – I think because I understood the pain that was making her try such a winsome tone, and yet still, that tone only made me hate her more. I say hate but of course I also adored her.

— You, fuzzy bear, she continued, — are all dopey because you love me.

— Yeah, I said.

We had slightly moved apart from Epstein and Romy, perhaps with some inclination to find more alcohol and snacks, but I think also we were audible, and that's never a situation I like although Candy seemed never to care: her lack of embarrassment in the social world extended in every direction, so she would happily cry in public or have major conversations on crowded metros whereas me I prefer the sequestered grove and wilderness mountains if my feelings are to be discussed.

— They're so happy, no?

— Who that? I said.

— Epstein, she said. — And Romy.

— Sure, I said.

I was trying to seem cool in case Romy was definitely

listening, and presumably she was, after all, so I also offered something that was meant as a joke for possibly her ears only.

— Although you just wait. Soon they'll go with other people, I said.

— Like you? said Candy.

— Like what?

— Do you ever think about other people?

— Other people? I said.

It's really terrible when a joke for another person creates a situation in your own routine. Obviously I was trying to understand what possibly Candy had understood or known about Romy. I had no idea. If she was saying it so directly, presumably it meant the question was innocent, or perhaps it was some intricate deceitful invention designed to blur every level of the real. I could not know, because it's never easy to know what is happening inside a conversation, especially one like this where major things are being said without you in any way being prepared, as you would be for the ideal interview, with your notes and new pens and other aids. For while it might be true that miscommunication is in some way the motif of our age, I think in some way this does not do justice to the true happenings, for miscommunication implies some kind of arrow that goes missing or misses its targets, whereas the true problem is that neither the arrow nor the target is aware of its existence, since we are using so many lies and problematics with each sentence. Or so I now think, when I think about the end of this fiesta, so many sad things were being said and as if without hindrance or control. And also they were being said very loudly and that's interesting – I mean it's

interesting when you become the centre of attention without
wanting to be. But there seemed no way to stop this. Each
sentence created another sentence – so that when my query
to Candy created no reply, I did not soften things or end
them which would of course have still been possible, but
instead invented some other line, something like:

— You don't feel lonely?

Violence in arguments is one thing that previously gentle
people are good at. Or at least I find that's true for me.
When I'm frustrated I can throw things and Candy has
been known to ruthlessly slap me in the face. But also it
is violence just when two people begin to shout without
embarrassment or shame. And to have a vision of Candy's
rage was truly terrible.

CANDY
Lonely? Why would I feel lonely?

ME
Hey, don't shout.

CANDY
I'm not shouting.

ME
OK, OK.

CANDY
What do you expect? You think people who've been
together for so long will be like people who've just
met –

ME

Sure, no sure –

CANDY

I think our sex life is good. It's sometimes even delicious, boo.

ME

OK.

CANDY

You think we need to talk more about it?

ME

It should be easy.

CANDY

No one finds it easy! Ask anyone!

Certainly the loudness with which Candy was talking was making me nervous and ashamed, and I am not sure that is really so wrong, not to want to be the film stars who are drunk and screaming at polite parties . . . Perhaps, I was suddenly feeling, the problem was that we had still not yet had children: without children, I was thinking, it was like you are creating all the energy in your house, like some animal that's being forced to go round and round to keep a motor running on electricity. It means that all your other energy is dead or otherwise dying. Or that was something I was thinking. I don't know why. I was often wrong.

that then escalates

Definitely it is no fiesta that does not alter your existence.
And yet as always, even amid the most serious things I
was being distracted, and I think somewhere I was having
this backdrop thought as I listened to the songs that the
problem with modern pop music was that it all got ruined
by just the odd bad line. No rigour, that was the problem
with pop music, and then I realised with surprise that I
was saying this to Hiro. I had no idea where he had
arrived from but also I was glad, because if Hiro was
there then possibly this discussion with Candy might
stop. And Hiro in response just gave me another upper
to calm me down. I wasn't so sure it was a good idea but
I did it anyway because Hiro wanted me to stay as
cheerful as I could. And I was thinking how this fiesta
situation was like one of my bad dreams. I was having
bad dreams every night – unlike Candy, who just has
lovely dreams, like a shoe is there and she examines it,
or a sundae, whereas me I get all feverish and crowded
with demonic shapes. But I had no time to analyse this
sensation because Candy was back there with me. This
constant substitution was exhausting, no doubt. She'd
taken something, like maybe coke, and she was also
turning serious which is a definite recipe for conflict.
That's the problem with drugs – they make things happen
but then you do not know what precisely they will have
concocted until it's too late. What happened next was
that suddenly we found ourselves the usual stoned
minicab driver with views on the music of the 1980s –
and to your surprise in such situations it turns out that

you do too, and then you are back home in your parents' living room and listening to music that is perhaps just very loud, or also you are shouting in the kitchen, observing the neat arrangements of pots and pans and it is as if you are examining your childhood from the vantage point of some Swiss mountain sanatorium.

CANDY
How can we improve if you don't want to try?

ME
Maybe we shouldn't talk too much about this.

CANDY
Maybe I've never had amazing sex.

ME
Great, petrushka, thank you.

Yes, violence in arguments is definitely one thing that previously gentle people are good at. Not that it needs to be like Kayvon, who argued with his wife with a gorgeous passion, so much that each time she would throw his clothes out the window of their apartment, not because she wanted him to move out but just for the pleasure of seeing him go down and gather everything up, or not even for that pleasure, she once told me, but for the pleasure of seeing his embarrassment at being observed by the friendly Shahs on the third floor, looking down at him from their window, and to whom he would each time just offer a small but amicable wave. It's incredible the amount of violence that finds its strange ways of emerging, I was thinking, as suddenly Candy emerged onto a new plane of hatred, like in one of those ancient video games where you jump from rising platform to platform in your effort not to fall.

CANDY
Do you even love me at all?

ME
You just said that was my major problem.

CANDY
Fuck you, OK.

ME
Babe –

CANDY
Like what, really, are you doing here?

ME
Hey, calm down –

CANDY
Calm down?

ME
I didn't mean that. Just come to – come to bed. Or let's just sit down.

CANDY

You don't think you want to make me be like this? You don't think you have models?

ME

Who?

CANDY

Your *mother*, sweetness, your mother.

Zigzags occur always in conversations and zigzags are a problem. And yet in depicting such a zigzagging conversation, I think, a lot depends, because in such a conversation are all the problems of being me and the people like me: I mean all the people who go about their business in island cities, going to restaurants and concert halls and supermarkets in circles, those people who find talking difficult but also necessary. That was the class in which I have to claim my inheritance.

ME

Why does this always have to be so difficult to talk to you? You're shouting!

CANDY

I'm not shouting. I'm not shouting at all, kook.

She was crying and I did that face which is always depressing to produce, the kind which is softened and worried and hesitant because it is not the right face and you cannot locate the right face, it is somewhere lost among your collection of Pierrot masks and other carnival accessories. And it suddenly occurred to me that perhaps the problem with every amour in history is that you know everything you need to know as soon as you meet someone, but then also you can live with knowledge for a decade and still do nothing with it.

— I'm really sorry, I'm an idiot, I said. — I love you, you know that.

— I don't need this, she said.

Always we were good at these conversations because we could make each other less hurt, even while we had hurt each other gruesomely.

— I do love you, I said.

— I know, she said.

— So much, I said.

— I know, she said.

That was how I managed to get her to our bedroom, and could even believe that I did not notice that the light was visible in my mother and father's room, as if I were way above such small concerns as other people. I was concentrating on Candy instead.

until the thoughts of blood return

Every conversation is a world apart, and I think I mean that as non-metaphorically as possible. That's why when I considered if perhaps I should just confess to everything, I was also thinking: Why hurt her more? There's something so very convenient in all confessions, when really things could be much better managed in silence, by keeping all the different worlds apart. Yes, I was thinking, as we got undressed, I could be a better person by saying nothing at all. Even if the prospect did leave me very frustrated, that I had not managed to make a larger impression on the world. Oh, it's appalling the positions you end up in, it feels just sometimes too impossible to continue! But then wasn't this impossible structure what I also always liked when it came to the movies and pictures? I was just less happy if it was all for real. But I really had always liked those impossible objects where things happened in one medium that couldn't happen in reality, the more dreamlike the better, I always thought, and so I always loved the images that included impossible tricks, and in particular the technical ones designed to demonstrate errors in perspective – where a man's fishing rod loops up and into a faraway mountain lake, or a traveller on a distant hill is lighting his pipe from a candle held out of the window by the mistress of a hotel in the foreground, whose sign is hanging somewhere in the middle of a very far forest. Just as my ideal raconteurs were the stand-up kind who talked like those water slides where you descend one chute but emerge head first from another – the way I emerged from this fiesta on my bed with everything awry, or askew.

— We could have sex now, said Candy, — if you want.

— It's OK, I said.

— OK, she said. — Well, you can't say I'm not interested.

I did my small usual smile but the interior of me was very sad. Everyone dresses in teeshirts in bed and we were no exceptions.

— So, shall we go to sleep? she said.

— Yeah sure, I said.

— Have you set the alarm? I said.

— Sure, she said.

I am trying to think how to put this – the way I was thinking about events, in the pale darkness. I was thinking about my horoscope and how I would ever know if it had come true. It's something like the problem of volume that is a rooftop swimming pool – that when you are in it and lissom and supported, your own transformation from solid into liquid makes it difficult to believe that this element in which you are drifting is also massive weight. Or no, perhaps it's better to think in other liquid terms, I mean not of water but of blood. Sure, the absence of blood is one of the strangenesses of my former history, my history before this history began. But sometimes the blood does emerge, after all. It emerges and there seems no way to stop it overflowing all the carpets and the curtains. Even if you had no idea that this would happen but just thought that you would be carrying on for ever in such lovely surroundings, like a pasha or state councillor from the old regimes, you never thought that in one conversation certain things would suddenly become tinged in your head with blood. But still, there it is: they do.

6. TROPICÁLIA

& once again he enters another world

And so it happens that someone falls from a window or into the sea and into another world. They just fall and are suddenly among the butterflyfish and blue-striped snappers. That isn't so strange, or what I mean is that certainly it's no less strange than other events that you might think are normal. As one guru has it, if you say *A man is sitting, there is a ship overhead*, that's at least as real and maybe more so than the sentence *A man is sitting and reading a book*. But also I think this could be described the other way round: you are sitting there, at your kitchen table with a bowl of nectarines and prickly pears, or wherever you want to sit, and then the sea falls in. That's possibly how it feels more often, whether what you are doing is bargaining with your dealer to let you have a rock of crack at a temporary discount, or trying to locate your elbow and wrist in among the auto wreckage. The outside just falls in on you.

which can happen anywhere

But did I know this or not know it? I mean, let's just consider the situation of your hero. Here he is: unemployed, with various women who love him, plus a friend who is let's say a little crazy. Now what is this hero to do? Does he try to be the good prince like he always is, the baby son? Or does he somehow move from state to state, a clown donning his various costumes, until there he is alone against the horizon begging for his life while someone points a gun at him? And OK, it does seem like option number 2 is the one he's taken, but at what point did the true darkness become obvious? From this perspective of the future, I do find it difficult to say. Did I know that I was in the tropical sea or did I only know this later? Because definitely the outside can enter your life at any given moment, whether you are lost in the jungle among carnivorous plants, or watching from your presidential palace while the secret services drop bombs on you. Or there you are, in the snowy wastes, having got down from your carriage, waiting for the horses and kibitkas to be changed, so you stand there, and around you there's this whirling snow and beyond it the flat dark. And you know it. It is over, civilisation. It is totally done with and over. Yes, in all these places – whether in the jungle or your palace or the matte snow – you can feel exiled from world history. And me I was unemployed and deceitful and in love with many women, as well as minor criminal and warlord: and when you do that, you also tend to find that you are suddenly outside all the usual references you previously relied on. You end up with this discovery of pain and its other elements, suddenly buoyant and alone in the soundproofed metaphysical spaceship.

even if it may not be obvious in the present moment

You think this is no way to reach the dark metaphysical, to squander the money and opportunities my parents gave me? To be harmful to my wife with my sadness and deceits? It turned out that it was dark enough for me. In the end, wherever you are is nowhere and is the silent snow and the broken kibitka, and a man cursing while he tries to keep the axle steady on the greasy ice. But I do not know if I knew then what I know now. It did not feel like darkness and snow at all. Such confusion! It was all just bright and interesting to live among, out here on the edges of a giant city, and I did not realise that I was moving darkly into chaos. In everything I say, therefore, you will have to have these time frames very much in mind: that not only did I not know something, that I only understood much later – by which point that knowledge was irrelevant, or of no use to me at all – but also that the understanding was precisely conditioned by what happened later. For I have studied this phenomenon, and its official terms. And in fact I think it's possible to say something even stranger. It's not just what you know that changes, depending on what you discover at the end, when everything is over; it's what you intended to do, as well. Everything is retrospective, and that includes your motivations. Which doesn't mean, however, that everything you feel when something's happening is blindness or self-deception. If a motive is revealed in the future, it doesn't mean it was there to be intuited all along. Like I remember once an erudite friend trying to explain to me in some pub or other dive how there was a difference between the conscious and the reluctant narrator, the one who knows what they're revealing, and the one who doesn't – whereas I'm not so sure you can really maintain that distinction. No person who ever talks is quite conscious of everything they're saying. However much I have always been the shammes of my own head, the guardian of all its thoughts, sadly it's never been possible to be the true comprehensive. That's the basic problem I am having when I talk and try to describe these facts, because there are, it turns out, no facts at all: just signs and interpretations. Or just anticipations, and recollections, so that possibly the moment itself might not exist at all. There is no romance, or adventure. For I would happily bet in any world currency that no one has a clue about the kind of story they are currently inhabiting – everywhere they look they are muzzled and confined with no escape in sight – and so for instance nor did I, when I woke up beside Romy bleeding, or left a nail salon with cash triumphantly, or other criminal acts, I did not know what type of story this involved at all. I would only know when I could tell it, and I could only tell it when it was over: and what could it really mean, for any story to be over? I don't mean I'm some philosophy champ. I just mean I was very confused.

but only later, in the future outside the actual story

Because all along I have been existing way beyond the events I am now recounting, at this story's most future point, for it was only in the enclouded future that these thoughts really occurred, long after Candy and I had definitively separated, and I had left my parents' house, and our dog was dead. I was definitely very alone – in an apartment in one of the high-rise cantonments, out on the South Side of this giant city. Here I am, with the wound in my leg, and its comical limp, like any other marked seer. Maybe always now I will be this person with a limp, like I have suffered in great wars. My apartment was very bare and the night was coming on, and I was looking at the patterns the smog made on the sky, just as I was also watching smoke crawl out of a cigarette across the air and I think that in an interview I could have plausibly replied that I was feeling happy in the lightest manner possible. Or at least, I would have liked to give such a ruthless answer. But it's not easy to be as ruthless as you might like, always you can get overtaken and in my case it was by this nostalgia. Nostalgia was the illness of our time. Because whereas other generations have this ability to let their past and all its artefacts disintegrate into dust, we have this availability on every computer or phone we happen to own to go back over our entire past: not only, let's say, the endless credits of *Dogtanian* or the lovely *Pink Panther*, the items from our childhood, but also our entire backlist of correspondence. Every human is now more historically documented than Napoleon and it would be much to be regretted were it not so irrevocable. It means that depression and nostalgia and a whole rearranged way of thinking is the central fact of nearly everyone I know. And so in my case I was reading all the emails I had ever sent to Romy, and watching the way our friendship had then developed into our affair and then evaporated, and I was thinking how much I love friendship. It's a really difficult thing. It's as complicated as love and perhaps more valuable. Or at least, it's just as capable of colossal sadnesses. It is definitely a form of adventure in a life. Just as also I was looking over emails to Dolores, to which she no longer replied, and then also the emails from the early years of my relationship with Candy, and only now was I realising something that Candy had been trying to tell me, and it made me want to explain to her how sorry I was that I had been so stupid. That's one dark pleasure our technology affords, to be so quickly able to reread all the communications one has received, and understand where one has failed. And I was considering calling Wyman and just seeing how he was, or at the very least sending him a message, when my phone rang, and it was Candy.

— It's me, she said. — Is this a good time?

— Uh-huh, I said.

— Are you busy right now?

— Where are you? I said.

— Here, she said.

— What kind of here? I said.

— Downstairs, she said.

I put the phone down. And then I paused, while I waited for the elevator to ascend, and in that pause I was partly looking out at the balcony of my apartment, where I had hung a birdcage I had bought the other morning in the bird market, and my new backpack, or listening to a fly scribble its noise zigzaggingly all over the room, but also I was perhaps at last having the kind of moment where I did understand what had happened to me, or was still happening. I had in some way definitively aged. It was the time sadness you get in a plane when you realise that not only are the air hostesses on your transatlantic flight in no way comparable to the lissom pin-ups of your imagination, but that in fact they once were precisely those selfsame lissom pin-ups, but now time has passed and they are still up here, in the air, serving mini muffins and miniature wine, but simply older, with wedding rings, and a more refined idea of sarcasm, and everything has changed without anyone understanding how, or why. I could not say that I was happy Candy was here. In some way it felt like a test or torture and I did not know if I could bear it. And then there she was, in my doorway.

where he sees his wife for a final time

Of the many exquisite aspects of Candy's beauty, the aspect that struck me now, as it had often, obviously, struck me, was the very long length of her legs. There you all are, I often wanted to say to the world, when I was out with my wife, you look at Candy, you look at the grandeur and the beauty of her legs and then you think: But only a man with a humdinger, a baseball bat against his thighs, like something resembling an aubergine or pumpkin, no not pumpkin, a *baseball bat*, could satisfy a woman with legs as long as that. Her legs are these things of supple delicate extensive beauty that therefore lend themselves to imagining them in various angular poses, kinked around your thighs, or upright and resting on your shoulders, and when I saw them again I had such desire for her I could not think, because I could only think about the way those legs became her hips, and the soft skin between her legs and how it would go wet if I just touched it, as if something had dissolved. I watched her while she observed my bare apartment, with my single beloved backpack, and also magazines and books and cigarettes, because lately I had taken up smoking, a habit Candy had always disliked and so I had rarely done it, or at least not professionally.

— You're smoking now? she said.

— I didn't ask you here, I said.

— OK, she said.

Then I walked towards her, I think just to be closer, and she watched me walking, and then when I was beside her at the window she leaned towards me and too late I realised she only intended to hug me – for after all we are very different in our heights, where I am small, she is tall, where I am cherubic, she is elegant and lithe – and so regretfully I felt my lips meet hers. She kissed me very softly on the lips and I felt like the women are said to have felt in previous eras, the way you are kissed and feel like you are swooning. The lighting in the room suddenly felt wrong. The lighting was yellow because it was twilight but before I thought to improve it her phone rang.

— Yeah I'll call you later, she said.

— Who was that? I said.

— How long have you been here? she said.

— How long? I said.

— And why are you limping? she said.

— Limping? I said.

— Yes, limping, she said.

— It's a long story, I replied.

It was definitely difficult to talk to her. And that in itself was part of my new knowledge, that something irrevocable had happened, but not just that – that something in the past had definitively happened, because of what was happening right now.

& understands his transformation

Most stories are like the story of the man who threw away a date stone and then there started up behind him a muscular spirit, saying, *Get up that I can kill you, just as you killed my son.* And when the man said, *How did I slay your son?* the spirit simply replied: *When you threw away the date stone it hit my son, who was passing by at the time, on the chest, and he died. There is no help for you. You have to die.* And so he kills the putz, without mercy. I mean, most stories seem to begin with chance, with just a djinn appearing, and then they end up being destiny. I say destiny, but what I really mean is total unfairness and people being beaten to a pulp whether they deserve that fate or not. Because here's how I see the present situation. The universe is a total psychopath and bully, with paws and boxing gloves and whatever other trinkets it finds most useful for beating people into pulp. It is out of control, totally. It is a bully and I am its slave and that leads to different kinds of knowledge. One of which, for instance, might be that whereas you might prefer it that one thing follows another very normally, in fact it's like how a friend of mine once described it – that if a dog bites a little boy and gives him rabies, the illusion of a universal cause and effect is maintained, and order exists, and everyone feels happy. But if, on the other hand, the boy instead turns into a dog himself, by which I mean, if the story has some inexplicable transformation or hole in it, then the world is uncontrollable – and that scenario is in fact while improbable also much more likely – like all of our affections, our inability to live up to our own standards, and our undeserved misfortunes. And when that happens, and you have a story with a hole in it, then that hole transforms your story into a myth. So that the obvious $1,000,000,000 question, in my opinion, is therefore something like this: is there really any normal story in this world at all? Isn't everything at some point, if you make the frames go slow enough, going to reveal itself as mythological?

only when everything is over

— Are you avoiding me? she said. — Is it me you're running away from?

— I'm not running away, I said. — I'm just. I'm . . . You want something to eat? I said.

Then Candy kissed me again and this time it was real. It was in no way what I expected but also if it was happening I did not want at all to resist. I pushed off her leather jacket and she wriggled her wrists out and then let it splash on the floor, and she had a white vest on through which you could see the outline of her nipples – because Candy hardly ever wore a bra, she didn't need to, and this was something always I had found so erotic about her – and something about this sight made me terribly sad, it was so definite and also so elusive.

— Are you with someone? she said.

— No, I said.

— And you? I said.

Then I realised I did not want to know, at the precise moment when I also realised that she was not going to answer.

— I didn't hurt you deliberately, I said.

— I don't care, she said.

Then she sat down in a chair, in this pose of complete elegance and sureness, with her long legs angular beneath her, just ever so slightly gawkily, and I did not know what was happening.

— Come to the window, I said. — Look at the streets.

— No, she said. — Come here.

But I didn't want to do that. I was suddenly too sad.

— You know, I said, — you once said to me that we should maybe get together when we were sixty.

— I didn't mean it, she said. — I was being nice.

— How was that nice, I said, — if you didn't mean it?

— Don't be crazy, she said.

But of course it was not the words but the tone in which she said it, this flat thing where nothing was emphasised, that was what made me so terrified for what had happened, as if in that flatness there was so much knowledge about the world but in particular about me. As she took off her vest and stood there topless in her jeans so that her breasts were there, I looked at them and understood that never again would I know that beauty, because it was nothing to do with the physical breasts themselves but to do with the entire situation, this situation in which a goofy clown understood what precisely he has lost. For I would say: the basic moral problem is that quite obviously we are more than one person, and throughout our lives so many of my friends are ruthless to the alternatives, to the other options and arrays of Wyman and so on that they do not wish to bring into life. But why not? Why does the Wyman who is a drug addict not get owed as much as the Wyman who is a paralegal? Why should the paralegal be the only Wyman who is adored? When I feel guilt it is all for the things undone, the things I do not do. To which the only possible response is what Candy would say and it is one reason why I loved her. That there is no logical reason not to do everything, sure, and therefore if we take the matter of for instance sleeping with the girl in the cream tuxedo and leather trousers sucking suggestively on a bottle of beer, the only reason not to go into the dark bedroom light with her is no reason at all, but also it is everything – that in the manner of the most superfluous and beautiful artwork you have decided to say to yourself that you will not ever do this, and that is in fact a binding and wonderful place to be. For it is wonderful, the state of being bound. Except now I was not bound at all.

   — I'm not sure we should fuck, I said.

   — I don't care, she said.

   — Stop saying you don't care! I said.

   — I'm sorry, she said. — What do you want me to say?

But I did not know what I wanted her to say. I was remembering a little speech that Candy had once given, where she at some drunken point announced that her life was basically always the same thing. When she couldn't do anything, she was unhappy; when she could do something she was unhappy because there wasn't enough time to do it; and when she thought about doing something in the future, which should presumably give her some hope, she was then devastated by fear, giant and encompassing fear. *That doesn't mean, of course,* she then added, *that there aren't good moments.* I missed the speech of Candy very much. Outside it was the usual overcast atmosphere: the taste of ashes floating in the air, flowers steeping, a fine drizzle over the canals. While above us surged the military helicopters and the fragile commuter planes. And then I lay back on the bed and Candy lay beside me, in the expanding darkness, with fireflies mimicking light bulbs at the window.

which demands a new kind of thinking

What I mean is: at some point, I had been invaded. The outside had come in – whether that was when I woke up beside Romy bleeding, or Hiro moved in, or we began our involved commune of injured feeling, or just when I began this life of lethargy and torpor, or when we started playing around with guns and scaring innocent well-meaning people – and I was lost. Because no one is impossible – if the right combination of apples and pears comes to rest in the slot machine. And when that happens, you need as tropical thinking as you can find, in the manner of the old tropicália masters. If there was ever an artistic movement I could adore, the tropicália artists would be such a movement. They understood the basic tactic – you have to take whatever you can get, and not care about the question of provenance. That's what you discover when you are outside civilisation: whether or not something is truly yours is no longer a pressing issue. If you need the Kabbalah or the four stages of enlightenment, then you should take it and make it yours. Or so I was basically thinking. Eat each other! Be a cannibal!

If you are born in the middle of nowhere, and in fact that nowhere is wherever you are currently sitting, then you better find your nourishment wherever it turns up. I mean, who are the tropicália masters? Since these revelations, I have been doing my small research. There is that artist Oiticica, and his installation art: where the viewer sits there among some pot plants, and various bathing huts, and also pebbles and macaws, and finally, at the end of one miniature corridor, discovers a single TV set. But also there is my other hero, the poet Huidobro: who once recited his manifesto in a theatre in Santiago, on the edge of the known universe: and on the edge of the known universe our hero, who was bored with the realities that surrounded him, just batshit bored, announced that instead what he therefore wanted was no longer to copy the realities of nature, which after all did not belong to us, but instead to create realities in a world that would be ours, in a world awaiting its own flora and fauna. There's no need to be satisfied with what's there, that was the basic message of Vicente Huidobro: if you find yourself among lianas with heavy pendulous tongues, glossy like boxing gloves, then so be it.

& so he resolves to record it

No wonder, if you are in such a way-out place of tropicália, that when you come to describe it you end up with these repeats and mini fantasies of time travel, as if somehow you can recreate your innocence deliberately. Which is perhaps not such a mad ambition, since what you foresee or what you remember can be as important as what really happens. What else would you expect of this new habitat?

In the darkness I could hear some people walking past and I was up here in this bedroom with Candy. I wanted to say something that would make things at least better, for it's always best if something ends on a happy note.

— Really, I said to her, — I am in your place and have not ever left it.

— Darling, you're a sweet thing, said Candy. — But –

— I mean, I am constantly berating myself, I promise you, I said.

— You know it, no? None of your self-recriminations excuse anything at all.

— Then what can I do? I said.

— There's nothing you can do, she said. — You could have done things. You could have, for instance, just not let yourself be spoiled.

I considered this grave charge.

— But to be spoiled is a terrible temptation! I sadly said.

It was as if I could see her figure becoming smaller with distance, even though she was right there beside me on the bed. And while I did not blame her – since it must be so boring waiting for people to improve, I understand – it occurred to me that I would no longer be able to prove my innocence to her, and since she was the only person to whom I ever wanted to be proved innocent, I would never be innocent again. I was guilty for ever. Not, of course, that all my crimes had not been punished very severely by the many misfortunes that had darkened the recent part of my life. So that maybe you could even argue that since Candy had discovered so many avengers on her behalf, my guilt for having offended her was possibly much diminished. But also it was at this point that I realised that if I were ever to have an art form, it would have to be an art of full confession. Only a description of my profound *triviality* would be adequate to convey the magnitude of my perdition. My own corrida! – where I would hunt myself desperately down. I was so despicable it was wonderful. As I lay there with Candy for the last time beside me, I suddenly remembered the miniature sketch I had written after what had happened in the sauna, and was thinking that surely now I could carry on my task, as a new gargantuan version. I had this vision very clearly of a book in which I would record my total experience, and I knew how it should sound: with all the tones that no one ever admires, – the Gruesome, Tender, Needy, Sleazy, Boring, the Lurid and the Cute. In such terrible tones I would tell my kawaii tale, with no distance between me and the absent person to whom I was talking. I saw it as one continuous thing, a little cascade with eddies and swirls, or an endlessly fidgeting fire. For always, I had only wanted to live. And the true life – and this is no new discovery of mine, after all – the life that was at last discovered and illuminated, and therefore the only life that has been truly lived, was the life you observe in retrospect, from some way-off point in the clouds, and one word for that kind of look might possibly be literature. Or if not literature, then talking, at least. And if Candy was not there, I was sadly and delightedly now thinking, in the tropical air, I could still talk as if she were.

very possibly in a book

I don't know why people think that stories or pictures take you out of the world. My talking was the only route I had into it, like it was Velcro or a hinge. In the end, nothing can be taught: everything has to be learned. And you only can learn anything by letting yourself howl as many words as possible. After all, I considered: I was very used to writing down my own thoughts, or talking very fast. I was a prodigy! Always I did this talking to myself, without anyone there to listen, like some crazy man out in the park in the open-air afternoon. And yet, it now occurs to me, as I finish my endeavour, there is one final somersault that I had not in fact predicted. It's difficult now to write this all down and still believe that what I say is true, I mean true absolutely. I know some of that might just be laziness but also I do have this fear of betraying my ideal. For the dream is that everything you say will be complete, with absolutely every qualification docketed and allowed for, but of course this is only an ideal and like every ideal also unattainable, so that instead what happens is that you say something and because you have indeed said this you end up losing the thing you intended to say, for it is only replaced by the thing you have said which while inaccurate is also real, and therefore according to the law that what is there will always erase what is not there, that's all that in the end you can remember. I suppose on the other hand you could see this as a good thing too. For OK, perhaps you have lost the original import-ance, but when you have that sentence there before you it's also possible that from that point on it might be able to gain a new importance, that had never been suspected. What you say is never what you think you say. What you really say is said without you knowing. It's like how no one ever thinks they are of their era, even though everyone of course is of their era, except that it will only be when we are all dead that what is of our era in us will be revealed. Once you realise that, it's a very difficult problem for creation. For why begin something with any intention in mind, if that intention will in no way be the effect of the finished work? And yet if you do not begin anything, then nothing will be expressed. So that the only way of beginning is to begin with an idea that you know will never be expressed, in the hope that through it something else will be able to be expressed of whose existence or form you are not yet aware. It's not so much a record as a new experience entirely. I was falling asleep beside Candy, and when I fall asleep my thinking tends to become more frantic. I was trying to find an analogy or image for my ideal. For some reason my only image was a hamburger. My thinking was as vulgar as that – the last time I ever saw Candy, when I finally realised everything I had lost, in the dark metaphysical desert of an apartment whose air con runs through the night and is very loud. For books, like hamburgers, are both just things that are layered in groups. Yes, if I had a picture of my ideal method of talking, it was a hamburger with all its sauces: a multicoloured assemblage, sweet and greasy and delicious. That's what you need if you want to talk about what happened to you in tropicália, if you want to do all the tricks you might like with that horrible substance called time. And for as long as I could before I fell asleep I lay there contemplating this possibility, like the risk-analysis clerk or med student who for the very first time stands there longingly at the entrance to the hoochie-coochie joint, gazing up at the neon void.

7. THE THING ITSELF

that records our hero's unbound freedoms

From my future perspective, I guess I was not as in control of events as I believed. And yet it did not seem that way. After two or three bottles of bourbon our choices became freer – whether borrowing my parents' car to deliver fresh peanut-butter cookies to friends and local stores, or accompanying people to their employment tribunals and addiction treatments after Hiro had befriended them on the street. That's the beauty of the mind-altering and the world-historical. One minute you're in a peignoir, the next you're on the metro with your replica gun in a canvas bag, just one of your many possessions – even if admittedly you're also enjoying this new accessory, but only the way you might enjoy a new sneaker or mascara. In that way we visited the city's sights – the parks and avenues, the museums of banking and heavy industry – and felt very gleeful that with us was this object, like our surreptitious pet. Or we simply visited the stores and monuments of our locale and barriada, supplementing beer with various bottles of vodka, sometimes smoking fourteen or so joints while strolling with the dog in a happy small miasma. This really is the beauty of the mind-altering – it alters everything in the picture. For in non-real life you always would have the option of transforming into a zombie or some other animal or superfreak. Whereas in life what happened previously continues to happen, just maybe worse – like watching a movie, where all the fascinating business of getting from scene to scene is the seamless concern of someone else. Elsewhere, the season was at last beginning to disintegrate. Remote-controlled bees were being flown clumsily among the lavenders and other bushes. In the background you could ever so faintly hear the old dialogue continue: *Mrs Death! Mrs Death!* The sky was heavy and grey, as if the sky had some consciousness of its own farewell, and although I had written back and asked them to stop, sometimes I still received odd messages on my phone. But I insisted on feeling carefree because it's so easy to delete a message, it's as if it never happened, and so I did. And if I suddenly had this purchase on the world, I think only the hardest-hearted reader will begrudge me at least a small amount of exhilaration. I would not be downcast, even if among the bird reserves and estuaries the general monsoon murder rate was very high.

beginning in a cafe

The place we were in was one of the cafes beside the ice wharf and the canal. We had ordered blueberry clafoutis with cardamom ice cream on the side, or other delicacies. In my cup there was coffee, and beside us light illuminated the narrow perspective. There was one solitary person writing in a notebook, and I looked indulgently on her, for I had my own small experience of her tribulations, scribbling signs and messages everywhere. But otherwise this place was empty. Peacefulness was everywhere. And for a while this was how I liked it. You could hear the barges and the bicycles drift past with their different noises, and then the sound the general noise made, too, the surrounding noise of the city. There was a waiter who seemed to be loitering, just doing nothing but observing the general scene. But the problem with feelings is how quickly they develop, and I think that at this time a general time pressure and impatience was something I could feel almost every day. We were talking very gently about what we might do next, because as I said, the need for ready money was very present. We had been talking about this recently very much, and in Hiro there was a worry that our criminal mobster antics were no future.

— Is no career, said Hiro.

— What? I said.

— Stealing from people, said Hiro. — As a life.

And while I understood that perhaps we did not have the heart for it, to make the criminal a way of life, since to do that you need to use the most severe aspects of your personality, and also encourage a will to succeed that it was possible we did not quite have, still, I was more in favour of this pursuit and wanted to convince him. Because really – when you've done something once, then the possibility just becomes much easier. And so while I was always ready to follow Hiro into whatever endeavour he wanted, I also tried to encourage him into thinking that the street could still be a place for moneymaking. And I was pleased because he was not totally opposed. If I had this passion, he thought, then it was important to respect it. And yet to decide which precise location to apply our energies next was not so easy, for there were many competing options, either repeating the same exploit, or venturing into more recondite territory, like warehouses or factories, and as always we tended to lose ourselves in these reflections, like this lacklustre afternoon, watching the way the light developed on the stagnant metal water.

with a waiter in the background

Late Capitalism! Late! It had only just got started! The atmosphere was definitely lacking – like the city or epoch had just remembered another appointment and had left you alone with its distracted PA. I mean, did anyone ever *choose* the cafe culture? I do not think so. I think the whole bohemian vibe is just what happens when nothing else is happening, when you would much prefer there to be great events and meetings and appointments. The bohemian is a very noble aspect of *making do*. And so the sudden sense of freedom I now possessed was very enticing. More privately, perhaps, I was stuck –

(— But what can I do? I said.

— Well, said Hiro. — You need to be with Candy, or with Romy, or with someone else like –

— But I can't do any of those, I said.)

– but this only meant that the general inner freedom I now possessed was all the more welcome and convincing. The problem is in finding ways to express this inner freedom, in imposing your effect on the world at large, and this seemed to be a problem for me now. We had been waiting in this restaurant for a long while, and still there was no sign of our blueberry clafoutis. There were only these coffees which were making me as always just a little hyper. I tried to catch the eye of the waiter but he did not acknowledge me, he was just texting or talking to the barista, just lost in his little social cloud. And I thought this showed a problematic lack of respect – for if you are to work in this business, where your job is to serve other people, I think you should be pleased to do that, and take pride in your subservience. Whereas it was obvious that he wanted to signify to me that he felt humiliated, that he did not feel this was a worthy job for him – and even that he wanted to prove to me that in a moral duel between us, he was the higher being.

— Hey, cool, man, said Hiro, or other soothing words.

But I did not want to be soothed. When it concerns a matter of principle, I don't think one should be ashamed of making a scene. I learned this very early from my mother. I was only small, she would tell me, but that was no reason why anyone should ignore or overlook me. I had to stand up for what was rightfully mine. And so I always wanted to, but with maybe little success. Now, however, I felt more in charge of my own person. For why in the end should one always be made to feel guilty? I mean, guilty for being served? Always we had people cleaning our house, as well as the people in restaurants and department stores who were there to help me in my choices, and that always felt very natural. For the point of employing someone isn't for them to hate you; the point is to form an extra family, to have people around you who care for you and admire what you strive to do. That's certainly how it was when I was growing up. Always there were people in the background – and definitely without background you are lost, or are nothing – people who wished me well, and wanted me to fulfil my entire potential. Whereas here there was this man who did not care about me at all, as if he were animated by some much grander sense of privilege than I had ever known, and it distressed me very much.

who frightens our hero with his disregard

At first therefore I tried to wave at him, without too much wanting to make it look like I was trying, since I did not want to be observed by the girl writing in her notebook – I mean, observed in failing to make my presence felt. I could think of nothing worse. In the sycamore and orchid trees, pigeons were hiding their faces under one silvered wing. The world was as paused as that, and kept on pausing. I tried staring, or then ignoring him. It was as if the entire principle of a cafe as a place of refreshment had been just ever so calmly abandoned. Yes, this pause in which we waited was lasting longer than I had ever known, and it was making me almost frightened. That always happens for me if anything is just not the right size. I see in this nothing unusual. In the end everything we think is dependent on length and size. Meerkats for instance might seem very charming, but you only need to think of them enlarged to the size of even a cow or flamingo to realise how this charm is very much a category of their reduced dimensions. In the same way, a pause in a cafe that is not the right length can become debilitating or even worse. It can make you very fearful. And fear, I think, has this way of making everything seem different, so that all the usual behaviour seems less available when you maybe need it most.

which leads to improvised violent decisions

For instance, in my sense of disorientation, I decided to confront the waiter directly. I walked up to him and asked if we could have the bill.

— You don't want the food? he said.

— We did want the food, I said.

— But it'd be terribly sad if you left without eating, he said.

I suppose I should have not let myself be persuaded, but I always do want to see the good in people. So defeated I went back to my table, where Hiro was waiting for catastrophe. Then behind me came the waiter, with two plates of food. Except this was not the food we had ordered. Where we had wanted blueberry clafoutis and cardamom ice cream, there was instead a tempura of market greens, and mint sorbet – or roughly that, the precise details are not important. And it seemed to me that this was not at all something we should have to bear without any redress. To be insulted in this way was very sad. And absolutely, in retrospect I do now see these ugly feelings as not just pure, but also caused by other things, I mean not just the waiter's rudeness or indifference but also for instance the desolation I was trying not to think about when alone in the house with Candy. But then, this is the problem with motivations, they are free-floating and difficult to locate, or locate at the true location, which is why it's always important to be super-vigilant like a desert patriarch alone in his monastic cell observing all his reflections – because if you don't reveal all your thoughts to yourself at every moment then they can rise up against you. To be super-vigilant is basically to be super-vigilant of all the demons ranged against you, like inside your little self there are pupae with their individual moths folded up inside, waiting to unfurl, like pale umbrellas. And then these things do unfurl, after all. And one of these, I think, was this worry about my machismo and general influence. I was perhaps never as sure of my machismo as I might have liked – and I think that was visible in what happened next. As I looked at my tempura or mint sorbet, and thought that this was not at all what I had ordered, not at all what I had been excitedly imagining, I also remembered that, as usual, in our bag under the table was a very convincing gun. That's definitely a way of offering you more options in your everyday interactions. Also it seemed to me, when we had been discussing our future options, that everything we did should be done as morally as possible, because if you don't act like that, why bother? And here, it seemed, was one such opportunity. To take action against this locale was not at all an immoral act: it was instead a way of defending a certain ideal, for a world where niceties are not observed is not a world worth inhabiting. And while certainly I wanted to propose this to Hiro as a suggestion for him to approve, I also thought that there was very little time to act, since if the moment was lost then it would necessarily be lost for ever.

but improvisation is a difficult method

Unsteadily therefore I stood up with our gun. It wobbled in my grasp unsteady too, like a divining rod. I was not sure I was the man to choose for such a moment, being as it was devised without the meticulous planning we had previously employed. Still, one thing my schooling offered me was to put everything into the fight. I stood there with the gun and with much ferocity stared at the waiter, and did the usual thing of demanding money. And yet as I did so I was also aware that first there was the problem of what to do with the girl who had been solitary and engrossed with her scribbling and her notebook, since at this moment she was moving to the door, and I was not sure we should be allowing her escape, considering the possibility of police and other security measures. And yet I had no prepared way of forcing her to sit down, since I had no wish to harm or even scare her. Therefore I offered her more time.

— I'm going to count to three, I said, — and by three you need to be sitting back down.

It seemed a reasonable offer but she said nothing to me. She just looked at me, and I found that unnerving but I continued to count to three, nevertheless, since if you have made a threat you must always try to fulfil it, that's the basic rule of society, whether gangster or gallerina, and I was relieved to see that as I did so she began to sit back down.

— No, said the waiter to her. — You should go.

I admit I was definitely surprised. He had such assurance, and I would have been full of admiration, had it not been also such a delicate moment, and also had it not been one more moment where my authority was being questioned. It made the situation, I thought, much more difficult than was necessary and wistfully I considered once again how onerous is any form of work. There's no end to the complications. The same feeling must occur everywhere, not just for me or the editor of some local diario besieged by a violent mob, but also the collector of rare spiders and the assistant in a hospice. No one is exempt. But most of all I felt a righteous rage. Here was this man, without any sense of duty, with no sense of respect, and once again he was treating me as if I posed no threat. So that as if to contradict him, I found myself close to him, and pointing the gun in his face. And this was a very different feeling to what I had felt before, in the nail salon, where I had been anxious as much as possible to preserve everyone's calm, and not invade their moral space, the transparent envelope that I had assumed enveloped everyone. It was as if I had previously thought that everyone had this moral space around them, like in the grandest cable car or Ferris wheel, but what – this was the question now being presented, in a very violent form – if that wasn't true? What if everyone's available to everyone? I don't mean that's a world I love but that may well be the only one that exists, or at least that was how it seemed, with this sudden invasion I was performing of another person. As I said, I think that I was less in control of events than I might have thought. I could see the gun shaking in my hand and I knew that I was running out of methods to assert myself.

if it is to end well

But to be in a duo is always very restful – it enables each person to help the other out, and in many ways this duo

I formed with Hiro was the best society I ever knew. He always moved very deftly, and behind me I could sense him moving with purpose and a gentle grace towards the counter. I was trying to hold the eye of the waiter. I had no idea if other people were present, presumably there must have been a chef to produce the mismatched food, but I could not see him. There was just this Wild West idyll, while Hiro took the money and beckoned me to follow him to the door. Just for a moment I still paused, however, because I was momentarily shaken by the violence of my feelings and was in a stalled confusion. The woman's notebook was open on her table with the pen beside it, and I imagined it soon to be dark with her panicked writing. I think I wanted to apologise or at least show that I could calm down and was not a monster, because the expression on this man's face was not an expression I ever wanted to see, it was sickly and with all the pain of something melted or gone awry, the way a shoulder looks awry when it's been dislocated. I knew that I had caused this kind of pain and I wanted to assert that to do so was way beyond anything I had ever intended, but of course in these situations you do not get the opportunity for interviews and retrospective summations. Do the clothes you wear express you, as the underwear models and character actors believe? Do your actions prove anything at all? I had never quite thought they did – but now that I was outside in the fluorescent light it did seem I might have been wrong. And yet I wanted to still maintain that I had only meant very well. The ideal, and it was an ideal, was of a noble restitution – where we would assert our variety of justice, with no violence done to anyone. And should one really abandon an ideal, just because of local problems? I know my rages very well. They're like a pet whom people fear, but where the owner smiles encouragingly to other people – because she knows it will not scare, will do no harm. But also I can understand the arguments against that.

THE WAVE OF EROTICISM

& to a new high-energy atmosphere

For maybe just a few hours or days later I was once more filled with a gorgeous seam of energy, like I was on a megadose of vitamin supplements and antioxidants. Still I was oblivious to any form of imminent punishment. It really did seem that if we kept up this level of energy, we were on the brink of one final revelation, in the full pistachio light, and in particular it encouraged me to enlarge my personal recreations. I had never felt such power and talent for maintaining so many people. Our exploits offered a distinct sense of possibility. I became a monster of industriousness, as if everywhere opposing forces were going about their dire work, and I had to try to ward them off – like a game of computer tennis. Although if I really did sense that nothingness was depleting the world I lived in, the way the ghosts deplete things without you really knowing they are there, I cannot be sure. From this distance, it's impossible to know. So many time frames were occurring all at once! They overlapped and dislocated. But still, I was definitely occupied. Like any other utopian or tycoon, I was very busy with the problems of my communications. Sometimes for instance I wanted to write to Romy an email that would sound something like this:

Sometimes I wonder if I didn't love you so much whether I would therefore already have you. Because if I didn't love you as much as I do then I wouldn't be as much wanting to be your friend as well, to give you the best advice possible for your future happiness, and therefore would not say that of course it is not certain that I will leave my wife – even though I know I will leave her, because I no longer love Candy, not as much as I love you – nor would I be counselling you at least to reserve some doubt or hesitation. Whereas if I loved you less I would be promising everything for real, and so would have you. Because you would be convinced of our future together. I will lose you because I love you.

But even as I wrote that I knew that it was possible it was not true, that I was being sentimental, that the reason I could not promise anything absolutely, but only with small vaguenesses like commas or semicolons in my speech, was because I knew it was not true, I would not leave Candy, because in fact the love I felt for Candy was absolute and unmovable, which was precisely why Romy could not find it in herself to be convinced of our future together. I would lose her because I did not love her enough. Then neither of these possibilities seemed true. And that's just one example of a wider problem.

despite the multiple snags

Not that I am into total teletransportation and time travel but definitely I think it happens very often, that on an average day you try to make yourself into some backflip or loop-the-loop: to take one edge of the present moment and then fold it back over the other edge, just very neatly superimpose the whole design – the way I used to fold sheets with my mother to help her with the laundry, going forwards, then backwards, then forwards again to meet in the middle, while the sheet got smaller and smaller. Such moments happen all the time and I think that's how love works when it's at its height, or at its worst: it's like night school for the overworked, in a course on the true conditions of time and space. The true conditions of time, it then turns out, are always disappointing: snags, prematureness, belatedness, prophetic glimpses, misrecognition. Time, I would say, when I consider this account, is always in a strange and opaque state. No wonder, therefore, if it makes events very cloudy and also difficult to follow.

like the silence of Candy's conversations

And at this particular staging post of the story I was conscious of one particular opaque problem, the absence of one scene, which was the scene where Candy talked to me about what she had witnessed that night at the fiesta, the privacy she had encroached on between Romy and me. From Candy I now expected possible shouting and other events: spaghetti and its red sauce splurged against the walls. And perhaps I did want that, very secretly. But as always we said nothing. Which meant that from then on Candy had this silent power, if knowledge not deployed is a kind of power, which I think it is. The image I had of her was of a person enthroned: there she sat, holding the sceptre of her private knowledge, and I had no way of knowing what to do. Whenever Candy paused in any conversation I would wonder if what she was really contemplating was this image of Romy and Dolores, of Romy somehow talking about me in this manner that was rightfully only a manner that Candy possessed. It had only been a moment, like a sudden flicker of light – but a flicker is enough for setting your terrors into motion, for understanding that two people may be in more direct communication than you previously suspected or imagined. I mean, two people will seem all the more familiarly linked if that link or association is seen to be unconscious. And to those of you who are saying *So tell her! Tell Candy everything! You are a monster! She does not deserve you!* – like we are at a pantomime and I am the villainous creature – then I would say, I understand this argument, but still – is it really not possible to mean two things at once? At no point was anything I did insincere, with her or with other people. Perhaps to you this is already crazed, because what is more insincere than to lie or deceive but me I am not so sure, I mean, I am not so sure that deception is so wrong, if the alternative is to make a definitive end to something. For why shouldn't things happen simultaneously? While also, if I had to lie, could it be that Candy was to blame – for the fact that my small transgressions would be punished so mercilessly? If I imagined telling Candy everything, I mean about Romy and my infidelity, I felt that surely she would leave me and be angry and depleted – and therefore naturally I could not tell her. Surely her potential lack of forgiveness or understanding was part of the same problem? And it was meaning that, despite my best intentions, I just had this nagging feeling that I was losing the power to be absorbed – the way you might look at a portrait of a courtesan in some provincial museum just before that museum closes, when you are tired and you want to get out of there to find a beer or milkshake and so the beauty of this courtesan is powerless, because it is irrelevant to your current needs. And so I would lie awake in the night and list other things that had lost their one-time lustre: the old Coney Island, the old Soho, the old Kreuzberg, the old Belleville, and so on . . .

impasses of desire

For our dialogue was listless and happy, at the same time, in the manner of –

CANDY
You OK, cookie?

ME
Me? Oh fine, I'm fine.

CANDY
Because you seem –

ME
No really.

CANDY
Really?

That's basically a composite summary of our nocturnal interactions, like one of those puzzle pictures that the police dream up to catch the roaming killer. Whenever the real approached, I was very careful to remove it very gently from the area, the way you remove a child from dangerous machinery. To borrow from an old authority, we no more said anything specific than we let the hound off the leash on a busy road: for you had no idea what mazy craziness the hound of a conversation would lead to if something specific were ever said. I let her words just disintegrate into the open suburban air, out there among the hangars and the water parks in the distances, in this amphibian space, with its roofs and grass, pavements and furrows, shops and minia-ture sky. And maybe, sure, there are just some things desire cannot do and one of them is last, or last for ever, or in the same way. It's maybe as unlikely as the B-movies where the killer pursues his prey for at least three hours of screen time. It just seems improbable, I mean, to so continuously care. But still, it made me resolved to do better. Perhaps once I might have tried to explain this account of the powers ranged against our marriage with talk of angels and cherubs and cupids, I mean that might have been the vocabulary of previous gentler eras, but I think if I had to describe the new sensation I could say with more accuracy that the bedroom rarely now had that heavy clouding stink about it, the lovely sourness that is the proof that liquids of every kind are being produced underneath your duvet. We would kiss and kiss, Candy and I, and it was like one of those cable shows you come to late one night where you don't know what's going on, you just keep watching because it's late and you're tired and you are hoping that soon some minor plot moment will arrive and illuminate the whole perspective. And yet of course it doesn't. But I wanted to carry on because I did not want her to be sad, and so I would lick at Candy between the legs and sometimes look expectantly up, but her face was turned away and then it was me who felt sad, in my turn. I would stay there looking at her, just gazing between her legs and wondering what had happened to me, and wondering if even the way she tasted had changed, even though that must be impossible, like whereas before it had this penumbra that was mineral and soiled, now it was just the taste of itself, and therefore not dirty enough.

& other problems of ghostly communication

When I tried to explain this to Wyman, he blamed it on the ghosts. For Wyman believes in ghosts, it is one of his many outmoded charms that I appreciate, and I was starting to agree with him. Or at least, I was starting to understand how opposing forces might exist and once you admit that it's hard not to make them human in some way. According to Wyman the ghosts existed in every means of communication ever invented – including the carrier pigeon and gramophone – and perhaps Wyman was right. There were ghosts against me in particular in the telephone lines and in the wireless connections humming in every room. For the problem is that no one really exists when you write messages or emails to them, or talk to them very briefly on the phone. I'm sure in some way we do know this, which is why we think it is important to build fast cars, giant hovercraft, and all the other systems to bring people alone together in the same room, but at the same time you have to remember the far greater power of computer screens, miniature phones, and all their small developments. There are so many toys for making people disappear, and for making yourself disappear, too. My correspondences! Maybe it's possible that modern times are a perfect paradise of communication, but still, it comes with other problems, especially if you have a nervous disposition – like the various ways in which someone's privacy can be observed. And for me this centred on Romy and her mania for instant messaging – for I had never had this before, this love of messaging, and in particular I had not therefore known this particular form of anxiety about another person, where you could see whether or not they were there, or could see that recently they had been there and therefore seen your messages, and yet not replied, or even in Romy's case I would wake up and then be able to see that until four in the morning she had been messaging, but not to me, and that was a horrible worry, to be thinking who it was she had been writing to, and why she had been awake so late and never told me she was going out. Just as in particular if we were then arguing I felt so helpless, being able to see whether or not she was typing a reply, or waiting – and so time would stall there, just coagulate in pools – and these new forms of communication only made me realise how jealous I was of her, how avidly I needed her attention and yet had no right to this attention. Because it really is not a good feeling, to realise how jealous you can be, when you yourself have invented the situation. And so I demanded she do impossible things, like that she entirely stop having sex with Epstein, or only have sex in the most boring possible way (*How can I do that?* she said. *You know I like sex*), like I was the movie mogul who wanted to sign off the final edit. But I could not help it. The jealousy kept on working inside me, the way water keeps on rocking inside a bucket when you set it down.

ME
I don't want to control you.

ROMY
You just mean you don't want me to control you.

ME
I don't know. I mean, maybe. How should I know?

ROMY
It's like we're in some long-distance relationship. I never wanted that.

ME
But I'm here.

ROMY
But not really.

ME
There are some moments when I don't feel separate at all. Just moments when I hear your voice.

ROMY
We've never been separate. Not really.

I guess it's possible for there to be a happiness that is also an absolute sadness. For it was only with lying and secrecy that such wonders had even been allowed me in the first place – but at the same time it was this very secrecy which was now warping all the feelings, and not allowing them the usual relaxation of tempo. You could only have such feelings with secrecy, but the secrecy then changed them – it made them emerge slightly melted, like a plastic spatula you leave too long in the squelching pot of cholent. But still, the feelings were there – and what are you meant to do with feelings? They're very controlling, feelings: they make life very difficult and painful. To not include dark jealousy in my thoughts! How could I have been so careless? I had never thought in maintaining these relations how often I would think about Romy and imagine or know that she was in bed with Epstein or nearly. It was a tribulation. When I thought about Romy and how I would maybe never sleep with her again, that never would I be the one to push her mouth further over my red penis, or watch her come while she sprawled in front of me with her hand draped over her, as if in modesty or privacy, these things made me as sad as the ancestral pedlar on the boat across the Atlantic, never to see the shtetl again.

from which our hero tries to find erotic solace

I think it was to avoid such thoughts that at this time I also abandoned all restraint. Or possibly it would be kinder to me to say that restraint abandoned me and I could not get it back. I had this terrible weakness that I was still amazed by sex. For this I possibly blame the way there had been this whole new violence when I was in bed with Candy. It seemed to allow new depredations in my thinking. Because I so much thought of women as distant and in control, that every time I realised they were as much a mess as I was, and in the grip of some fantasy or confusion, I felt this mixture of tenderness and desire and the wish to see what happens next. It's a complicated position to be in because in general also I find it difficult, to know how to want to sleep with a girl without it being scary or very wrong, like I am the person skinning a woman alive and displaying her hide. I am the primeval swamp and all its swampiness. But still, I found it very easy to talk to people and to ask them about themselves, and when you do that after a while you can ask them to do anything, and mostly I think they will. To Wyman I explained it in cruder terms.

ME
Because I have this problem.

WYMAN
What?

ME
That I am really good in bed.

WYMAN
Oh sure –

ME
Is an affliction, or a curse.

WYMAN
Huh –

ME
I'm just saying. It makes life very difficult. It must be easier for the men who just lie on top of women and are heavy. I do think so.

Not that every scene was perfect, not at all, like for instance there was Shannon who due to a strange quirk of our timetabling was on her period both times we were in bed together, and while personally I adored this, I adored the viscous stickiness inside her and the way my penis emerged with its small tidemark of brown blood, it seemed to upset her, nevertheless; or there was Cassity who turned out to be a virgin and when I held her in my arms she trembled, but still I carried on; or Timeka with whom I did nothing but talk about our childhoods, and she haunted me perhaps the most of all – but nevertheless I was glad of all these experiences, however imperfect, I really was, I would not have given up this knowledge for anything. For when you are in that bar with the girl who has the ponytail and biker jacket and is very tall and gaunt and pale and therefore something you desire –

— Keep going, said Wyman –

– then it is much more of a temptation to sleep with her than not to sleep with her because you know in your heart that this will be a very interesting experience, and that in fact that experience is very close and possible, whereas the dweeb who has no such confidence will be experiencing in this bar many feelings of anxiety and worry that in the end the whole experience may not be so hot, for him or her, and then will be able to convert these anxieties into marble moral towers, columns of reasoning, such that when he leaves that bar without her he will in fact have really not experienced any choice at all, even if to him it feels like he has become the noblest stoic in the world. Me, I have no such luxury. I cannot help myself make her happy and eventually say something like:

ME
Maybe we should just go to bed and do crazy things. Like maybe we should just go back to my room and I can spend all night licking you wherever you want – like anywhere –

HER
Including for instance my asshole?

ME
I did say anywhere.

Perhaps many people know this situation often and are not moved by it, but for me the rush was overwhelming and delicious – that I could say such things and the object of your desire would not turn away. She did not turn away. She stared at me.

ME
And you?

HER
Me?

ME
What would you want us to do?

HER
Then, after you had licked me, I would want you to
bend me over a chair.

ME
Say that again! Whisper it!

She came very close and her breath was a vast temptation
inside my ear.

HER
I want you to bend me over a chair and fuck me very
hard.

Always, I thought, I will remember this. It will be like
this memento I have buried with me in my pyramid with
my million pottery slaves. That's how exciting the world
can be and I worry that my friends do not understand
this. Wyman, I wanted to say: do you really not know
about this? Have you never felt this mania for detail? I
do not know if you have. Or when you hear a girl swallow
your come, does it sound sort of breathy or is it quiet?
I know one girl who went very quiet but also I know
others who kept on sucking and made a slurping gurgling
noise which, Wyman, I can still hear. The gusto and the

joyfulness! And am I to abandon this for the pleasures of kindness and loyalty? Is that really how the argument is concluded? For surely happiness is a moral virtue, too? Surely, the true sin is ennui? Or so I tried to argue, with my friends and confidants. In my life I always want as much ludicrous intimacy as possible, when everything noble and normal gets melted. I felt such pity for the large heavy men, with their hair cut too short, in their pinstriped shirts and slip-on shoes. No pleasure has ever touched them! Whereas me, in the park I go walking and meet a girl selling antiquarian books and very soon she has invited me to her apartment. Or then there was the girl who worked in the children's puppet theatre, serving chocolate egg creams and limeade ice-cream floats . . . When things happen that naturally and inadvertently, I don't see how it's possible to use a language of blame at all.

— *Inadvertent*? said my mother.

which he tries to justify

I don't know why I always liked to confide in my mother, like I was the twelve-year-old bride and she was my aged nurse, but I did seem to have this need. Perhaps I wanted to be told that everything I was doing was correct, and of my many confidants my mother just might have fulfilled this role. But in this I was forgetting one important thing, which is that my mother loves me and to be loved is a place of many dispensations, but also she does not want to lie. It means that without in any way meaning to she is therefore the arbiter of the limits of my wishes, and that can make her difficult in conversation. Did I mention the shiny turquoise tracksuit my mother bought me when I was ten? I am not sure I have mentioned it enough – this tracksuit I had asked for, had begged for, with tears in my eyes, a shell suit that would make me look as gangland as possible, only for my mother to find a thing of turquoise satin, with flared trousers . . . What's a child to do with such a mother? She loves him so much and yet she will not overspend. Obviously it's in fact an excellent form of parenting but it still creates difficult dramas when really all I want is for all my wishes to come true.

— You think this is love, but it isn't, she said.

— So what is this?

— This is just sex.

— Oh really?

— Always you are thinking about just one thing, she said.

I am sure she meant this kindly but I felt just ever so gently belittled, and I did not like this feeling at all. If my mother thought I was not my own man, I very much wanted to prove her wrong. I wanted to be announcing my decisions to her, whereas instead there she was maintaining that this decision was not my own: as if I was the most imitative mimic in human history.

— You know we just want you to be happy, said my mother. — We love you so very much.

I understood the sadness in her voice, and her unwillingness to blame. I knew the sadness very well, since obviously if you give up everything and then have nothing you can show to other people, then there's no need for a commercial with screech trumpets and maracas to tell you that something might be wrong. But how could I explain my last resistance? These are delicate feelings, and while my parents always admired me for my daydreaming, still, I don't think daydreaming is given the attention that it's due.

— You remember Nelson?

— Nelson, sure –

— He has his own office.

— Oh because that's important.

— I don't mean that. Look how kind Nelson is, said my mother.

I understood her basic point. She appreciated Nelson's care for his wife. In some dark way I wanted to be like Nelson too. But I would say that Nelson had it easy in comparison to me. I mean, sure, I go in terror of being called bad. Like Nelson and all the others of my class, I go in terror of the adjective *selfish*. To avoid this adjective I will stifle many desires, or at least stifle them in public. But why should the single thing you most are scared of necessarily be the moral code to live by? It's not so obvious, after all. It was the code of the cloud in which I lived, absolutely, but what if this cloud was not the natural habitat – the way a fish might feel about its pitiless aquarium?

because it leads to utopian experiences

And what happened next perhaps only acquired its true significance because of this very bright tempest in which I moved, when everything was as sprightly as the emoji I adored. At some party or other gathering, there Dolores was again. No longer did she have Benicio with her, her boyfriend or putto. And as I saw her, it felt like a rearrangement had just occurred, for often perhaps when something with giant meaning occurs it has its mini prefigurations –

like someone trying to locate the correct code for the safe-deposit box. Or at least, what I mean is: if you think that everything has a cause, then you also have to admit that clairvoyance and other forms or horoscope are therefore possible. Yes, in retrospect I was thinking that I had definitely foreseen this, I had known we would meet again and also known that it would be perfect, even though at the same time I had to admit that she had only existed at the corner of my consciousness. And fittingly therefore when I saw her she was standing in a corner of the room – as if it might have been possible to just snip her out of the picture entirely, like the smallest nymph at the edge of a ceiling painted with faded allegories – and immediately we were talking and were smiling very much, like the most tentative clowns in the room. I was crowded with excitement, even if I knew that in many ways this feeling could well be an illusion and just some trick of perspective – and so as we spoke I was waiting for that realisation and yet not waiting, a little like hoping someone will text you and having your phone beside you on silent but trying not to look, so that every drifting cloud or shift of light on its surface makes you nervous in your peripheral vision. There was something in her manner that enchanted me very much. She had a grandeur, no question, and that grandeur was in how sure she was of herself and of her charm. She had this integrity that was endless, including her carnality. So that it was not impossible, it seemed to me, that she would offer some route out of this scenario I was in, something decisive and irrevocable, a mode of living that was completely outside the system of my life up until now. Such a possibility must exist, after all. I had been giving it much thought. For a moment it seemed possible never to feel anxious again. For in Dolores, there was nothing serious. Or no: in Dolores, everything serious was devoted to this question of precision.

— What did you most like about me? she said.

— About you? I said.

— When we first met? she said.

— At that fiesta? I said.

— For me, she said, — it was the way you were always looking at me.

And it struck me that this type of conversation was very difficult, since in a way I remembered very little of Dolores in that conversation, mainly in fact only remembering how difficult I had found it in relation to Romy and Candy, but now that she was talking I believed that I could remember, too – since who is to judge the past? The fact that she remembered so much detail was for me a tender thing, and it made me want her even more, including the past I could no longer remember. I was looking at her and thinking that never could I imagine not wanting Dolores's body: whether feverish with illness, racked with vomiting, crimson with sunburn. I could imagine our mouths all over each other, like intricate, intelligent animals. And even though we parted with no future plan or even appointment, every day I thought about her more and more, and this feeling felt like love: the way some pirate hackers take up crazy amounts of band-width without anyone's consent. That was how opaque the world was, how beautiful, how blocked – and I would like to record this, the future I imagined might be possible with Dolores, I would like to give this lost fiesta some memorial, just before the violence starts.

but then his utopia is interrupted

To be just a single person! What a disaster! I really do
think that the outside world is too small for the inside
of people, it's too definite and absolute. Who wouldn't
transform into anything else, into a piranha or other omni-
vore? Although already I was slightly like the other animals.
I was like some octopus with its tentacles around its
various saviours and adorees, around the bodies of Romy
and Candy and Dolores and the million other mirages.
But where would this melancholy octopus go? Events by
now were becoming denser and smaller. It was like everywhere the doors and windows and other apertures were
blocked, like those fake backdrops in the old theatres,
with endless streets receding in fake perspective. Even
the front door of our house now seemed like a place of
danger, or if not danger then entrapment. If you're given
to such thoughts, perhaps therefore it's only right that
what happened next will happen – that very early in the
morning, when the morning is also still the night-time,
but you are therefore not in any condition for such
philosophy, the doorbell rang very precisely and softly.
And so in the usual nightmare method I walked down
the stairs in my nightwear – some dead teeshirt, some
dead trackpants – to answer it. My mother and my father

were away on a romantic weekend together, removed from our festivities. If they were festivities, however, they were very mournful. They were people sitting in an endless tea party, with baking and other pursuits. It wasn't the zenith I had dreamed of – where in a commune or higher plane everyone would love each other and no one would be hurt, whereas increasingly it seemed that no one really loved each other, and everyone was hurt. As for whether or not it is right for someone to arrive very early in the morning, when the morning is also the night, I did not really consider. Perhaps of course I should have done, although whether or not such protective thoughts had occurred I am still not sure how much protection they would have offered – since when danger approaches it will still approach, however much you have worried about it earlier. But anyway, I did not think about such danger. When you are woken from difficult dreams – like in this dream I was tucking into my own torso, like an ice cream, and when such are your dreams you are happy to be woken up at all – then your sense of perspective or usual danger is maybe momentarily suspended.

by armed intruders

Also after the macabre scene with the boy selling dusters and other kitchen items I had this resolution that in general I would not be so fearful of those who came to our door, the extras and deadbeats. I would lavish attention every-where, on every member of the cast list, wherever they happened to be placed in the general composition. And so I opened the door and immediately discovered that I was letting in two men to our house, masked in balaclavas. Also they had these accessories that very much resembled guns. I realised that I was shouting something – not so much articulate as just a noise, and so no more useful than the cries of any other language, like if I had said *oyé* or anything else. I was being walked backwards from our hall and into our living room, and as I walked I was trying to think at this very late point in the night both of lighting and of the telephone, just whether in either case I could reach them and try to make the situation better. But also I was feeling very scared and my body was lighter than it had ever been, and softer. I was not really sure of the language I should use. Definitely I was happy that my mother and father were not here, because no one should see their house invaded, and not only that, but also see their child menaced in this way in the morning/night when everyone should be sleeping. The balaclavas in particular did upset me. After all, Hiro and I had been very careful not to use such threatening items ourselves, and now I did feel vindicated, because the effect was horrible and upsetting. Certainly it made me scared but the more scared I became also the more angry, even if at this point I did understand that to be angry was no solution. But still, a sense of humiliation was inescapable and I let it marinate there. These two people had dressed their faces in balaclavas, although as I say this I realise that *dressed* is perhaps not right, but I do not know the verbs for balaclavas, just as I only know that fear it turned out was new and very sad, because it was like a whole body had disappeared, like I was about as strong as the drape of a curtain as it hangs there, perhaps not even as strong as that.

— Sit the fuck down, said the second man, and as he did so I realised he was a girl.

Not only that, but at the same time I also realised that there was something in their tone of voice that indicated a possible uncertainty, I mean a lack of practice or of being duped by their own role, and that's a problem, because one thing that is true is that you have to sell your role to yourself and know it before anyone else will be sold and know it too, but whether or not that calmed me I do not know, I think it didn't, because in many ways the gangster who is nervous is much more dangerous than the gangster who is a professional and knows what they are doing, just as you do want your mortgage adviser to be seasoned and basically bored by the job they have to do, that's only human nature.

THE GIRL
I said, sit the fuck down.

So I sat. As I did so I saw Candy standing in the doorway, and she looked so vulnerable, in this black vest, and shorts, this vest that displayed the pale surface of her skin and the beginning of her breasts and I felt such love for her – such bravery in unknown circumstances! – and wished that I could cry out how much I loved her, but decided sadly no. And so instead I let the scene continue as its starlets wanted: with much terror and fainting and blood.

& very gently terror enters the picture

No doubt there are always people – as the poison works its way into their liver and veins, or they press the trigger tight as they aim it at their heart, or see the truck approaching on the wrong side of the road with its horn sounding across the empty plains, or while the girl who on reflection now seems possibly illegally young is unzipping them and whispering that no one needs to know – who have their doubts as to whether the real is as real as it tends to think it is. That's just the natural consequence of seeing blood or guts or other gunk. It's just what happens when gore is present. Because no one was expecting it they do not know what to say or how to describe it, they have no references and when you have no references it becomes difficult to talk – it's like when people after witnessing a car crash or drugs shooting or plane disaster say *Hey it was just like a movie* whereas they really mean of course that it wasn't like anything they've ever seen before. But the gore is a much smaller subset of the lurid than people ordinarily think. The lurid can occur at much smaller moments. Because I don't think it's so unusual to expect that the lurid and the normal might just happen to never coincide, no it's not so lunatic to imagine that nothing strange will ever happen in your life because of course most of the time it doesn't – but then the extraordinary isn't what never happens but what sometimes or very rarely happens, which means that it does happen, in the end. And one conclusion that can possibly be drawn from this would be that the lurid and the ordinary are in fact only different descriptions of the same thing, like they're the low note and the high note and in between is the sliding glissando scuzziness of an electric violin. The movement from one state to another can be therefore very small – as miniature as crossing over from Mexicali to Calexico, or, for instance, letting in two people who seem to wish you harm, with deep malignity in their postures and their tone of voice. And in fact maybe there's not so much difference between the benign and the malign. In the end you cannot separate any event into any category at all, since everything is just a succession of singular things.

— This is only a warning, said the man.

— OK, I said.

— Is kind of your own fault, the girl said.

— We're being nice, said the man.

— You shouldn't take what isn't yours, said the girl.

— But what have we taken? said Candy.

So much communication was occurring between Candy and me that it was no doubt marvellous, if what you are interested in is the wonder of human consciousness and its ability to exist as this kind of ectoplasm between two people, but I was trying not to think about what Candy might be thinking. And also I was at the same time interested in the fact that these two gangsters did seem very unsure. They were picking things up and smashing them but in a slightly listless manner, like they did not quite believe in this as a gesture. It was making me sad because now all my suspicions would return again, and never would I trust people, I mean the people I did not know – for always now I would feel justified to refuse the people who came to my door, demanding things, as if they were just criminals or lunatics rather than hard-working honest people. Little by little, they were taking the room apart. Everything that had previously been in the room was still there, sure, but now it was in more pieces than it should have been. And I think it's quite unusual, to see a room that's minutely multiplied like that. Only a few people will have seen this phenomenon – when a room in your house is completely and very beautifully destroyed, in one systematic tableau.

in the form of a destroyed room

Up against one wall, the twin cushions of the sofa were now standing, in a slack and improvised V, and each half had been slashed like the canvas of one of those modernista paintings so its foam was visible and you realised just how dense the foam inside a sofa is, like *foam* as a word in no way does its deep density and honeycomb kapok justice – and these slashed cushions formed the backdrop or central motif to the general scene, in the foreground of which was the smashed form of my banjo, whose pieces were now haphazard around the room, the left-hand side of which was marked by a chest of drawers, except now every drawer was pulled out in an irregular stacked fashion so that its profile was more like an art deco building, and while most of these drawers were still in their containing chest, with the stuff inside them strewn on the floor or collapsing over the rims, two of the drawers had been entirely taken out of the chest and turned upside down, so that out of them had tumbled a selection of old photographs that were now in a spilled heap, including the ones

from my father's business visit to an unidentifiable city
when I was five, and also photos of me sporting a space-
man's helmet and space cadet's shirt, while on the other
side of the room, by which I mean the right-hand side,
the wall now had a small smash or dent in its plaster,
maybe related to the fact that a mirror had been pulled
off the wall in the process of which the hooks had ripped
down two strands of wallpaper that was printed with
ornamental roses or tulips – I have never been good
with the language of flowers – which now descended flop-
pily to the floor where they caressed a pile of my old
Super 8 films and a broken Polaroid camera and a smashed
pair of Hiro's glasses: yes, this was the basic set-up on the
floor, over which was now scattered my backpack that
was now torn, and some of my mother's shoes, which she
had left out, maybe to clean them or reheel them or resole
them, which included a pair of gold sandals with high
heels, and two pairs of black stilettos, and as I looked at
all this it struck me very forcibly how easy it was to make
objects into garbage and I think that's an interesting
phenomenon, that everything ends up like this, I mean
just sad and badly made, unusable like my banjo, dirty,
it's their natural fate, there's no meaning in anything at
all, I suppose – an example of which, for instance, was
one of the toys that Hiro had bought for the dog which
had once resembled a spirited rabbit but now no longer had
the stuffing in its legs, and the stuffing itself was revealed
as a mess of cotton wool that was a pile of clouds on the
floor, while its felt eyes had been ripped out and were on
the floor among its entrails and its arms, although I think
that in fact this destruction had been there already, and

was not these gangsters' fault but the dog's, but as I looked at this bright tableau I was also thinking that while this looked like total mess the amount of actions that they had really performed was strangely smaller than you might think, the effects were much grander than their causes because there are only so many objects in a room that can be destroyed and in fact the most confusing and perplexing to the eye was the most minute, by which I mean the new surface on the floor that the girl had caused by just upending some quite small boxes of my mother's in which she kept whatever she had no idea of classifying, a surface that was soft and sharply glittering and was made up, for instance, of two pairs of folding sunglasses, but also some plastic and silver rings and a set of picnic plastic cutlery, under which were draped one striped silk scarf and one chiffon scarf – printed with what I think was a floral design but I wasn't down on my hands and knees among it – along with some hair grips and a miniature pill box with a beaded design on its lid and some old beer-bottle tops that were presumably souvenirs, one fried-chicken menu, then various chain necklaces tangled up, I think in fact there were more rings than I previously thought, as well as a flyer from one of the bars that we had visited, and then also a pile of now-defunct fairy lights to light up any home which I had never ever noticed but now realised they had been hung up in our house for all the major festivals, because I suppose in the end what people mean by an unknown reality is just the real you haven't noticed, like the image in a microscope or the mess that's created by just making a pile horizontal, a pile which further contained, I finally noticed, not only a bag of weed but also various other empty plastic sachets, and a felt-tip pen which I think was the one Romy had once used to do up her hair, though how it had got there I had no idea, and then another pen, one of those pens where inlaid in the holder is a panorama, and this particular panorama was a miniature ferry that slid to and fro in front of the Manhattan backdrop while I definitely thought that if you could only look closer then you would see the hopeful faces at the ferry windows and then the mascara on the women's heavy eyelashes, if you could only get even closer, but I couldn't.

& a gun

It was at this point that in wandered our curious dog. And I was very glad, because a dog is always a distraction.

— What's his name? said the man.

— Sidney, I said.

— It's a girl? he said.

— No, boy, I said.

— Fuck you, he said.

— How is it a girl's name? I said.

— Obviously it's a girl's name, he said.

I had no idea what to say to that and so I just said nothing, because possibly this was just the menacing crazy talk that was prelude to us being dismembered or other violations. Or maybe in fact every name is double, and philosophically he was right, which I suppose is possible.

— Sydney, is with a *y*, he said.

— Oh, OK, I said.

Always in life it's good to humour people and especially

when they mean deliberate violence to you – for obviously I was not convinced that you could spell Sydney with a *y*, not as a name, but then in life there are so many names and in the end a name is just not important, it's just a means of identifying something with one sound when that thing is in fact multiple and not really to be identified at all. And if this were all that were to happen then I did think we had got off lightly.

   — The money, he said, — is to be paid tomorrow.

   — What money? I said.

   — Really? he said.

   — What money? said Candy.

   — The money is not important! I cried.

   — No? said the girl.

And she presented a definite gun.

which he cannot deny is in some way a just punishment

I felt a wild smearing sense of injustice inside me, or perhaps more precisely this sense surrounded me, like a cape, and maybe in fact that sense was also fear. When I was criminal myself, I had not been so fearsome! We had been very careful to avoid harm! When we entered the nail salon or canal cafe with our gun we knew that definitely it was not real and also that even had that gun been real we would not have been capable of using it. Whereas this was a very different proposition, it turned out, just because this person was not me. There was no way of knowing how far this gun was just a gesture or a true instrument of massive harm. In general I did feel that people were not such maniacs as to shoot in domestic areas, but obviously I did not know what she was thinking, not at all. Of course I was therefore scared! But not just scared. I was many frequencies at once. Anger certainly was something I was feeling, or a sentiment just like it. And also at the same time I had some expanding sense of karma. For the provenance of these people was very mysterious and could not easily be explained, or at least, there was more than one possible explanation and they were giving me very few clues. But whether they came from the nail salon or cafe or even the small bodega from so long ago, it was obvious that at some point we had made one fatal miscalculation, which was to think that that salon or cafe or bodega would be run by conscientious citizens with impressive insurance deals, rather than, as was perhaps becoming clear, criminal organisations who very possibly were using these operations to obscure their secret financial misdeeds.

— I think, I later said to Hiro, — we made a bad call somewhere.

— In what way? said Hiro.

— I think we may have got mixed up with very bad people, I said.

— It's possible, agreed Hiro.

— Yeah, maybe, I said.

But then, you can never know, when you enter the world, what dealings the people you are dealing with now have. That's a principle of all business and in particular perhaps the gangster style. And in this state of large revelation it began to occur to me that the cast list for grievances against me was so vast I did not really know where to begin, like I was responsible for a swarming muddled series – as if everything cartoon on the surface was linked in some vast network of transversals. There was definitely a very long list of people I had wronged, like Candy or Romy or even Dolores – whose messages I did not always reply to, or not at least with the correct adoration, if I was busy with my wife, or my lover – even if obviously I was not thinking that any of this trio were responsible for this armed invasion, but the realisation of the harm I did every day then led to the darker thought that also there was then this additional list of extras to whom I had not done the right thing, like Quincy and Osman and the maid at the hotel, or Caycee, or my friend Shoshana whom I no longer see, then also Shannon or Timeka or Cassity, or the woman in the burger bar with her many children, or the girl in the cafe, or the boy who came to our door with feather dusters, not to mention the owners of the bodega and nail salon and cafe, and their various terrified employees and customers, just as also there were so many people I had not correctly tipped or thanked or remembered their name at gatherings, and it made me frantic not only with guilt but also a sense that therefore in some way they might not only have been wishing me harm but even causing it, and that was why my life was such calamity. Not every light in the distance is an automobile on a distant freeway, and not every fear you can feel approaching is so easily explained. Some fears may have very formless sources – and in this case I was wondering if in fact the entire backdrop of my life was really a vampire waiting to strike. Many people did not like me. They were on the outside, and they wanted to come in. I guess it's difficult to use words like *enemies* but I think these sad people should be considered as my enemies, and in fact not just mine but those of everyone around me. For perhaps they were right to hate me, the ghosts ranged in opposition. I was feeling very philosophical in a manner that reminded me of my father, who was given to repeat snippets of his reading like an old-time sage, the whole fortune-telling routine such as: *Whatever you imagine is real.* Or, perhaps, *If you're thinking about it, then it must be meaningful.* My wisdom I think was tougher. Why wouldn't people want the things that I had? That was the single question and I think it is still the single question. Why should you have what you have for ever? Once you realise that, it's very hard to think of other people as unjustly envious at all.

even if it becomes far worse than he could imagine

The surprising thing was that normally if a dog walks into a room that's a cue for general adoration and gasps of joy. Oh such loveliness! Look at his four paws! Whereas now I noticed these two phantoms in balaclavas were eyeing our dog with much malice. The girl still had the gun raised, just precisely raised in my direction, and I was looking away because the spectacle was scaring me very much.

— You don't seem so very sorry, said the girl.

— Me? I said.

Because I was keen, if possible, that Candy should not know the precise facts of my recent criminal activities. Definitely I was keen, and I think perhaps however this keenness for privacy within my marriage looked different to the people who wished us harm. It looked, I think, like some insouciance or misplaced lack of remorse. And had I known this or foreseen this of course I would have tried to convince them otherwise. But who is able to foresee anything? So that then the girl just turned slightly so that the gun was pointing down at our dog, and the dog was looking up at her in its usual manner, because that is what dogs do, they are not attuned to social precision, they think that everyone loves them. Until the man suddenly said:

— What the fuck, man? Not the gun.

— Good point, she said, and pointed the gun away.

— I mean, he said, — don't shoot it.

Then the man took the gun from her and just clubbed our dog on the head and our dog fell over, just very awkwardly tumbled, like his body fell before his legs could crumple, and as he did so he made the strangest noise, a little like the noise he made if accidentally you trod on his paw, but much more terrified. Then everything went silent. I mean, he went silent, but it felt like the whole room was silenced, too. There was blood gunked over his eye, and also his mouth went strange, as if to match his voice – like it went slack over his teeth in the way it sometimes did when he was asleep. I cried out but I did not cry out, because Candy was crying more than I was and I wanted to stay strong and brave. Instead therefore I stared very intently at the way the blood was forming from his skull. I know the usual phrase is a *pool of blood* but I am not sure that pool is right. It was more like now there was an extra surface beside him and that surface was viscous and a deep brown shade of red. Or maybe only red, I can't be sure. As before, blood was indescribable. It was brown against the green carpet of my parents' living room and everything was horrified.

— You give the money back, the man said. — In twenty-four hours. And then we can all leave each other alone.

& darkness descends

It was maybe five minutes later when Hiro finally descended, for which I don't think I can blame him since sleeping pills were playing a useful part in his existence at this time. I suppose what he found was like one of those scenes where the eunuchs are engaged in destroying the sultan's possessions before his fall, right down to gouging out the hearts of the luscious screaming concubines – scenes where the whole previous construction is just meticulously dismantled.

— Hey man, I said.

— Fuck, he said.

— Yeah, I said.

I was just stymied and quiet and this seemed to make Hiro pause. It was like he was seeing this scene as dimly as when you first try getting into Bangla, or like the way at four in the morning you are looking for cold takeaway, maybe fish-fragrant aubergine or bear's paw bean curd, and the kitchen's just vaguely outlined by the sad light from the fridge.

— What the fuck? said Candy.

— I really, I said, — have no idea.

The basic realismo principle, after all, is people's readiness to be duped. If you say a thing with enough conviction, they will never ever doubt you. Or no, I think that's too much. What I mean is that in such a state of trauma and of shock, no one is so interested in precise explanations. They just want to feel safe as soon as possible. So that if I could maintain that I did not understand, yes, maintain that this was some horrific act of random violence or mistaken identity, it would be possible for Candy to believe me, or at least believe me for a while. I wasn't sure. *Just call the police, OK*, she said, then got up and walked upstairs and covered herself in our duvet. And as she did so I think I did just possibly know that finally the cloud in which I floated was about to descend to earth. But I did not think about that, not at that precise moment. I sat there staring at the wrecked room, and in the middle of that room our savaged and beautiful dog. I think what makes something a pet is that we live longer than it does, which I suppose means that maybe to the trees we are also just pets, too. But never had I thought I would witness his death as violent. He had very sad eyes, and was very thin, and did this skittering thing when he ran like he was made of mercury. And I was thinking how always he could make things supersad. He would stare at me with his triangular ears straight up and his eyes unblinking as if thinking worried thoughts and when that happened I got worried like a reflection. Then I just started to laugh hysterically. It was zany like that, like some comic film for children that is showing in the citron afternoon when the only people who are watching feel just desolate and crazy and alone.

8. TIME SADNESS

THEIR FINAL ENTRANCE
INTO THE PUBLIC WORLD

then much later they wake up

When we woke it was already dark. The day had been erased, and it would have been no surprise to perhaps just hear vast guns booming exorbitantly on the South Side. To clear the house up and decently dispose of the body of our dog would have definitely been the obvious next element in the sequence, but I did not know if I was equal to such a clean-up operation, and Candy seemed no more able to cope with it than I was. Not that we wanted to go to the balloon festival in the park, or sunken trampoline display, but I don't think it was strange if we just wanted other distractions. That night there was meant to be some happening that our friend Tiffany had organised, a discussion of inequality in some outdoor impromptu cafe. We knew that Romy would be there with Epstein, not to mention groups of other and interesting people, and as always we had a wide selection of narcotics, and also we had promised we would be there – and so this seemed a better option for the moment than considering what to do with a destroyed room. Our souls were exhausted. I carried the body of our dog outside and shrouded him in a towel, so that later we could bury him and try to make things right, and then with Hiro we made our way over to the gathering. I would not say that the conversation between us on the metro was easy or delicious but also I think that's normal after such violence. One of the major problems with the telenovelas is how tough people are, how easily they cope with rape, embezzlement, gunfights, and so on. Whereas any one of these would be enough in real life to make a person a total breakdown and always weeping. And I did feel like weeping, very much. But also I wanted to be faithful to some idea of style. If people were ranged against me, I intended to face them with calm.

& decide to enter the public world

When we arrived there were fairy lights strung in the trees and someone had made latkes. But also there were many pamphlets, and leaflets. This particular demonstration was designed to encourage a new way of relating to each other, a digital project to promote exchanges of little acts of kindness. There were movements like this everywhere – libraries in tents and other inventions. And I did approve of this desire for a larger community. All of us were trying to divest ourselves of our power. If we had discovered that we were occupying powers, we were very regretful, and I think that's noble. We wanted to create different loyalties, and it meant that often I would argue with my mother and my father. They tended to see the right community as our general ethnic group, and I disagreed.

ME
They are not my people!

MY FATHER
They are your people. Your people are your ancestors –

ME
I'm not so sure.

MY MOTHER
Not so sure? You think in the last century they were not
so sure? You think in a pogrom you would be so –

ME
That is not a right comparison!

MY MOTHER
So who are your people? Tell me.

ME
Whoever I choose to be among –

MY MOTHER
Nonsense.

ME
I think it's true.

MY MOTHER
You have no idea what's true or what isn't.

My mother, folks! I wanted to gesture to the TV studio
audience. Always I have thought that I never knew my
mother well enough, even though I love her so very much.

Always there is this imbalance, and difficulty of communication. Perhaps I should have met her as an adult, except that then we would have had the friendship of two adults, which is not at all the same. For what did we have in common with the immigrants and kibbutzim, the learned scholars and the crazed politicos? I could not see it at all, among the barbecues and swimming pools. But while therefore in theory I did sympathise, definitely, with Tiffany and her dreams for a better society, whenever I was there among the revolutionaries I always found it difficult to feel as one with a crowd. It's much more difficult than it seems. If I saw just one activist with a pet squirrel or new ideas as to how to signal agreement or disagreement, such things bothered me. It didn't seem to me to look like true revolution. Not that I want barricades and blood, but ideally we would at least form some giant transport system for the sick, and escalators in favelas, but we tended to talk instead. If we were like a monk who righteously sweeps the path in front of him, it was only if that monk mostly does the sweeping in his mind, which is probably not so good. But then, this was how we lived: the world was multicoloured. There were palm trees in among the monkey-puzzle trees, and monsoons in the summer. Parakeets descended in the parks. In the gentle rain, kids were out drinking on the sidewalks. Probably in the tea rooms the more furious boys were eating tea cakes and planning a future coup d'état. Others just played ping pong. At least, I suppose, it was an idealistic time. The global project was for demonstrations and occupations and I knew that in some of these my friends were filming and writing slogans, including Candy and Romy and Tiffany, but also other friends like Bjorn and Shauna and Trey, and I tried to follow their progress intently, even while I was preoccupied. They had their stories too, my friends out there in the world. The story of Bjorn is that he went to take part in the occupation of a bank. He arrived one night and realised that although his hunger was intense he was too scared to go back outside in the illuminated dark to find a chilli dog or shrimp taco or cheese slice. So very hungry he went to bed. That was his story of life among the occupiers, or so he told me later. In general, people's stories were getting smaller and smaller and were ever so toy-like, which was not, perhaps, the exactly perfect size. Tonight however I had no opinions of any kind, all I wanted was to be with people who were safe and did not want to harm me. Although also I knew that this current mood was not a good mood in which to see Romy. For a while now we had not seen each other on our own, just increasingly sent each other messages or emails that were very difficult to gauge, sometimes full of love and devotion, sometimes curt and only information. And now there she was, talking politics and when she does that often we do irritate each other, we can't help it.

ROMY
No let me tell you why there will be no revolution –

ME
OK –

ROMY
Because if you are one of the people who owns an iPhone or likes to pizzatweet and so on then in any rightful revolution you will be a target –

ME
Uh?

ROMY
Sure, the ones who have multiple private bank accounts
and speak fourteen languages can get the fuck out and
will be safe on Mustique. But the happy person who
just happens to have enough to live on but not, let's
say, *escape*, will be hunted. They will be hunted down
and massacred. And the happy people know this –
they know this very well which is why they stay very
quiet and why there will never be a revolution in our
lifetime.

The problem is that such conversations can so quickly be
conversations about other things. In some way, I knew, if
she was talking about the lack of revolution then there
was a way in which this was not exactly what she was
saying. And I did think also that I possibly understood
the implications.

where Romy separates from our hero for ever

For of course in the end Romy was tired of this, and tired
of us. I understood that and I was tired, too. I would have
liked to propose that maybe we could all live together, in
some commune reminiscence of the orgy which now felt
so long ago, but it seemed not the ideal moment to make
such a proposition.
   — You understand me, yeah? she said.
   — I think I do, I said.

— This has to stop, she said. — I'm not waiting any more.

It was very obviously the opposite of any commune proposition, and yet I was surprised to discover not only a wild sadness in me but also possibly a sense of relief, not because this situation was now over but that in some way it was simpler. Very neatly therefore I replaced my vision of a commune with a vision of private happiness. Perhaps, I was thinking, this would mean that I could become a new thing with Candy, a way of being that would renew our vows and make the entire past different. Perhaps utopia had all along been present, but in a different way. This was also possible.

— But we can still be friends, I said.

And Romy looked at me.

— I don't know, she said. — Like, maybe we shouldn't talk for a while.

— For how long? I said.

— I don't know, she said.

I was trying very hard to think because perhaps she was not as definite as she seemed, in which case I could at least keep in some form of communication with her, and if we could communicate then possibly my sadness would be less, and that was very important to me at this time. But also I did have no idea, because the problem is that people are often very nice, especially when they are saying things that are hurtful and causing harm, which only means that the harm then takes much longer to be understood, and therefore is maybe more hurtful.

— I mean, I'm supposed to rescue you, is that it? Or you're supposed to rescue me? she said.

— I never said that, I said.

— Look at you, she said. — Just look at you.

It was a very difficult moment, when suddenly everything I thought I cared about just vanished. I could see the living room of my parents' house and my dead dog and I wanted to tell Romy this, I wanted her sympathy and understanding but I suddenly realised that in fact we would never talk again. Darkness was descending everywhere. It's baffling when you consider how trivial you might seem, just by imagining your future self considering your own past. I was trying to remember only a few days before, when I was considering growing a moustache that could be ideally Mexicano but maybe more realistically one of those Sichuan glamour moustaches from the early twentieth century – just a slick line like a kid's drawing of a wave or the flourished squiggle of mustard on a hot dog. I mean a moustache like a cubist quotation. That had been my pastime, and now these pastimes seemed just old and very fragile. Like also I'd been listening often to pirate radio on the Internet, which was very absorbing until the DJ at the end of his show explained that he was going to be lonely, with no one to talk to at home until his mother got back from work – and *that*, machacho, I thought, is what is meant by sadness, when it turns out that even the DJs still live at home with their parents – or so I had wanted to tell Romy, or Candy, or anyone who would listen. Whereas now such reflections seemed rendered insubstantial.

— Well, how long? I said. – Like a week?

— Yeah, maybe, she said.

— Well, OK, I said.

Because I did think that maybe this would be OK. I could understand if she only wanted a week in which to spend some time apart.

— Or maybe longer, she said.

— OK, I said.

— I mean, a week it wouldn't feel real, or maybe any definite time, she said.

— You mean for ever? I said.

— Yeah no I think so, she said.

And I was just about to howl or yelp or yowl – because the discovery that everything is temporary, or that everything can be made temporary by the will of another person, that's a terrifying discovery, however much you know it is always possible – when Candy arrived with Tiffany, with boxes of manifestos and declarations that required immediate sorting, and so I could not howl because that is not how these things happen. Instead the conversation continued, and we talked about other things, and Romy was gone, for ever, the way a marble sculpture might have been lost in the more classical times – just tipped overboard from a trireme in the process of some shipjacking by a bored and overworked Viking.

& so in his anguish he tries to talk about suffering

To watch her disappear like that was a terrible experience. I wanted to talk it over very fast with Hiro, in very deep breadth, but instead we had the wider distraction of a conversation, and to have your attention divided in this way is never a restful situation. It creates a small persistent sense of difficulty. Nevertheless, I tried to understand the general tone – while around us accordions were being played and a stage for lectures was being constructed out of cardboard. How will we help people at a distance? Tiffany was saying. Because that really is a major problem, perhaps the major problem of our time. How will we think about the suffering that we are causing every day? And I did, of course, agree with her concern.

— Like what? said Hiro.

And Tiffany took out her phone and showed him a movie, for everywhere on the Internet were these camera-phone movies from our war zones – and they were total snuff movies, absolutely, except not in the manner of hutong violence with people's nails ripped out or eyes made into jelly. I mean if your idea of gore-fest is when you see a man bite out his tongue or there is brain on somebody's brogue, then this was nothing. The scene that Tiffany showed us was more like one of those ski slopes beside the autoroutes, if you also allow that this particular slope was inside a concrete hut. Four men were practising their skiing technique, with their arms outstretched and invisible sticks in their hands. They were just practising but with real goggles on. Also beside them were two other players who had given up the game, and were now lying on the concrete floor – and what was strange was how familiar it all looked, this scene, with these two people lying down exhausted. It was like twilight at a music festival, or the horizontal soccer players of a tragic penalty shootout. Possibly if you looked very hard then the neckline of a man's white vest was really red but it was difficult to see. And then among these men a soldier moved, encouraging them with a helping hand or cheering backslap to resume their skiing position, but instead he only seemed to manage to transform them into an atonal avant-garde choir – emitting sad whimpers and groans, small noises, the way our dog would whisper like an elf throughout the night. It was very disturbing, the way these movies on the one hand showed nothing at all, and on the other hand you knew that this seemingly innocent surface was also total pain and suffering. It meant you found yourself asking crazy questions like you might ask about a sex scene in the old movies, e.g. *Are they really doing it or not?* Yes, the whole real thing was very unclear. And according to Tiffany, the only way to refuse this was to make the audience part of the picture. For we really are all film critics and in a mute parenthesis I considered Dolores and our conversations, and wondered what she might say. Because in the end, Tiffany added, the basic problem is how to live in a community. And of course, absolutely, I agreed. I thought that this project was magnificent. But I was not so sure that large-scale projects were always possible. Even politics, when you think about it, is so much smaller than you first assume: it is you in a public square, with a megaphone and a felt-tip placard, or one person in a suburban apartment being tortured, handcuffed in a bath, sprayed with a hand-held shower. Or not even that. I mean, I continued – trying not to think about Romy or about Candy, and yet only thinking about them both – because I was starting to lose the noble line of my reasoning, and wanted to resume it – the world you ever inhabit is very small and limited.

— Can I interrupt? said Candy.

I was kind of glad, because I definitely was worrying that I was not expressing myself correctly, and was interested to listen to Candy always, and in particular to her theory that she now proceeded to outline, according to which we would all have to accept the possibility that the best you will ever do in imagining the suffering of other people is to imagine it as garish, with very gruesome blood effects. Whereas the real truth of suffering, in Candy's opinion, as she described it, was so much more everyday and dull and difficult and inescapable. But that was much harder to imagine and so we tended not to do it. And I wanted very much to show that I agreed with Candy, that the lurid is the best the cute can do in imagining such suffering, and one way you can show your agreement in a conversation is to extend another person's reasoning, and so I tried to do that. It seemed to me, I added, that the problem of what to think about should be much more personal. Like often I sit there thinking how I only have one life and do not know precisely what to do with that.

— Darling, said Tiffany. — It's not about you.

Always, I thought, I am fated to be the one who is not understood! But still, I carried on. Here we all are, I said, in a panic about suffering, but what about death too?

— I do not see you, said Tiffany, — being currently scythed down.

— The *currently*, I said, — is not the point!

For I could not understand, I tried to explain, in my own private panic, at what point you can think about both suffering and death – I mean think about them equally, with equal weight. It's like you cannot concentrate on both, and both seem worthy of my full attention. If you concentrate on the suffering, then obviously you must tender to the needs of other people. But if you concentrate on the death, and the fact that every single person in this gathering right here is going to be a corpse, and possibly very soon, then the urgency of suffering perhaps disappears, and the more imposing question is the one about you, and how much pleasure you should get before you die.

ME
Like maybe the severest question you can ask is whether you are in a happy marriage.

CANDY
You really want to talk about this?

ME
I'm only saying.

CANDY
OK then, OK.

I could see that she was smiling despite herself, and that she was possibly angry or on edge. It would have been useful to determine the precise depth of her irritation, but I felt unsure as to how to go about that, and in company. Always it's important to be as gentle as possible with other people, and in Candy I often felt that it was also important to acknowledge this giant pressure all around her, that was not of anyone's making. It was the atmosphere in which perhaps everyone now lives, a giant weariness – considering how many demands were being made on everyone's time, not just developing the correct sex life and career but also needing to know the right crèche or massage place in a curious out-of-town location. How in this time will anyone ever be blissfully lazy again? And so once more I felt a tenderness for Candy that was like a burden I carried with me, and I would have liked to say this to Candy but to say it in front of all these people seemed impossible or improper, so instead I came out with something wilder and more general.

ME
I mean: what's destitution?

CANDY
I'll tell you what destitution is. It's when a person is watching some daytime soap where two women are arguing over a parking space – and this spectator cannot comprehend such a situation – a situation where there are *too many cars.*

even if he is no expert on the subject

It wasn't that I disagreed with our grand desire for justice – I just doubted how to change the situation. Definitely it's noble to want to divest yourself of your colonising power, but to do this might need much more drastic schemes. To care so much about the people far away! And with such limited achievements! The problem with these kind of woes is that they're basically as otiose as the single honest policeman inside a giant police state. Just look at me, and my utopias! Certainly if people wanted to accuse me of black crimes, I would not resist – and not only for the obvious crimes that were now occupying my conscience. To think of the money spent on my education! On the paints and paper I liked to play with, and on my toys! It just seemed natural never to think about the factories and the workers in those factories who produced such things. Most of life I think is like being in the restaurant of your dreams, where the waiters are attentive yet invisible. That's basically how we want our world to be run, and it's amazing to what extent it really is. You are always spared the oil extraction and other tasks. I used to be told off by my mother for telling people how easy I found everything, at school, or in my job in the city. My mother seemed to think that if I pointed this out too much then I would maybe be detested, or possibly even worse – that I was giving away a secret which should be kept among ourselves. For the problem is that to live in this way is totally delicious. That's why, I think, to abdicate your power is so much harder than it seems. However much you might have beliefs and consciences, it turns out you only have them in the way you own anything else: they're very easy to ignore. It's so much more difficult giving up what you already possess. For many are the princes who wake up in the favela suburbs – but if they have a choice they do go back to the palace they once enjoyed. It's in their nature, to prefer the vaporetto and the dawn satsuma sky.

but more like an imperial scribe or defendant

I have come to know a vast pity for the scribes on the edges of dark empires. I can understand how that schmuck might feel, the functionary out there among the swamps and reeds, not concentrating on the work at hand but devoting himself instead to pointless exercises in calligraphy . . . That's just one of the undignified poses time will conspire to force you into, and I do mean you as well, not only as you read this account but in your private and public life. It's impossible to describe how mistaken we always are, it's more like air or food which is why all time is wasted time, it can't be otherwise. For one thing I had never imagined, no not ever, was that in my quest to make this world a better place I would not have Candy by my side. I could not picture that at all – not, I think, because in my arrogance I did not think that it was possible for her to leave, but only because she was simply always a condition of my thinking, which was also why it had always been so difficult for me to live with the various consequences of my behaviour. If you had ever asked me nevertheless to picture what it would be like, for Candy and me to break up, I suppose I would have said that it was only imaginable after months of conversation, a period replete with reprieves and future possibilities, and no setting was ever possible, or adequate: it existed in some high and abstract state. So that if now it did seem to be occurring, on returning home from this demonstration, here in our kitchen in the outer suburbs, with the room next to us destroyed, it also felt like there was some extra backdrop, like an echo – like we were in the midst of some vast courtroom out of the ancient revolutions, and behind Candy were serried ranks of other judges and executioners, the gleeful voyeuristic public.

— I just keep thinking, she said, — what choices were the wrong choices?

— What does that mean? I said.

For it really did seem as if I was being sentenced or condemned.

— I don't know. I don't know, she said.

— OK, I said.

— No I do know, she said. — I think we should break up. I'm done.

— Really? I said. — I mean –

— I think we should, she said.

Then she started to cry, but without doing anything about this – she just sat there crying and letting the tears emerge and disappear very slowly, and it was the fact of not doing anything about these tears, not wiping them away, not smearing them across her cheeks, that seemed most delicate and bereft. So I decided that I should at the very least look after her and not be the one to cry myself. If to be noble was my ideal, then to maintain some self-possession was the best course I had at my disposal.

confronted with his fate very unexpectedly

For if she wanted to leave me, I could understand this desire. Probably I had made life very difficult for Candy, if I thought about it from a certain perspective. And I began to wonder if perhaps I had therefore deep down wanted this, yes wanted our marriage to founder and my happiness to be destroyed, yet even as I thought that I also knew that if this was finishing, and even if I had wanted it to finish, now that it was finishing I certainly wanted it to begin again, and the possibility that I might be logically inconsistent in this way pained me very much. It was like the way in your remote childhood when you are going out to some party to drop acid or methadone, and you have lied to your parents for a long while to bring this situation about, but then as you are about to leave, in the early evening the house suddenly seems so comforting, so happy, with your parents consulting the takeaway menu and a selection from the video store, and you do not know why you are going to leave it for the dark large windswept night.

> ME
> Don't you think every first marriage needs to end? I mean, no, that's not what I meant. I mean: can't you be my second wife?

Furiously I was trying to argue with myself. I was trying to maintain that the liberation I had just been envisaging could still exist, and I did believe this, since why should it not be possible on my own? And yet I was sadly realising

that all my liberations occurred with Candy as the background, and the prospect of having this backdrop torn away,
like the end of the studio system, seemed to render everything
inexplicable. Like for instance now Candy did not however
smile at my small witticism and attempt at lightness; she was
only in her own careful world where she said exactly as
much as she could, like tell me how bad she felt about my
parents. And I wondered if I could seize on this as some
concession, and change the subject to the possibility of us
seeing professionals for help, if that would change her mind,
but brutally she shook her head softly no.

CANDY
I want to leave now.

ME
I want to talk to you. You're who I always talk to –

And then I could not continue. Regrettably and despite
my best intentions I started to cry. Then she started to
cry again, too.

ME
This doesn't feel real.

CANDY
I'm sorry.

ME
Are you really leaving?

CANDY
Yes –

ME
I feel like I'm dying. Like totally –

but also very definitely

I wished I could escape it in some way, this fate of mine –
that I could just stop off in some desert diner and stuff
myself on jalapeño poppers and ranch wings, or at some
hill station cafeteria, with pickles and chapatis, but overall
I realised that this vision like most visions was sadly unattainable. I had to carry on. From now on, I would have
to carry on and I would have to do so on my own. The
prospect was so painful that I really did feel that I was
dying, it was no exaggeration, even if as I said it I also knew
that it would only sound like an exaggeration and melo-
dramatic, but still, I had to say what I felt. It was as if I
could feel inside me all the molecules of my body close
themelves gently down. While at the same time it surprised
me to realise that, painful as this was, it could have been
even more painful, if I had suddenly confessed to Candy
everything that I had been doing without her knowledge,
or if not without her knowledge then without her acknow-
ledgement, which is a slightly different situation. Whereas
instead for ever we would continue in this small enclosure,
where not everything would ever be said.

CANDY
We needed to do this for so long. You've wanted this, too.

ME
How long?

CANDY
Well, months –

ME
This is horrible.

CANDY
Look, we were dying here. You know this. This shouldn't make you so sad.

ME
Hold me.

It was very strange. I was making these sad noises like I was groaning or keening, because definitely I was feeling like everything was dissolving beneath me, the way the floors dissolve in horror films when you are trying to escape, yet as I did this I was also thinking how I needed to preserve a pleasant cheerful tone. If this was going to be the finale, then it at least needed to be treated with as much lightness as was possible. For everything can be made into a toy, if you only choose the correct viewing position. Or at least I hoped so.

in one more of time's catastrophes

From this position therefore I tried to create a small stalling of Fate, however miniature – the way a cartoon genie might raise his hand to trap a malevolent spirit in a freeze frame eternally.

ME
I thought you were going to be there when we were old. I thought that we'd have children.

CANDY
Really? Did you really?

There was a long pause.

CANDY
Maybe we should just try again when we're sixty.

I was grateful to her, because it was surely a way of showing that perhaps this was not for ever, that always there exist other possibilities and byways. The fact that it might not be true or only gentle was too sad for me to contemplate. And I know that people think that if you're young, or recently young, then the tricks of time are not available to you, not really – but I was discovering that the fact of being young or almost young simply means that these tricks are just more compressed into a smaller span, like computer models of constellations. All of time's disasters can occur at any moment, and nostalgia for instance is no different, it can just graze you in its gentle flight – as for instance at this moment when I was losing Candy for ever, but also when you find yourself calling every film you watch a video, even though it is only digital on a screen, or, to give you a larger example, when I had recently been with Hiro, passing a cinema, a multiplex of which I wasn't even fond, and it occurred to me that it was in this cinema that I had first seen the foreign and stylish movies, almost exactly half my life ago. Back then, I thought there would be many such great works that I would see or read and that they would have a major impact on me, and I would of course become an artist myself. But in the event there were rather few. And the only art form I achieved was this swarming account, all bright and sincere like the paintings people hang on the park railings. As nostalgia, I understand, it's perhaps smaller than a man about to die seeing a vision of his first love, but so what? The feeling is the same. And I was having another such moment now, as I felt the entire future disappear. Suddenly it seemed very important to memorise as much as possible, of Candy's face and everything she said, just as often I found myself remembering aspects of my past – like for instance the room we slept in had its window over the drive. Although by *drive* this doesn't mean it was some hacienda in which we lived, no this drive was the length of a car, and it had gravel in it, poured out by my father. When I was a child I used to stay in that room if I was sick, as a treat, and I heard the milkman coming down the drive. And now I woke up in the dawns and realised that there were no more milkmen. The only keeper of the sound was me.

ME
Could we start again?

CANDY
I can't –

ME
Why not?

CANDY
Let's not do that –

And suddenly I had nothing else to say. For obviously, she was right. She was the noblest person I knew.

— Go, I said. — It's OK.

It was really very sad, to think that there would be no second chance, and to suddenly see the entire recent history of my life, as if from a great height: to realise, in other words, that the judgement of time was now definitively against me. It's like those history paintings which up close are all swarm or splurge, with gouts and gross enlargements, but when you move back far enough you see the grand coronation, or liberty at the barricades. Or like one of those blurry crowds where only if you get back far enough do you see they're holding up those electronic flip cards spelling out the name of the immortal and only leader. For a long while after Candy had left, I sat in the kitchen, looking at this room. I had nowhere else to go. I was like a pond or pool, where all of time was eddying and stilled. Then finally I went upstairs to bed, and for a moment was confused, because something else was missing but I could not name this extra absence – and then I remembered that, of course, the dog was gone.

9. NOIR

from which he wakes up transformed

When I woke up the next morning it was very peaceful. Life was just immobile, like a field. It had no ZOOM! or WHAAM! My mother and father were still away. Candy had left for Tiffany's apartment in the hot polluted city. I did not think that I would talk to Romy again, or certainly not soon. And the dog was an absence, too, but in some way the absence of the dog was worse because he was gone for ever, so that no longer was he breathing on my face in the night, or moving pensively around the bedroom. His paws were not at my nose, with their warm milky smell. Our dog smelled of rice, or toast, or sometimes vanilla frosting. Our dog smelled supersweet. Only Hiro was still here, snoozing in the spare room – and I was pleased that at least I had that company in the world. Always I was used to the attention of other people – and so I did the only thing I could think of, which was to wake up Hiro and together have a larger narcotic breakfast than was usual even for us, with white powder to make things seem more electronica and carefree, then the white pills to even the sensations out. It did seem to make things better and I could reason much more clearly. Even if traumatised and terrified and alone, that's no reason to give up on one's ongoing projects. Very obviously we needed to return the money – and even if I was not entirely sure where exactly this money was due, it seemed most likely that the nail salon was where we should go, since it was from the nail salon that we had taken the most money, and it was the nail salon that seemed to me the most likely to have sinister violence hidden behind it. I had no idea if that was in any way a correct line of thinking. To make things right was such a burden! It was such a bundle of decisions. And yet also it was delightful if I could think of doing this so that everyone else could live carefree, while I alone knew no rest from morning to night bearing other people's burdens. And one further task, I realised, in trying to continue to make things right, was to give our dog a burial. The previous day, we had put him outside in the garden, and the thought of him lying out there overnight, while Candy and I argued and cajoled each other and separated for ever, this was a melancholy thought and left me ill at ease. And so in my pyjamas I went down to the garden, and that did feel good, I mean to be at last taking control and doing the right thing. It was one step at least towards a better life. I wanted to bury our dog in the fields far out, on the edge of the city, in the woods, among the breadfruit trees and oaks, where he so liked to roam. But when I walked down into the garden and stood there, with the backdrop of one plum tree and one chirimoya tree, and in the distance the noise of the autostrada, I could not help a sort of terror. I had forgotten the violence that had been done to our dog, the violence and its effects, so that his skull had this depression in it, the way a button might jam on some ancient tape deck and never return to its right position, and his jaw was awry so that his teeth did not match up, like he was grimacing, or smiling very clownishly. Blood was now brown and biscuity all over his muzzle and fur. And it was as I looked at this blood on his muzzle and also on his paws, because some had dripped from his head to his front paws when we had lain him down, that my feelings in some way changed – because our dog was always very clean, he liked to lick the mud off him or any other dirt, in the manner of a very houseproud person. Never would he have allowed such staining to his paws, no never, and it was this staining that suddenly made me feel enraged, and I paused there, in this bright stain of my own fury, and was only woken from this daze by the sound of my phone.

rejecting all guilt

Once again, I had a message from this number I did not recognise. I sent a furious reply, and received no answer. And while I understand that once again such a message could have a very innocent explanation, it seemed to represent a major problem that I needed to confront. It was as if the world would never leave me be. Always, I was thinking, I must be the one who goes in fear. And while I was willing to accept that there was a case to be made against me, I also did feel that there was much to be said in my defence. And I still do not think that perhaps it was so wrong, to want to question this assumption of my guilt, since this is surely very intricate and infinite to answer. So that if now as my historian I was looking for reasons to explain this whole catastrophe, then I would have to begin very slowly, like it would need to include also other people around me in the background, like the man who walked his Rottweiler in the local parks and did not like me letting my dog off-leash at the same time as his because my dog annoyed him, because he was too quick and upset his slower beast, and also the woman who used to tell me not to let my dog mess her dog around like that, *He doesn't like being messed around with*, she would say, as if my dog were a paedophile or delinquent. And then also there could well be other causes, like the way the first girl I ever kissed never spoke to me again, which did make me very sad, or perhaps I was sad already, and therefore in this picture of those to blame I would have to include also my dead and absent grandparents, yes, I would have to go back very far, perhaps as far as my swimming instructors at the municipal pool, who let me leave school without ever learning how to swim, and my dentist who removed a milk tooth and then never replaced it, so I had this wonky gap in my teeth, then the teachers at my school who would not give me the magic mark which would allow me to use a fountain pen, which meant that technically I am still forbidden from using anything other than pencil or biro. And then the other children at my under-14 county athletics trial who upset me with their speed. In fact the more I think about my entrance to the adult world I am amazed at the handicaps I was born with, including the chance procedures that had gone into the make-up of my body, and especially my skin. Ever since birth, my skin has been inadequate, luminous with rashes and little weeping cuts. And this means, I'm just saying, that most things associated with pleasure become a problem – like beaches, for instance. I go to the beach and I develop heat rashes and my skin is finely speckled. In the children's hospital, they swaddled me in bandages, to try to stop me scratching, and later I learned to bathe my hands in chemicals, so that they might harden. Or also we would try the various mixtures of twig and bark provided by the Chinatown apothecaries, even though neither my mother nor I believed that they would work – and they tasted very disgusting, and did not work. Yes, you really could continue very minutely, when you started thinking in this way. It was like two facing mirrors. Or like the way once a muezzin begins it starts off all the other muezzins pre-recorded muezzining.

as an avenger

The end of guilt! If I had a battle cry, perhaps this could be it. For was I not going to pay back the money? Was I not also preoccupied with the demise of my marriage, the death of my dog, the happiness of my friends? Not that I did not think I deserved dark punishment. I was very much aware that punishment was my due, as just one more of the powerhogs and warmongers. But at the same time I would argue that I always tried to act from the best of motives – I really do dislike harm in all its forms, and surely that's a form of purity, even if what happens seems to have this impure tone? – and if unintended consequences ever occurred that were shameful, then surely this was not the only way to judge a person's life? Totally, I had entered a world I did not understand and when that happens perhaps you will have to accept some violence as your due, and it was true that the violence used against me had been quite small, involving as it did only one member of the animal kingdom, and not for instance the severing of my wife's ear, or clubbing me in the legs with a metal baseball bat. From that perspective, sure, the violence was quite delicate, but then I think it's important to remember how vast such smallness feels. And why should it be our dog to suffer? Our dog was the most innocent creature I had ever known, the kindest, with the saddest eyes. I began to lift him up, just very gently take him in my arms, and as I did so it was like my arms remembered what it had been like when he was miniature and a puppy, when I would take him in my arms so that he could go outside into the garden, for the single step down to the patio was too much for him and alarming. It was really not to be endured. Everyone had disappeared. Everything had gone. But therefore I would face this situation with some kind of grace. I would face the violence with grace out of love. Because to be a dog is a terrible situation, you are dependent on the protection of other people and always I had taken this protection very seriously. Absolutely, I had done something wrong. But did that mean the punishment itself should be so grotesque? If they thought that it was easy to be fearsome, then they should surely be taught that this was no way to behave. If I had to, I would defend my territory with aplomb. Whether such a decision constitutes a spiritual life I have no idea, but for me it was enough – like if now it were the día de muertos I could acquit myself with bravado. Suddenly I understood the material, the way the best movies are the ones where at a certain point you can see where the film-maker has understood what she is doing, a moment of pure clarity, and *that* is when she transforms the whole shebang into something live and fragile and unfamiliar. I would face violence with style. And surely that's something? Surely in the history of the saints there is one who does not seem so saintly, whose saintliness does not take the form of performance pieces like sleeping on a bed of nails, and so on, being tied to a wheel and spun? And if so, then maybe I was one of these less obviously saintly saints.

together with his sidekick Hiro

Very softly I laid our dog down, then went inside to talk to Hiro. Because if you are in the business of revenge, you generally need weapons, and a sidekick.

— You still with me, yeah? I said.

— This is crazed, said Hiro.

— It does seem so, I said. — But this is what we are going to do.

Probably it was good we had already entered a narcotic atmosphere but I also think my plan was justified. For what I was proposing was no mayhem and multiple murder, it was only something very simple and not necessarily violent at all. I wanted to bury our dog out in the fields, in the woods, where he so liked to roam. But first I wanted to go to the nail salon and return their money – because although we had spent that money and although the idea of stealing from my parents did not excite me, still, I knew where my mother kept a fat pile of notes in the freezer, for emergencies, and surely this did count as an emergency. But also I thought it was important to do huge violence to the nail salon's premises: not to anyone personally, but just an act of vengeance that would show I was not going to be perpetually accused.

— That your plan? said Hiro.

— It is, I said.

— OK, said Hiro. — OK.

And I was very pleased that this operation would be conducted with Hiro, because angry as I was, I still understood that maybe this plan would not succeed, for many things can go wrong when you introduce violence to the world and are not practised in it, and that worried me, but I tried to keep that worry as small as I could. It existed in my mind like a patch of sunlight through a window on a floor. I mean it does and does not belong to the floor you're looking at.

— Then, said Hiro, — we only need ourselves a hammer.

— A hammer? I replied.

— Sure, said Hiro.

A hammer, he continued, was very frightening to people and you could pick it up in every home, which is an advantage if you are new to the business of revenge. And of course he was right. We have this category of *weapon*, whereas so many domestic things are weapons if you use them differently: knives, forks, hammers, hooks, tongs, shovels, spades – these are all you need to behave completely manically. And that, he concluded, was how we would manage this conundrum. It was all very neat and very intelligent, the way Hiro planned it out. We just gathered up our dog, the money from the freezer, two hammers from a cupboard in the kitchen, then took the keys to my mother's car, and drove up to the parade. That's how easily things can happen when you're thinking clearly. Just as also thinking clearly has its advantages of complication, too – because as we drove Hiro suddenly said: *The spade*, and I had to admit he had a very good point. Because it is not possible to dig a hole among leaf matter or mud with your own hands, it's just not possible at all. For a moment we terribly paused, and I worried that all my planning would disintegrate – but then, in one of those moments of inspiration that must mark the biography of a person destined for great things, if they were not often forestalled by circumstances and practical details, I remembered the warehouse emporia, out by the motorway.

a revenge from which they are briefly sidetracked

For something noir can still be very bright. And so we drove back out past the vacant apartments and chop shops until we found the home-improvement store. It was opposite the hypermarket where ever so long ago, or so it felt, I had sat in the car park and felt this encroaching doom. And maybe after all *doom* was not so wrong. But I did not want to think like that. The light inside was even brighter than the bright blocks of cars. It was made of plastic multiple chandeliers, teardrops, copper wire, with a fragile tinkling when the distant air-con fans approached them. But me I was making for the garden section, with such opposite softness, such scent of wood in the air, of garden twine. And it was only maybe now that I was discovering that terror is a drug, terror is an atmosphere you acquire. I was on a mission to buy a gravedigging spade for my beloved dog, this dog who had been killed in revenge for my own misdeeds, with hammers concealed on my person. And perhaps one reason why it was so enticing was that to the outside observer there was nothing fearsome visible at all. And so it was occurring to me, because I am always given to seeing myself in or as other people, that the woman beside me, testing a range of ornamental garden forks, was maybe buying a fork to bury the bloodied root of her husband's penis, or that the man looking at urns for shrubs or herbs or other foliage was in fact assessing if it might be large enough to plant his child's beheaded head. That was how I thought, with maybe wild eyes but still a softness in the sneakers, while I contemplated the garden tools. The spades that I had been thinking about it turned out were very big. They glistened and were stainless steel and so heavy that I wasn't sure if I could wield one. But nevertheless, I bought one. I had no choice. And so we went back on our way.

before executing this revenge with miniature violence

Of course I wasn't sure exactly who had threatened us from the salon, and it was possible that in fact neither of the choppers who had attacked us were employees of the salon itself. I knew that my revenge might not have the perfect symmetry that the usual revenge should possess, but I couldn't help that: I had to make do with what I had and I think in the end that's enough, or at least it often has to be. And so we entered the salon like some nightmare scenario, bearing hammers, and a spade, and a dead heavy dog. I was surprised by this, but now it could not be altered: Hiro had perhaps inadvertently – since the dog had been lying on his lap, in its shroud – just brought the dog in with him. Certainly it was interesting to notice the effect – where the single customer just stood there with her mouth open, then

— Scram, said Hiro, cradling the dog, and she did go –

and the receptionist who owned the lovely portrait of a saint began to tremble, very fast. There was deep fear on her face and I must admit I liked that. Once again I was having a miniature glimpse of the power that maybe gang leaders feel or mad dictators, the total power anyone can have if they can abandon all their restraints, just take them down like dismantling a Lego castle – if, I suppose it needs to be added, they can also do this without any fear at all. Fear of consequences, I think, tends to obfuscate the picture. If that's something you can reconcile, then it really does allow you a tremendous range. And so with that power deep inside me, I began the scene, while Hiro placed our dog very gently on the floor. In moving him some blood had slightly squeezed out from his wound.

— The fuck? said another girl.

— Shut the fuck up, said Hiro.

— Here, I said, — is your money.

I placed the notes carefully on the desk, because I did not after all want to lose any. I wanted them to see that we had paid them back in full. And it seemed to me obvious that it was the right place, that this was indeed the correct object of our vengeance, by the very fact that they said nothing. It was exactly, I was thinking, as if they expected it. And therefore with this doubt resolved I smashed the hammer down onto the receptionist's desk. I was exulted. I was very large. The silence that followed this tumult seemed very long, and I understood it was because no one knew how to respond, and that did please me, very much. Also more kinds of liquids were emerging from my dog's body, and the effect was very gruesome and upsetting. Then I smashed the telephone with the hammer and it slightly broke but mainly slipped to the floor, where it fell noisily and with some impact. The receptionist bent to pick it up and I understood that she seemed to be testing or using it, just talking very softly or at least seeming to do so, but I did not quite understand this because at this point the violence inside me was totally huge and I was not sure how I would stop it. There was a small hand mirror and I smashed that too, and it was making me wonder if I could smash the mirror in front of each customer's chair. I had no idea how much violence that would require. I did regret now that we had no real gun. If I could have fired bullets into the ceiling, and made holes in every possible surface, I would totally have done that. But then slowly, very slowly, with this grace in her movements which I now noticed for the first time, the receptionist moved from out behind her desk, and into the middle of the salon, where she kneeled down beside my dog. Then she took a towel from a pile in front of one of the mirrors, and wrapped him, and she did this very gently, and I appreciated that gentleness very much. It was like something now was understood, even if perhaps she did intend it as rebuke. Her face was very grave. Then she handed me my dog, and he was totally swaddled and ensconced: only his black nose was protruding, the way it used to protrude from the bedclothes when he was sleeping under the duvet. And suddenly I felt no power at all. I felt very sad and very tired. All I wanted to do now was bury my dog somewhere, quietly. I understood that people were staring but I did not care. A fine rain was falling, very faintly, at a slant, like the most invisible curtain, and in this rain we made our fast escape.

that is surely our hero's right

In the street, happy people among the damp palmettos were shopping or speed-dating and were delighted. In a parked car a man was sitting, listening to some cool jazz, tapping drumsticks on the steering wheel. Whereas here I was, with a dead dog in my arms, and Hiro sparkling and beeping beside me. It saddened me how I could not be absorbed in the verdant scene at all. There I was, in the same street, and I had forgotten what happiness was. I hugged this thought to me, as if it were some hot-water bottle to soothe me in the dark. The only possible conclusion was that a cruel injustice had been done to me. Why had these last few months been so exceedingly complicated for me? If you thought about it long enough, it was all incredibly unfair. I really did deserve, it seemed to me, a small vacation, perhaps panning for gold, or exploring the South Seas. I owed myself, I thought, at least that much. It did not seem unreasonable. For perhaps, I wondered, as we slammed the car doors shut, it was possible to do good in different ways? The effort that is necessary to create a better world! No bravo in a mass brawl in a pastiche hostelry had it worse than me . . . I looked at Hiro beside me in the car, holding the dead dog very tenderly, and I felt so tenderly about him too, just as I tenderly also remembered the similar way in which Candy had carried our dog home, in the car, when he was only a month or so old, and she looked into his eyes with love.

or so it seems

To drive at high speed in a built-up area is a very specific thrill. To complete the mafiosi picture, we only needed to be shooting out the windscreen from inside so it crumbled up, like icing sugar. And if in the annals of history other children have been transformed by time into drug baronistas, or hit men, why couldn't I be transformed too? I felt like an outlaw and in many ways, I reflected, I think I was, if by outlaw you include those excluded from their normal world. I was so grand I was benevolent, and it occurred to me that in this matter of trying to restore some calm, before I went out to the woods I could take this sorry car, whose paintwork might well be briefly stained with canine blood, to the car wash. And this was especially generous because that kind of situation is never one I like – to be served by sad waterproofed people who do not disguise how unhappy they are to serve you. But still, I will let myself be served, after all, even if this kind of practical situation always perplexes me with the various things I do not know. Behaviour is difficult, and perhaps the difference between those who can do things and those who cannot is one of the hidden divisions of our time – much more than capitalists and workers, or blacks and whites. Like for instance people were tapping on the bonnet and asking me to open it, while looking concerned at some miniature piles of sodden leaves that had gathered in the well in which the windscreen wipers sat – but I had never opened the bonnet before and did not know how it might happen. So I gave a gesture that was intended to mean that really I did not care, but they did seem still to care and I cursed this obsession with professional appearances. So to indicate how unimportant these leaves were I tried to move forward but this only made them shout, and therefore I tried to argue that it really was no bother but they were implacable and so finally I admitted that in fact the task was beyond me, and with this admission I thought that this would disarm or charm them, because in general such honesty is to be admired, but instead a man just opened my door, a gesture I found perhaps intrusive, especially in my nervous state, then leaned down beside my leg where the catch was, and in obedient unlikeable response the bonnet gave its miniature sprung spring. I did a gesture of thank you but it was possibly too late, if by that gesture I intended to imply a kind of level between us, a sort of flatness of equality as men. Silently they opened the car doors and then vacuumed the inside edges. Then silently they were putting the bonnet down and telling me to be on my way, and in good-bye I raised a confident hand. For I was trying to maintain a careless blissed-out mood, the kind of equable excitement that makes you basically divine, according to some philosophers and sages – even if, talking of such sages, what I was about to discover in the environs of Toy Town was how many more depths and darknesses in reality existed, as the talmudic sages have known all along. But then, to understand the workings of Fate, it needs no study of the ancient texts. You can do it with that cartoon – where the cat relaxes and is all happy before being malleted by the mouse. I think such cartoons should play on endless loops in every high school and other college.

even if Fate seems also to be lurking once again

For the wisdom of such cartoons is the only wisdom that might prepare you to survive such terrible things, as when for instance you are driving out to the woods in the suburbs of a giant city, in order to give your beloved pet a decent burial, and are in your mind just trying to maintain a small bouquet of happiness, and then in the rear-view mirror you minutely notice that one car seems to have been on the same journey as you – the same mini roundabouts and traffic signals, the same views of tennis courts and funeral parlours and vegetable markets – and while I suppose in every city there are people mimicking each other's journeys, that's just one feature of a giant city and its mania for multiple coincidences, this one did seem strange to me. Not perhaps so strange that I had to consider it a threat, but still, it seemed of let's say *interest*. I could not after all forget that we had just done much violence, and I suppose no act of violence can be assumed to exist without its consquences, possibly no act at all. Although to be chased still seemed a little exorbitant, for surely in paying back the money we had done what we needed to do? So that it was also possible, I had to admit, that if we were the object of a pursuit, the range of our pursuers could be much more vast than I had first considered. And I would argue that in such a situation the best thing to do next is to do outlandish things, like explore a train station forecourt or make a reconnaissance tour of the area's business parks. And if the same car keeps on following you then perhaps the chances of this being a giant coincidence are maybe slightly diminished. With such thoughts in mind I drove zigzaggingly and disordered, with Hiro just slightly querying the general sense of direction and my possible concentration.

— Kid, said Hiro. — Let us keep our eyes on the road.

It was very good advice and very sober. For to be chased in these places is not the exciting experience the video games and other educational environments have imagined. It requires a much more stressful concentration than the videastes seems to think, since while they imagine constant bursts of speed and a grand disregard for the safety of others, I found that it was not possible in any way to reach the desired acceleration I might need. There were old people crossing roads quite slowly, a funeral cortège involving a Caddy Hearse filled with flowers, and then roadworks with temporary traffic signals, or also at one point a procession for many saints, which made me pause for at least ten minutes, with a Jesus carrying a bright white helium cross on his shoulder. Such a chase is more like the complications of a driving test or proficiency exam, and not some pixelated swirl.

in the guise of an adversary

And also it forgets that if this is an area you know well, then it will have some sad connotations. There was one point when we zoomed down the underpass, then up alongside the hospital and away down the street with the eastern restaurants, then the street with stores for sewing-machine parts, past the zoo, and it occurred to me that this was always the route I had taken with my parents if we drove into the city. It had always been the most romantic route for me, and it still was, even if now it had such danger and tempest attached. I wondered very fleetingly if my parents ever knew, I mean knew how tenderly I thought about this small collection of streets. The nostalgia was very great, even if really I was just one car among the many other traffic items, the ambulances and caravans and bikers in scrambled formations. Beside me, kids were in trucks smoking weed while in a more compact sports thing a probably coked-up girl was probably going to see her orthodontist who was probably superhot. While it was also possible in this system of blockages and slowness that in the limousine behind me a philosopher was being driven to a conference where he was going to prove the non-existence of time, which was one thing I would have liked to believe as I very slowly entered and exited the outer lanes. I do not recommend it, a car chase in the megalopolis traffic. I think to be in such traffic makes it even more difficult for the beginner hoodlum, especially if driving was never that hoodlum's thing. Had I been choosing a location for my first ever car chase I would not have chosen a major city in the twilight, but something more akin perhaps to a deserted freeway in the steppes at night. There was a vast gap as usual between the real and ideal – about as wide as in that story of the screenwriter who wrote down his dream ideas one night on a notepad beside his bed, only to discover in the morning that his

big idea was Boy Meets Girl. We were on a road somewhere between the city and the suburbs and not really in
the direction of the woods, since that destination was
for the moment just suspended while I tried to lose
whoever was intent on hunting us down, and I realised
that our journey had led me to go past the hotel where I
had returned to find Romy bleeding, and yet as I examined
it with its pool and palmettos, I could only assume that
something was wrong, that to search in this place for
that previous time was not possible: since the fact that the
time had passed meant also that the place had disappeared,
as well. It was the same and not the same, which was just
one more demonstration of the world's non-existence.
Meanwhile I was feeling more and more frightened and
distracted. At the junction for one of the largest shopping
centres in the world, I did not make for the quieter roads
but instead entered the funnel to one of the city's outer
speed routes.

— Well, it's an adventure, Hiro said.

He was so cool it was extravagant. And if perhaps, in
retrospect, I could have finally paused, then this is where
I would have paused, at this moment of the highest speed.
Just look around you! The stars were starting to get scattered in the upstairs loft of the sky. Beside the autoroute,
in the distance, the paintball signs, in the twilight, were doing
this stammering thing in neon. While below the underpass as we zoomed onto the freeway and into the sky,
some tired men who presumably probably came from
distant war zones were selling a range of remote controls
for absent televisions and a few dead video cameras. Far
away, beside the canals, grasshoppers were probably

folded up like nail clippers. But the sad thing is that you cannot pause. Because you really cannot avoid a fate. By which I mean, the method by which you avoid it in the end will be the means of your destruction. You prove your new machismo and the very means you use to prove it will be that machismo's takedown and general beating. That's how it is. The dog-god in the end will hunt you down.

pursuing them in an auto chase

We were up there on the Presidential Freeway and to go at the turbo speed I was going made me very much afraid. Whereas the car which was following us was in contrast a very happy automobile. It was careering joyfully among the other cars with a freakish allure of abandon. There were moments when I began to worry that I would soon confuse the accelerator and the brake. I was overwhelmed. The entire scene was so much action that I felt just felled – the way you feel when you've forgotten seventeen appointments and then as you remember them you feel them descending on you just like the lava descended from Vesuvius to Pompeii, or maybe worse, because unlike Pompeii the petrified inhabitant of such everyday cases does not have the luxury of being immediately calcified and therefore excused from further diarising. You have to continue instead, amid the continuing disaster, and for instance try to figure out exactly who this car might be, and why they had such an interest in our persons, since in general I think it's fair to say that most people are able to live very much obliviously to other people, and that's in general the perfect state in which to live. But also as well as thinking these impossible thoughts I had to make many quick decisions, and the decisions I then made were maybe not the best. That should be no surprise when you consider how confusing thinking can be. Now, of course, as I consider the matter from up here in the dulcet clouds of the future, it might well appear that the best would have been to drive for ever on the endless highways until this car behind me disappeared – I should have relied on the gift of speed, and also for safety kept to the open and public roads. But that was not what in fact happened. I was very scared and confused and not after all sure that the acceleration on my vehicle would match that of the car that was so patiently behind us, so that is not what did in fact happen. What happened was that in my panic – and this whole account if it is anything is a description of a panic – I took the very first exit off the motorway and went back down into the ordinary roads and roundabouts. I wanted to make for the woods, after all – for if you have once decided to do the right thing, then you should do it, despite all present dangers. Or at least, I think that's why. I can't be always sure of my motivations. And maybe this absence of a deep reason is just natural. Maybe always when the end point finally comes, and it always will, you will think that it arrives for no good reason at all. I think I also had the idea that in such wilderness and suburb undergrowth I might have the upper hand, because in such a competition it's important to choose your territory, and in particular to choose a territory where you feel at home, the way other creatures choose a burrow. Quickly I entered smaller roads, looping round the cemented village greens, past the water troughs and the mini golf courses converted into car washes, until again we were out of the urban system and instead in some kind of greenery. We were driving through the outer villages that were really just ferocious roads. Still behind me hovered the terrible car. It was a very interesting experience, to know that you are being followed and chased and not have in any way the capability to stop it. I was pausing at every zebra crossing for pedestrians and when I slowed this car slowed as well – which gave me hope because I thought that if you are doing this then you have some respect at least for civilised behaviour. You may not be all blunderbuss and death squads. I wondered if in fact such obedience to the law might represent my only chance. There was night just softly descending its million nets over the houses and the breweries, and I accelerated through the cross-coming traffic with the klaxons doing their diagonal streaming thing behind me, and for a moment I believed that I was free. We were speeding along and I turned down towards the forest and I was thinking that perhaps as usual I would be exempt from major trouble. Then in the mirror I saw that behind me still followed this terrible car.

— What you going to do? said Hiro.

I considered this and found no easy answer.

— You think we should stop and talk? I said.

— Perhaps, said Hiro.

That was how he was. Always he was open with many people and I think that's cool, to be so open to new experiences.

– It seems to be their intention, said Hiro.

He had been taking a cocktail of small pills while we

were on our car chase, and now he took some more, presumably for the hours ahead, complete with a bottle of water. There was something very homely in this gesture, I considered. It was very domestic and very homely, in some indefinably consoling way.

which ends in a forest, or common ground

The forest outside our suburb was one where I had once roamed with my father when I was young, looking for dead leaves to take home and use as mulch or fertiliser or other garden terms. The ghost of my father was everywhere, even though he was not dead but then that's not impossible, that a person who is alive is also something that haunts you. As usual, I suppose, I was wanting to live up to my responsibilities – for after all, what's growing up, in the joke of the old master? It's to be allowed to crack that whip, your will, over you with your own hand, which was something I was doing as I parked to the side of the road. The other car mimicked me, if perhaps with more precision of manoeuvre. And I guess my plan in coming to a halt had been to begin a benign conversation, something in which we would simply come to conclusions about mistakes and misunderstandings made, then slap each other on the back and go our separate ways, but the problem was that no one wanted to talk, or certainly not talk in that way. I don't know how unusual that may seem. I've always thrived in atmospheres where people are quiet and respectful. Instead they preferred to shout which always I have found completely distressing, and it meant that I was scared and seemed to feel myself consenting, as if I were no longer concerned about the precise reasons or motivations but only the issue of my safety. I was surprised to see that all three of these pursuers, now that they had stepped out of the car, were women, but that was not so much interesting as the terror of their equipment: ski masks, wipe-clean leather, that kind of terrific accoutrement. I determined not to be scared, or at least not to show I was scared, because if you show you are scared then you're finished, and I did not want to be finished, not just yet. To Hiro I gave a confident smile and I could see by the way his face moved that this somewhat reassured him. He was communicating to me something like: *You want us to sort this out? We will sort this out, and it will be a very easy thing. Just as easy as the way I took those pills back then, just as fast and slick as that. Don't be scared, amigo!* You could tell he was saying such things just by the way he was feeling in his pocket for a cigarette and lighting it with untrembling hands. It was kind of him, because I would say that I was currently feeling scared, not just of the people in front of us but also in particular the setting. It was difficult to tell where one fear ended. They seemed to swarm together. For I had only to think of how I really was unsure as to who these people might be, and what wrong I might have done – since after all there was a wide selection to choose from in my past and recent past, like the problem in the old game shows of choosing the most desirable reward from the goods arrayed on display, like some portrait of the trophies of the hunt – that I necessarily also became confused and worried in my thinking, a worry that was difficult to distinguish from a worry or presentiment that all around us now in this forest were insects and also animals, possibly aliens as well, as I had once believed when I was younger. There was a rustling that was like the way you might imagine language rustling, if it were a thing, which I suppose it is, or also danger, in so far as danger is also remote, miniature, desolate, and very close. And so as usual I tried to be the one to speak first, because in the end this is how you control a situation, so in my head I prepared very carefully the right things to say, such as how sorry I was, and also how I would like to know exactly why it was they felt this need to direct us into the dark of a roadside woodland or forest, even if I suppose in this I was wrong, since I was the one who had chosen this location, and yet in some way I was very convinced that things were happening without me being able to control them at all. But one of the women was quicker than I was.

— What do you want? she said. — What did you think would happen?

— I don't know, I said.

I wanted to ask if also she had been the one responsible for destroying the objects in my house, and also for the unusual messages to my phone, but at the same time I was feeling how suddenly I did not know how to be in such a conversation, I mean one in which all the responses were unpredictable. It was obvious that they were talking to us in code, like the ghosts talk to their mystic Dictaphone at the Ouija board in tongues, and as with every mystic the whole problem is decoding the mystery in time.

— There's been a mistake, I said. — We mean no harm.

For if she intended to intimidate me very quickly I wanted to point out that whether or not I had grown up in the same kind of circumstances as she had, I was still my own person and had a certain courage.

where a conversation takes place

But instead I found that I was burdened with a heavy silence, with no more words left inside me at all, which often happens when people shout at me, it silences me completely. Like for instance there was this one time when I was in my infancy, when I thought that I had locked myself into a room, that I could not open the door, as if it were too high above me, which I did find very perplexing. And when I called, eventually my father came, and opened the door with ease, because it was in fact not locked at all – but instead of reacting with tenderness and care he only seemed angry, and shouted at me, while I stood there, my trousers round my ankles, and I felt a total silence and injustice, which always happens to me whenever I am berated. I cannot avoid it. And so I was grateful when I understood that Hiro was now doing the talking for us, even if also I felt a regret, since I had always promised myself that I would be the one to protect him, and yet at the highest test it had turned out I had failed. But then perhaps that's not so strange, that in extraordinary situations the familiar structures might impossibly mutate. I felt this tenderness for Hiro that was a terrible sensation, given the invisible weight of such a feeling and how little prepared I was to bear such a weight myself. It had never occurred to me how good-looking Hiro was, with his unlined skin, his natural quiff. I was half in love with him. He was talking quickly and at some length, and while I knew that many of the reasons

for this were only chemical, and that if you got to know
Hiro you would understand that he meant no harm, he
simply did not mean any harm at all, but still, the problem
with life is that so many times we are making assumptions
based on very limited information, and I could see that
these people here were precisely doing such a thing, they
were judging Hiro and finding him difficult on the basis of
an interpretation that was certainly at least a little unjustified. When Hiro informed these individuals that he saw
no reason to be scared of them, that in fact they did not
scare him, that they should probably pack up their masks
right now and disappear into the sunset, there was no need
to see in what Hiro said anything arrogant or untoward.
Not of course that I did not realise that to others he could
seem just unpredictable. To me he was only vulnerable
whereas I suppose it seemed to them that a certain cool
bravado was the real machine for his actions.

— So maybe, said one of the women, — you should
just stop talking, yeah?

To think that in this country there can be death squads
and other torture organs! Not that in a way I disagree, since
I can understand very well, from this long distance, the desire
to put me on trial, but still – we had got so used to the idea
that we would never have to face up precisely to what we
had done. It seemed so beautiful, that kind of life. I never
thought I would have to meet my enemies. And if this word
enemy seems to you old-fashioned, if you are puffing out
your cheeks or laughing like a putto, taking another bite of
samosa and in triumph at my stupidity, I do think that's
unfair. The old words can maybe be useful. For here were
people demanding that Hiro should stop talking, and one

thing which is always true of Hiro in these moods is that he does not like to stop talking, especially when asked. Such misunderstandings perhaps happen all the time. To Hiro, he really was a person with so many intricate thoughts and opinions and tastes, he really did think that his love of green-tea ice cream was something that made him very rare, whereas to these people I understood that if they were seeing a human at all it was the most abstract version of a human, a person who simply does not understand what they are about, who is a problem for them and quite possibly needs to be eliminated – and to explain the one to the other would be almost superhumanly impossible. But well, not everything can be explained. Some things are spidery and private. There's always this giant mismatch between the large interior and the small outside, and in fact sometimes I think the distance between the two is so gigantic that there's no possible way of relating the one to the other. They are the pure incommensurate.

which becomes more violent

But at the same time, it turns out to be very easy to make someone very small, just as large as the largeness of their body and no more, as demonstrated by one of our adversaries, who stepped forward and placed a holdall on the ground. Then very gently, and I was impressed by the way she did this, how smoothly and how at ease, she then removed from this holdall a gun. She looked at us and it was the kind of look that says *adios, compadre*, in the very fact that the look is so blank it says nothing at all. The problem was that I saw no way of understanding what would be the way to take myself out of such a situation. I did not know what was wanted, whether money or attention or apology or promise to flee the country. I wanted to plead and offer anything at all. To think how angry she was! How angry someone must be with you to bring out a genuine gun – and that it was genuine I had no doubt, it was just something in the way that she was holding it, and I realised that this was a very useful knowledge for the future, if I had a future, and if that future involved me being confronted with a gun, which I hoped would not be true. Everything inside me was scrambled and in despair. No wonder I was admiring of Hiro's courage! I knew that in some way there was a relation between his sprightliness and the pills that he had taken, but still, I don't think it's possible to reduce anything to anything: all behaviours in the end are a total mystery.

— We should totally calm down, said Hiro. — We should absolutely sit down and talk about this, maybe over coffee. Wouldn't that be a better plan? I'm not meaning to impose, I'm just –

He gradually stopped speaking and I understood, because it's difficult to maintain your poise in the absence of an understanding audience. To try to diminish such disquiet I tried to look around me at the natural beauty. It had rained so continuously that violent flora and fauna had emerged: new beetles, and savage kinds of kale. The last sunlight was making soft columns among the trees. I think I have no interest in natural beauty, or at least I didn't then. My interest very strongly was in something my mother had once said to me, which was that I deserved everything that happened to me. She meant that I deserved all the good things and the prodigies, but I was wondering if also I did deserve this too, as punishment for all my million misdeeds. And if so me, then maybe Hiro deserved such violence as well. And yet what kind of violence, I did not know. A small animal was staring at me from a tree and a vast terror overtook me. I really did not want to die, out here, in terrible pain. I am used to telling my innermost feelings to people and having them respected, and so I did this now. For I really was not ready for death, to go down into the underworld, into the hall of two truths and weigh my life against a single feather. I know you are meant to be ready for death at any moment, but what does this really mean? Certainly I am not ready for death – with so many secrets to be discovered in my email, so many projects left unfinished and indecipherable in my notebooks. I had no wish to become a body, with around it crouched my nervous first responders.

— I'm afraid of you, I cried. — I'm really afraid.

For if you say such a thing, surely this is a signal that you mean no violence to anyone and deserve to be pitied? And also I did want to emphasise that even if they were murderous and like a firebrand from the ancient myths, I did not judge them, since I think it's a basic principle that if you are inside a situation where you may have been to blame, you cannot blame the people you might have hurt if they want to take matters into their own hands, however objectively bad they may be.

— You see? said Hiro, in a gesture of amenable supplication.

And then they shot Hiro very gently. It was a brief

moment but also irrevocable, about as small and irrevocable as the moment whenever the instrument known always as the bonjo acquired the new name of the banjo, and all previous musical history came softly and precisely into focus.

& placing our hero outside all his usual categories

Everything was creaturely and disintegrating and wet around me, like suddenly I was part of the natural world and that's always a disturbing feeling. It was no longer just a history of some uptown hustle. Presumably thousands of miles away in a brown swamp somewhere on the outskirts of town a green crocodile was submerging its one good eye, and me I was crying very much without being able to stop it. Had you ever talked to me about gun violence, I think I would have said that the true guns would have been terrible items, complete with dazzling sounds. I expected flame and burning maw, but instead it was much softer. The gun flinched but her arm didn't. Then after a very small pause, certain reds were slowly everywhere on Hiro's sleeve and I did not know where to look or how to feel, except my feelings very strongly were occurring without my knowledge. I say knowledge but I mean control. I think they had shot Hiro in his outstretched arm but it was difficult to know. I was screaming many things inside my head but outside I was silent. Or possibly I managed something very small and meek, but righteous, like:

— It's not right. It's not right.

Or something roughly like that. I thought that then

Hiro had scrambled away into the dark forest before realising he had simply lain himself down very simply on the floor. And I became very afraid. I think that fear has been one of the lessons I have learned from this season, and how you cannot find the way of being equal to it. It's just the natural reaction when everything is sweet and there is no mischief in you, yet everything you do tends to create these ancient consequences, like you are in the amphitheatre with the wolves and the lemurs. For since this moment in the woods I have often dwelled on this finale. Never have I felt so single and alone, and suddenly I thought of our dog in the car underneath the salon towels and how he was alone, too, just as Candy was somewhere in the city and alone. When I used to wake up in the mornings, I would lie there and consider the fringe of light below the curtain. And I always knew that my mother would be in the house and everything was safe and that was always a relief. To know that safety was always possible was a lovely form of knowledge. And it occurred to me that in fact until this moment there had never been a point when my mother did not know where I was. This was the first moment where I was completely outside her orbit, and it was very sad. I mean, it was sad to discover how this sense of safety was just one more of my illusions, that in fact I was not exempt but like every other animal in the world I was *killable*, just like my dog was, too. It was really amazing and terrible. But still, I was trying to keep thinking because I had this instinct or superstition that if I was thinking then I would not be in danger, and the hyper was as ever my only mode, like thoughts were leafing from me and gathering at my feet, like pencil shavings. You always do whatever you want, said my mother. Always you do whatever you want and that is OK with me but it is going to upset other people, she said. I had always disagreed with her. I thought that instead you had to have some faith in people because otherwise why continue? I mean why continue in society at all? – and everyone in some way is in society, they can't help it. Except that possibly right now I wasn't.

in a small delirium of language

Then I heard a noise and felt something on the inside of my body that was a pain more than I had ever known. I guess I knew what must have happened but also still I was hoping that I did not. I did not want to think I had been shot. So many images of dismemberment and maiming were inside me. Still, it was undeniable. It felt like all my legs were gone except they were also still both there, and one of them was frantic, as if in panic. I was thinking things through as belatedly and slowly as the people on the sidewalks whose umbrellas are still up although there isn't any more rain. There was a crumpled liquid soft implosion in my thigh, like a starfish. I felt like I was not precisely here but everywhere else, which was complicated, so I closed my eyes to concentrate.

— Yeah it's done, said someone above me.

I thought she was talking to me before I realised she was talking on a phone.

— No it's sorted, she said. — It was nothing at all.

Then they walked away, leaving us to our sad devices. Everything was over and empty, the kind of emptiness the station boulevard has, at night, when all the minicabs are gone. And I was trying to hold together this conversation I was trying to continue with myself, since no one else was trying, and I was saying that of course I couldn't be sure that this wasn't dying. I might be wrong that I was going to live. It was my old *Madama Morte* fear, but this time perhaps more rational. For presumably, I thought, in fact I would never know if this was dying, because if in the next four minutes, or twelve minutes, I find that I have died, this will be a pure delirium of grammar, unless it turns out that in fact I will be able to just leak out of this body and observe the scene, and only then I suppose will it turn out that grammar was not delirious at all. Hiro was moving very slowly and I hoped that he was smiling, because I did think we had reached some resolution, and that was definitely a relief. It was like finally all the pirates had arrived at once to claim their merited revenge. And perhaps, I suppose, they had.

from which our hero surveys his recent history

One thing I had been considering a lot in these nightmare times was that story from the classical era about the famous sadhu and the flute – that as the poison was being brought to him in a bronze cup to effect his immediate execution he was learning a melody on the flute. And when people asked him what the fuck he was up to he said: *At least I'll have learned this melody before I die*. And while I know that this legend is meant to be a legend proving how noble the sadhu was in his adherence to an ideal, I think it also helps to make something clear that is usually very difficult to think about – because I don't see why the fact that this sadhu is about to be executed should make any real difference to the degree of his nobility. Every child who ever learns a banjo or piano scale in suburbia is being as noble and as grand – since after all proximity to death is just an effect of proportion: and in the scale of the vast long shadowed centuries we are all just as close to death as that pre-executed sadhu, or almost. But whenever I had thought like this, it had left me very anxious, since while one interpretation of the story of the sadhu was that this represented a noble adherence to the value of things that cannot be priced, there was also the possibility that in fact this just represented a total pointlessness, that this story was in fact not a parable but a black and gargantuan joke on all human endeavour. What I mean is: if it seems point-less for the sadhu then, why not for all of us now? Why do anything at all? That's a difficulty that seems to me far easier to dismiss than ever solve but also, I was suddenly thinking, among the lianas and ivies and streamers, it was liberating, too. I mean, it really is impossible to know what's truly real, or at least I sometimes think so. If you were to ask the prince which state was real, the slumming or the palace, I think he'd find it difficult to answer. All of which must mean that it's not impossible to change one's life, as in any Technicolor sequel in the tropics – or that if the world you believe in was lost before you ever entered it, and is only an illusion, that's no reason not to preserve that lovely illusion. To have lost everything, I just mean, may be a disaster but not all disasters are catas-trophes. And when I thought about it like that, it made me very hopeful for the future.